Scarred City

Book of the Huntress, Volume Three

Joshua David Bellin

for L.F., who took a chance

The darkness drops again; but now I know
That twenty centuries of stony sleep
Were vexed to nightmare by a rocking cradle

—William Butler Yeats, "The Second Coming"

Prologue

The Skaldi chieftain stood at a shattered window high above the city, gazing westward over the desert.

For millennia, travelers heading in that direction would have arrived at one of the wonders of the western world: a great saltwater lake that stretched for miles across the arid landscape. Migrating birds had congregated there in great numbers; tourists and photographers had reveled in its warm waters and stunning views. But like the city that had taken its name, much of the lake had been swallowed by desert in the past sixteen years, shriveling to a vestige of molten gold against the red-brown earth. Though its depth had always fluctuated in response to cycles of rain and evaporation, now it was on the verge of vanishing entirely, leaving only a shallow bowl as a reminder of the deceptive oasis whose promise had never been able to quench the wanderer's thirst.

The Skaldi turned from the unappealing vista to face the empty room. The creature had taken the form of a man, but it was not a man. The eyes that flicked restlessly this way and that saw everything their long-dead host would have seen: the broken glass, dust-covered table and chairs, and scorched walls of this boardroom in one of the few remaining skyscrapers of the bombed city. But the creature also perceived traces no human eyes could see—paths of organic molecules floating in the air, webs of movement emanating from living things far distant from the city. Human beings thought Skaldi detected prey by sense of smell, but they were wrong. It was in the Skaldi's nature to feel the presence of life energy and be drawn to it. From miles away, they tapped into this living force, an irresistible lure that alone could fill their empty bodies.

Today, the chieftain had no time to search for the vital energy it craved. The sickness had come upon it, as it did in every Skaldi's life cycle, and the creature ached with hunger so keen it could barely concentrate on the task at hand. If food did not come to it within weeks—possibly days—its body would simply disintegrate, melting into the common dust that covered this shell of a city.

Its eyes turned to the door as others of its kind shuffled in. There were ten of them, a core group their leader had assembled from the hundreds that still dwelled in the city, themselves a mere fraction of the swarm that had descended on this place years ago. Many of the original host had departed months earlier to search for food; many more had died the final death and faded into the general dust. Those that entered the boardroom wore the body of the last victim they had consumed, men and women and children they had found wandering the city and attacked without thought or remorse. Yet even those that had feasted on young humans bursting with vitality had turned listless and gray, with skin drawn tightly across their faces and eyes that bulged from the unbearable hunger inside them. None had reached their desiccated final state, but they maneuvered carefully around the husks of furniture lest an accidental bump or jostle cause parts of their bodies to flake into dust.

Once they had settled gingerly into their seats, the chieftain stepped forward, riveting their attention as it stood at the head of the table with the shattered windows as a backdrop. The Skaldi shared no love, but they were capable of coordination, teamwork, collective decision-making. Insofar as their leader could read their minds, it judged that they were committed to a common purpose. The sickness had come upon all of them at once, and there was nothing to feed it—nothing their own bodies could supply. If not for that fact, they might have turned on each other, but as it was, desperation united them.

"My kindred," the chieftain said, and the others bowed their heads.

"You know our situation," the thing at the head of the table continued. "The city is dead, its population decimated. Without a new infusion of life, we will pass into nothingness like the great majority of us that came before."

"Could this not have been foreseen?" one of the others spoke. It was tall and thin, a woman at one time; now it seemed a shadow thrown by chance sunlight against a wall. "Could the Skaldi not have anticipated that to feed so recklessly, so wantonly, was to doom ourselves to nonbeing?"

"What else could we have done?" another retorted. This one was shaped like a child, and it spoke in the piping voice that had cried out in fear and delight when it was alive. "We are what we are, and must feed."

"Until nothing remains to feed upon," the woman-shape replied.

"Something remains," the chieftain said. "If we have the wisdom to obtain it."

The others looked at it, quivering at this mention of fresh food. The chieftain bore their gaze for a long moment, drawing out their hunger almost to the point of madness before continuing.

"There are human life forms beyond this city," it announced at last. "Small colonies that roam the great waste to our south."

"We know this already," the woman-shape said. "We cannot reach them."

"Then we draw them to us."

"And when we exhaust them in turn?"

The chieftain snarled, its chest scar opening. Instantly, the others responded in kind. Retaining the veneer of humanity had become increasingly difficult as their hunger deepened, but the headman chastised itself for losing control. Tamping down its anger, it forced its stolen face into a conciliatory expression. When it did so, its chest scar closed, and the others in the room relaxed.

"There is yet something we can do," the chieftain answered the skeptical one's question. "Something that may enable us to escape our past, and secure our future. It will not come without struggle and sacrifice, but if we succeed, it will give us a chance to earn immortality rather than crumbling into worthless dust."

Its eyes wandered to the door. Turning, the others became aware of something outside the room, something they had never felt before. Even with their innate capacity to detect the life force of others, the thing beyond the door eluded them; they could sense its power, but could not grasp that power's nature or dimensions. They knew only that it was a power far greater than their own, and, for the first time in the succession of lives they had stolen and lost, they felt the cold grip of the thing their host bodies had called fear.

Their eyes returned to their leader's. It smiled, and as it did so, the scar that ran down its chest opened to mimic its smile.

"Let us begin," it said.

Chapter 1

Aleka lowered herself into the dark.

Her climbing rope ran through the ancient descender clamped to her harness, while high above, she'd anchored the rope to the protruding end of a girder where the tunnel had collapsed. Between the girder and the pit below, she dangled like a spider on a string. She owned gloves, useful for friction on long downward slides, but she'd tucked them into the harness and concentrated on the burn as she rappelled into the depths. No helmet; that hadn't been part of the gear she'd scavenged from the rocky terrain where they'd made camp two years ago. Her long, dark blond hair was tied back in a ponytail with a scrap of cloth. The air was cooler down here than topside, but sweat licked her eyes and slickened her hands. She tightened her grip on the rope and arrested her descent to check below; seeing nothing in the weak glow of the junky lantern clipped to her belt, she swore softly and relaxed the tension. If the rope ran out before she found a surface to land on, she'd have to haul herself back up, hand over hand with no one to help her control the climb.

Damn Mouse.

She'd arranged this climb with him earlier in the day, when he followed her belowground to the juncture where the tunnel broke. Mouse had been suspicious when she proposed a limited partnership, but she'd talked him into it, assuring him they would find more salvage in a day than the other tunnel rats had found in the past month. Part of her had been reluctant to include him, but once the words were out of her mouth, she couldn't take them back. She'd gathered her gear and returned to the spot to wait, but after an hour of waiting, she'd decided he must have chickened out, so she'd tied off her own anchor. A tandem climb would have been easier, but on the plus side, whatever she found was hers alone. If she found nothing, the humiliation and wasted time were hers alone, too.

The rusty descender stuck, and she swore again as she swung out of control, cursing Mouse and Auntie and all the rest of them. The gear was who knows how old, abandoned by some climber who'd bit the dust years, maybe decades ago. That explained the absence of a helmet; the fool had probably cracked his head open when he fell. If she wanted to avoid his fate, she had to get the descender unstuck before she bashed her brains against a girder sticking out into the dark.

Her hands scrabbled with the mechanism. It bit her finger, and she yelped as blood slickened the metal. Her feet, swinging wildly, touched ground, the momentum carrying her forward to land painfully on her knees. At that moment, the descender popped open as if to mock her with its metal half-smile.

She unhitched, left the rope dangling. Removing the lantern from her belt, she stood to take a look around.

Another tunnel, featureless as any. Gray cement, bits of trash and rebar. No lights. Tunnels like this ran deep beneath the desert, level after level crisscrossing crazily like hollow bones through the earth's body. A world beneath a world, one that belonged to climbers like her. How much of it had she seen in the past eight years, since she'd gotten big enough to dodge Auntie and strong enough to hand climb? How many tunnel rats could say they'd seen more by the age of sixteen? You could barter what you found down here for food or gear, but even more important, you could claim bragging rights over the other foragers. More important still, you could get out from under Auntie's eye for an hour or an afternoon or a whole day. It was a pretty poor substitute for freedom, but it was all she had.

She held the lantern high, willing it to shed more light. Like the tunnel she'd started from, this one was badly damaged, snapped off at the end where a pit yawned too deep for the lantern's feeble glow. It seemed as if a whole series of levels had collapsed, the topmost layer setting off a chain reaction in the ones below. She was in no hurry to delve deeper; she could scout this one for a good distance, see if there was anything left over from the time before that she could barter or hoard, then figure out a way to descend if she came up empty. No one would seek her here, no one would find her if they did. For as long as she chose to remain, her time was her own.

She set off down the tunnel, the small circle of light bobbing against the bare gray walls. It got colder the deeper she went, until she wished she'd grabbed her jacket when she ducked out of camp. Other than that, nothing much changed: a tracking light or two flickered, a puddle wrinkled from a drip in the ceiling. A pile of refuse attracted her attention, but when she squatted to sift through it, she found nothing of value, only scraps of flaky material like the skin-litter Skaldi left behind. Too dry and scaly to be fresh, so she didn't freak out the way Auntie would have. Demand was high topside for anything with a modicum of use remaining in it: strips of cloth, cups and containers no matter how chipped or broken, plastic casings that had probably belonged to computers or phones. Lots of the stuff she found in the tunnels had no discernible purpose, bits of metal and plastic that looked no more plausible than children's toys from a time when things like that mattered. But she never left anything behind, because people in camp broke it down, put it back together, repurposed it in any way they could: to carry water, tie down tents, craft weapons. True weapons were almost impossible to find, and the people who owned them—like Auntie and her guards—weren't about to give theirs up. Aleka had been thankful no one was around when she came across the dead climber's gear; anyone else in camp would have jumped at the chance to acquire rope, clips, anchor pins. She had initially considered trading the gear for food or possibly a knife, but in the time since, she'd been glad she kept it.

She heard voices, and she froze, cursing her luck. Something moved in the lantern's beam: a flash of brown bodies, their shadows blurry against the tunnel wall. The voices shouted in protest, and Aleka quickly diverted the light, relief flooding her that it wasn't who she'd feared.

"Petra? Tyris? What are you—"

"Baking cookies," Petra's rough voice floated back to her.

Tyris giggled. "Ding!"

Aleka was glad for the dark so the two of them couldn't see the bonfire of her face. "Sorry," she mumbled.

Tyris sat up in the nest she and Petra had made from one of the camp's tarps. She rested her head on her hand and eyed Aleka languidly.

"Is Auntie still on the warpath?" she asked.

"No more than usual."

"Oh, dear," Tyris said. "I figured you came down here because you knew."

Aleka's heart skipped. "Knew what?"

"We vamoosed before she finished dressing everyone down, but your name was a big part of it. Something about…"

"*That girl*," Petra said, her shaved head popping up beside Tyris's reddish curls. "And I believe the words *tan her hide* were in there as well."

"Great," Aleka muttered.

"If I were you, I'd steer clear of camp for a good long while," Tyris said.

"I can take care of myself."

The two yawned, stretched, settled back into their makeshift bed. "Well, if she asks for us, tell her we're … indisposed," Petra said.

"For an hour," Tyris chipped in. She gasped, giggled. "On second thought, make it two."

"Days," Petra guffawed.

Tyris joined in, and their laughter followed Aleka as she fled down the tunnel.

When she slowed enough to realize she wasn't hearing their voices anymore but the echo of her own feet, she shook her head in mortification. *What are you doing down here?* she'd been about to ask. What did she *think* the two of them were doing down here? Petra and Tyris acted like they were the first two people on the planet to discover sex, and they weren't shy about showing the rest of the camp how into it they were. For them to have sought refuge all the way down here, Auntie must have had the whole camp in an uproar. Aleka wished she could believe the old Indian was merely having one of those days when she couldn't stand the sight of anyone doing anything they enjoyed and was determined to make everybody as sullen and surly as she was on all the other days of the week. But if what Tyris said was true, and Auntie had charged everyone in camp with looking for one person in particular, the one person she loved to hound the most…

Aleka's stomach tightened with fear. What could Auntie want with her today? What had she screwed up this time? There'd been no sign of Skaldi for weeks, so there was no need for any of the camp leader's innumerable drills, much less for an evacuation. Why was it that, even when Aleka thought she'd found a place where her godmother's eyes couldn't penetrate, the woman followed her anyway, a presence she could never shake?

She looked back toward where Petra and Tyris were bedded down. She couldn't see them in the darkness, but she whispered, "Have a blast," envying their age and independence. There was no way she could risk returning to the surface now, and even when she did go back, she vowed not to tell Auntie where the two had gone. Let the old witch find them herself, or die trying.

Using her sleeve to try to clean the lantern's smudged glass, she started down the tunnel again.

More emptiness, more garbage. Possibly Skaldi dust, possibly plain desert dust that had leaked in from above. Whenever she came upon a pile, she set her lantern down and ran her hands through it, but she always came up empty—not so much as a thumbtack or a shard of glass. Still she kept going, determined not to show her face in camp until after nightfall, when the old woman's anger might have partly burned itself out. Maybe she could find some out-of-the-way corner and spend the night. By the time she had to face tomorrow, she'd be better prepared with a story or an apology to soothe Auntie's temper, at least for another day.

She was searching for doorframes or fissures large enough to accommodate her body when she heard something else moving in the tunnel, and she jerked upright, holding the lantern as high as she could.

"Who's there?" she called in a tight whisper.

A maniacal laugh rolled out of the darkness. Aleka released a breath.

"Damn it, Mouse, where've you been?" she asked as his shadow fell athwart the lantern's glow.

"Oh, how you wish you knew," he said.

He came fully into the light and leaned casually against the wall. With his fuzzy brown hair and large ears, he looked enough like his nickname to make it funny. He'd accepted the name from the more experienced tunnel rats because he'd had no choice; only his mother had called him Marcus, and she'd died of fever when he was no more than three. For the ten years since then, he'd been tagging along after the older teens, lately settling on Aleka as the most daring of them all. But being a mouse had its advantages in the world of the tunnels—more than once, he'd entered breaks in the walls she couldn't fit through and emerged with his meager share of plunder—so she let him stick around.

"Find your treasure trove?" he asked.

She spread her arms wide. "Look at me. What do you see?"

"Empty-handed tunnel trash," he said with a laugh. "Who's lost her gear."

"I didn't lose my gear," she said, annoyed that she let this pimple-faced tunnel brat get under her skin. "I left it at the head of the passage, which I wouldn't have had to do if you'd showed up like you were supposed to. How'd you get down here, anyway?"

"The mysteries of the Mouse Clan are many," he said. "We don't spill our secrets just like that to you paleface squaws."

Aleka bit back a retort. Mouse seemed to think it was some special badge of honor that he had Pima blood, but the fact was, half the people in camp were Indian or part-Indian. The western reservations were some of the safest places in the country when the Skaldi wars started; no one bothered to bomb them. *Red Man's Revenge*, Auntie called it, though as she added with her best Diné scowl, it was just like white folks not to give the country back until they'd turned it into a wasteland.

"Well, I'm getting out of here," Aleka said to Mouse. "You come to team up, or are you going to scurry off again?"

"I come with news of the world above," he intoned. "And with a warning of dire consequences for those who stray from the fold."

"If you're talking about Auntie, I already heard."

"Ah, but did you hear that she's dispatched her disciples to hunt you down? Even as we speak—"

"They have to find me first," she said. "Now come on. You in or out?"

His nose twitched like his namesake, then he pushed himself from the wall. Aleka realized that the leaning posture hadn't been just to make him look cool: he'd hurt himself somehow, couldn't put full weight on his left leg. It wobbled like it was made out of water. She shook her head, wondering why she'd thought it was a good idea to team up with him in the first place.

"I'm in," he said. "Where's the rope?"

Aleka led the way back, Mouse gimping beside her. As so often happened in the tunnels, she'd underestimated how much distance she'd covered, but she ignored her partner's complaints as they passed one identical pile of garbage after another. "Don't waste your time," she said when Mouse pounced on a particularly large heap, the same one she'd gotten excited about on the way in only to find that it consisted of nothing more substantial than powdered concrete. Almost impossible to work with, not worth its weight to carry. Last year, one tunnel rat not much older than Mouse had fallen to his death with a sack tied to his waist, and when they found his body wrapped around a girder, Auntie said the paltry amount he was carrying wouldn't have been enough to build a decent planter, much less to erect a barrier against desert raiders or Skaldi.

"How much farther?" Mouse whined.

"I didn't invite you along for your dazzling conversation."

"You didn't invite me along, period. You the queen of the underworld now?"

"Shut up, Mouse."

"Or was this the plan all along?" he taunted. "What did you think, if you found a big enough strike, you'd be able to leave Auntie in the dust?"

"I said shut up."

"That's what I don't get about you white girls," Mouse babbled on. "You think anyplace you're *not* is bound to be better than the place you *are*. You should learn from the Akimel O'otham. You know what we said when we emerged from the place before and took a good look around?"

Aleka breathed through her nostrils to calm herself.

20

"We said, *Huh*. And then we stopped feeling sorry for ourselves and got to work."

"You certainly are wise, Stealthy Rodent Warrior of the Great Western Desert. Hey, Petra? Tyris?"

They'd reached the spot where she'd stumbled across the couple. Aleka figured that Mouse, all thirteen years of him, would have a heart attack if he saw what the two of them were up to, but there was no response from the tarp where she'd seen the lovers tangled in each other, unless you counted Petra's peaceful snores.

"Petra and Tyris are down here?" Mouse asked, looking puzzled.

"Forget it."

She strode past him, moving faster now that they were close to the end. Mouse hurried to catch up, but his leg was obviously troubling him. He looked like he was running in thick mud that affected only his left foot.

"Come on," Aleka said. "I don't have all day."

There was a moment when she was sure he was going to remind her that all day was the only thing she *did* have, but for once, he kept his wit to himself.

The rope dangled from the end of the tunnel where she'd left it. She tugged on it to make sure it held tight. Mouse looked over the edge and whistled. "What do you think it is to the bottom, fifty feet? A hundred?"

"Why don't you jump and find out?"

"Ha, ha."

He uncoiled his own rope from his belt, lips moving while he silently counted it out. Aleka could tell by sight that it was more than she had left, enough to lower them another two levels, maybe three if they were lucky.

21

"Now the big question," Mouse said. "Who's climbing and who's belaying?"

Aleka sized up her companion. She knew that the only thing that made sense was for her to anchor him; Mouse was stronger than he looked, but not strong enough to lower her into the pit without the full use of both legs. But letting him go first meant trusting him to be honest about what he discovered, and trusting Mouse to be honest was like trusting the mirages that danced across the desert. "How are we going to divvy up the stash?" she asked.

"There's a stash?"

"Come on, Mouse. If we find anything."

"First come, first served," he said with a smirk.

"Not a prayer." She leaned over the edge, and was almost convinced she could make out dim shapes just beyond the lantern light, no more than twenty feet below. Her heart raced at the thought that they might be closer to a landing than she'd realized. "I'll go. It was my find."

"Our find. Lest you forget."

"Where were you when I needed you?"

"We've been over this before," he said. "I've got my secrets."

He stared a challenge. Aleka knew he wouldn't give in. "Go to hell," she said.

"After you."

She gripped her rope, threaded it through the descender and clamped the device in place. Then she hooked her lantern to her belt and walked to the edge of the precipice, glaring back at him.

"You serious?" he said, just as she pushed off and dropped into the void.

She braked with her hands to stop the fall, then looked up at Mouse in triumph. His face appeared over the edge, wide-eyed and filthy-cheeked. Something about the lantern's wavering light or the steep angle made her vision swim, and she could have sworn she saw a reflection cross his forehead like sunlight off water. Where her hands gripped the rope, it was suddenly slick, and she began to skid.

"What the hell, Mouse?" she called up to him, but he was gone.

She tried to haul herself up the wet rope, only to feel its taut strength turn limp. In the half-second she had to wonder about anything, she wondered how the painstaking knot she'd tied more than a hundred feet above had come loose. Then she fell.

Chapter 2

Her first thought when she woke was that hell was no worse than anyplace else.

She was lying on her back, a rough bundle of cloth pillowing her neck and head. The cloth stank of sweat and piss. Five feet away, an antique lantern whose square panels were grimed with smoke and grease sat on a table made out of a busted crate. The lantern beam backlit filmy strands that fluttered above like webs spun by wolf spiders. Beyond, the room was cavernously dark, so much so that Aleka wondered if she'd fallen to the deepest level of the tunnels, or even to a level *beneath* the tunnels, however deep that might be. Her body didn't hurt, though, so she couldn't have fallen that far. The memory of Mouse's staring face returned to her, along with a hot burst of anger.

The little sneak, she said to herself. She wasn't sure how this was his fault, but she was sure it was. She was preparing to climb out of the nest and figure out a way to track the dirty rat down when she discovered something that turned her anger to ice.

She couldn't move.

Nothing held her, not that she could see: no straps, ropes, weights. But when her brain sent the orders to her arms and legs to push her from the floor, nothing happened. It was as if a solid wall stood in the way, blocking the signals from reaching their destination.

Cold sweat broke out on Aleka's face. She strained, her teeth grinding together and the cords of her throat tightening with the effort. A memory of sharp, jabbing pain just before she blacked out came to her, but she felt nothing now, and her eyes were the only thing that told her she still had a body.

"Lie still," a soft voice spoke from the darkness beyond the lantern light. "Any movement may worsen the damage."

She peered into the gloom as a shadowy shape materialized. It came forward and hunkered down on the floor several paces from her. Aleka eyed it fearfully, but it came no closer. "What did you say?"

"Your neck," the person said. "The fall was not far, but your head must have snapped back when you landed. Can you move your arms at all? Feel the tips of your fingers?"

Aleka concentrated, trying to propel her thoughts physically to their termination, but there was nothing, not the slightest tingle. "I can't—"

"It is as I feared, then."

Though she had no sensation below her neck, it seemed as if her entire body were trembling violently. "You mean I'll never be able to—?"

"To walk? That is the customary prognosis, yes. Provided, that is, you survive at all."

The person stood and moved into the light. He was small, not much taller than Mouse, but he wore a billowing black cloak that made him appear much larger. A black keffiyeh was wrapped around his face, only his dark eyes showing through. The wrinkled skin around his eyes convinced Aleka that he was

25

old, but she could tell nothing more about his appearance or expression.

"What do you want?" she asked, a quaver in her voice.

"To help. Drink this."

A hand as cracked and lined as an arroyo after a rainstorm emerged from the cloak, holding a glass beaker filled halfway with an almost-black liquid. Aleka's eyes widened. "What is it?"

"It will help you heal."

"You said my neck..." She couldn't speak the words. "Nothing can heal that."

"This can."

He raised the beaker so it caught the lantern's light. Aleka's gorge rose when she saw that the fluid wasn't black but a deep red, the shade of fresh blood. "I ... I can't."

The man cocked his head, his eyes shining through the mask. He took a step toward her, seeming to tower above her despite his short stature.

"I am not going to harm you," he said in a voice as soft as a purr while he knelt by her side.

She tried to retreat from him, but her limbs refused to obey her commands. All she could do was turn her head from side to side, which sent daggers of pain down her neck where they died in the numbness of her back. How far belowground were they? If she screamed, would Mouse hear? Would Petra and Tyris? Even if they did, they'd never be able to reach her before—

His hand gripped her throat just beneath the chin. With his fingers holding her head in place, he pressed the beaker to her lips. She gagged as the fluid filled her mouth, its taste as foul as the water that pooled in the tunnels. She tried to spit it out, but that required more muscles than she could summon to her defense, and before she could think what to do, his hand sealed her nose and mouth, forcing the liquid down. It burned all the way to her stomach, a feeling of inner fire that was worse for her body's inability to react to it.

When he was done, the man moved away. Through tears, Aleka watched him sit, hands on his knees in a posture of meditation. She tried to form words to curse him, but her throat rebelled, squeezing shut without expelling one drop of the blood-red drink. She sobbed, and had the horrible feeling of drowning.

"You ... bastard," she managed to choke out.

"Wait a minute, Aleka," the man answered. "And then you may charge me with anything you wish."

She cried quietly, too stricken to ask or care how he knew her name. The man watched in silence. The rancid taste in her mouth had just started to fade when he stood, raising his cloak with both hands like a pair of giant bat wings. She flinched reflexively.

Her mouth fell open. With wonder, she lifted her hand in front of her face and wiggled her fingers as if they were pale underground creatures she'd never seen before.

"So," the man said as he seated himself again, "what was it that you wished to tell me?"

Aleka could only stare at him as she felt her body come to life, warmth and sensation spreading through her like a rising sun. She sat, pulling her long legs to her chin; the muscles she'd built over years of hiking and delving tightened at will, without the slightest quiver to remind her of their awful absence. She saw that her pants were torn, her knees scuffed and bloody from the fall. But there was no pain—not in her knees, not in her neck, not anywhere in her body. Whereas a moment ago she'd been as helpless as a stink beetle flipped on its back, now she felt a surge of energy running through her veins so strong it seemed mere flesh could barely contain it.

"How do you feel?" the man asked.

"I feel…" *Wonderful*, she wanted to say, but she couldn't say that to this masked stranger. "Better."

The lines around his eyes crinkled. "I thought as much. The elixir is potent, the more so in the young and strong. Yet I must confess that your recovery is even more rapid than I anticipated."

He relaxed his position, stretching his legs in front of him and gathering the cloak in his lap. His eyes traveled calmly over her face as he spoke.

"My name is Aesir," he said. "I have lived the solitary life of the desert wanderer ever since the Skaldi robbed me of the only home I knew. For long years, untroubled by my fellow man, I have labored to gird myself against further loss, and in some respects, I have met with success. As you have seen, my elixir possesses curative properties far beyond anything presently known in the camps. Your own healer—Tyris, I believe you call her—"

Aleka kept silent, determined not to let anything slip.

"She would give much to acquire this serum," Aesir continued. "She might even find it proof against the despoilers."

"You mean the Skaldi?"

"Indeed," he said, his eyes growing wistful. "Though that test has yet to be conducted."

"If you have something like that," Aleka asked warily, "why don't you share it with the camps?"

"Ah, but my supplies are limited," the man said. "And you are mistaken if you assume me to be a philanthropist. I have

28

shared this formula with you, but surely you do not expect me to part with such a gift and expect nothing in return?"

The words had no sooner left his mouth than she was on her feet, stooping in what she discovered to be a low-ceilinged chamber. It surprised her how quickly her body had reacted, as if the action had preceded the intention. She was debating whether to take his lantern and run when Aesir held out an age-wrinkled hand.

"You misjudge me, Aleka," he said. "What I would ask of you is nothing you need fear."

"How do you know my name?"

"Ah," he said, resting back on his hands but keeping his eyes on hers. "If you wish to learn the answer to *that* question, you must ask your mother."

"Auntie? You mean my godmother?"

"Your real mother."

"My..." Aleka kept a careful watch on him as if he might pounce, but he remained completely motionless, not even his eyes moving. "My mom died when I was born."

"That is what the Indian has told you. I happen to know that it is not true."

Aleka returned to her seat among the piles of dirty cloth that filled Aesir's den. Auntie had told her nothing about her mom beyond the circumstances of her death and the fact that the two of them weren't really sisters; she'd provided a name, or an alias—Diana—to the phantom who'd bled out giving birth to Aleka, but she'd offered no pictures, no stories, no memories. That had left Aleka to imagine all kinds of lives for the mother she'd never known: she was a commander in the Skaldi wars, a foundling like the twins, a pregnant drifter who'd been picked up by Auntie's camp. If it was true that she was alive, and her godmother had lied about something as important as this… Aleka's body, dead to feeling just minutes ago, burned with anger at the thought.

"How do you know about my mother?" she asked.

"I met her shortly before you were born," the man answered. "I was there on the day she delivered you, and I can assure you that she did not die. If the Indian has told you otherwise, it is for purposes of her own."

"But then … where is she now?"

He waved a hand vaguely in the air. "That, I do not know. But it may be that, working together, we can find out."

"So you fixed me up so I could help you look for my mother? That's the payment?"

His eyes roved over her face. She'd gotten better at reading what lay behind them, and she perceived the amusement of an adult answering the question of a guileless child.

"Determining your mother's whereabouts is not my primary purpose," he said. "And yet, I possess resources that might be of assistance in your search. I would be willing to help you find what *you* seek if you agree to help me find what *I* do."

"Which is what?"

"A means to defeat the Skaldi."

Aleka threw her head back and laughed. "Good luck with that."

"It is not luck that will determine our victory," he said. "In the past several months, I have begun building a team to achieve my objective—an army, one might call it. An army of soldiers like yourself, who know that nothing they face in my service could be any worse than what they leave behind."

His characterization of her present life stung, but she laughed again. "I'm no soldier."

30

"You lack the necessary preparation, it is true," he said. "But you have drunk of the elixir, and already you begin to feel its power within you. Is it not so?"

His dark eyes flicked over her. When Aleka reached inside herself, she felt the energy thrumming through her veins, and she knew its outward signs must be visible in her flushed face, her tapping feet.

"And so it will continue until your full potential has been realized," Aesir said. "But time is short, and the despoilers will not wait for our plans to mature. Perhaps you do not know what it is that they intend."

"I don't know anything about them."

"Then let me tell you that in my wanderings, I have seen what no other has. I have learned that the Skaldi mean to unleash a new terror on this land, and I do not expect the camps to withstand them if their efforts prove successful."

Aleka looked away from his penetrating gaze. Everything about this man made Auntie's voice screech *danger* inside her head: how he'd found her down here, what he'd already given her and what he was offering now, his idea of ridding the world of creatures that only the craziest of colonists, the ones who'd lost their families to tragedy and their own lives to drugs, talked about overcoming. Not to mention his knowledge, or part-knowledge, or claim to knowledge of Auntie, Tyris, her mother, herself… And all this with him dressed up like some kind of Hopi witch doctor, lacking only a staff and a rattlesnake to complete the picture. She should thank him for fixing her neck and then figure out the fastest way out of his burrow. She should leave the tunnels behind, track down Mouse and give him hell for whatever stunt he'd pulled up above, and then try to forget that any of this had ever happened.

31

"You remain unconvinced," the man said softly. "Perhaps this will change your view of the matter."

A hand emerged from his cloak. Something black and lumpy sat on his palm, looking like it had come from one of the charcoal deposits the camp was sometimes lucky enough to find for fuel. Only, as she watched, the stuff *moved*, first wobbling and then stretching as if some small figure inside of it were trying to break free. Aleka stared, equally fascinated and repulsed, as Aesir tipped his hand and let the mass fall to the floor between them. She yelped reflexively, pulling her foot back as the thing crept across the ground for a short distance, seeming to be searching for a way out of the cavern before Aesir scooped it into his palm and stored it once again beneath his voluminous robe.

"What was *that?*" she asked.

"The beginning," he said, "and the end. A substance engineered nearly four decades ago by those who founded the Skaldi experiments, and who brought these dire beings to our world. I had thought it dead, or at least dormant. Now I know that it has returned."

"And what exactly does it do?"

"It breeds," he said. "And spreads. It is the Skaldi's life source, the seed of their existence. Should this birthing agent come once more into their possession..."

"And you're walking around with it?" she asked. "In your pocket?"

"As a safeguard only."

"A safeguard? How safe is it going to be when the Skaldi storm this place and take it from you?"

She rose to her feet before he could answer. Strong as her legs felt, she couldn't stop them from trembling. She stared at the man's eyes, but she could no more see through them than she could see through the deadly black mass he'd held in his hand. She spoke in a voice as measured as she could manage while she stepped away from the lantern light.

"I appreciate what you've done for me," she said. "But I can't get mixed up in this. I don't even know who you are, and if Auntie found out..."

"Yes," he said calmly. "The Indian would not wish her godchild to talk to strangers."

"It's not like that!" she said. "I'm a tunnel rat, not some kind of mercenary. You said you've already got others. Let them fight your war. I'm having enough trouble just trying to survive."

"The moment we stop fighting for a goal more worthy than survival," he said, "is the moment the war is lost for us all."

"Tell that to Auntie," she said bitterly. "I'm sure she'll give you an earful. But I'm going."

She backed from the lantern. He'd returned to his pose of inward concentration, eyes serenely closed, and he made no move to stop her. For a second, she considered jumping at him and tearing off the mask, but then his eyes flashed open, and his quiet words shivered up her spine.

"Where will you go, daughter of the desert?" he said. "Without rope, and without knowing the way?"

He stood in a fluid motion, his cloak swirling about him. Short as he was, it seemed as if he were enveloped in a sea of shadows that would engulf the small room and everything in it. She steeled herself to fight, but as her fist drew back, the cloak settled and its owner threw her a look of great weariness and sorrow.

33

"I will show you to your camp," he said. "I am sorry that you cannot find it in you to do what I ask."

She swallowed a rejoinder and accepted the neat bundle he held out to her. Rope, harness, descender, gloves—everything except her lantern, which must have shattered when she fell. Taking up his own lantern, he led the way from his lair, and she followed a step behind.

He took her through secret ways she had no idea existed, though she'd been exploring these tunnels ever since Auntie established camp here. Ladders led to staircases that led to bridges, tunnels angled in ways that looked more like chutes or slides than passageways meant for human travel. Aleka began to wonder how much of the hidden world she would never witness, no matter how long she searched. Aesir toiled tirelessly up the slopes, his robe flapping in gusts that rose unexpectedly from above, wailing as they went. Wary of her limits when they first set out, Aleka soon discovered that she felt stronger and more vibrant with every step they took, as if she were drawing energy into her body rather than expending it on the climb.

Along with that unaccustomed vitality came an unaccountable urge to explain herself. The events of the day seemed unreal: had she actually fled from camp, quarreled with Mouse, lost her ability to walk? And then, against all hope, met a man with the power to restore her—a man who claimed he could help her find her mother? Having lived through all that, had she actually turned him down? Her head spun with apologies and excuses, but she couldn't bring herself to say them to him, so she voiced them silently to herself.

You don't know Auntie, she said. *Or maybe you do, but not like I do. She'd never let me go, never stop hunting for me if I left. Even now, she's going to read me the riot act for sneaking away for a single day. And she'll be watching me like a hawk from now on, so unless this army of yours is ready to fight her whole camp, you're better off leaving me here. I'd be more trouble to you than I'm worth, plus I'm not convinced there's anything out there to find anyway. The world's dead, and my mother's gone, and neither of us can change that. I wish I could believe differently, but I just can't.*

They emerged at last in the early morning hours before sunrise. The exit Aesir had chosen wasn't the same as the place she'd entered the previous day, but the stony outcropping behind which camp lay was visible from where they stood. Aesir stooped, his cloak spreading like a pool around him, and passed his hand over the dusty ground the way Navajo healers did while preparing a sand painting. He lifted a handful of earth and let it shower from his loosely held fist, then turned to look up at her.

"This ground has known Skaldi," he said. "Recently, and in some numbers."

Her heart sank. "Are you sure?"

"I am, and I will leave this place so soon as I gather my forces." He struggled to his feet, seeming old for the first time. "You will leave as well?"

It was hardly a question, but she nodded in response.

"And where will you go?"

"Wherever Auntie says."

"She chooses your path?"

"You know she does," Aleka said. "She's camp leader."

"Still, it must feel strange," he said in a musing way, "not to know where one's steps lead."

Anger rose in her again, but she didn't know whether it was directed at him, Auntie, or something else. He never gave her a chance to find out, as he turned with a flourish of his cloak and vanished into the predawn darkness.

"Farewell, Aleka," his voice came to her. "Wherever you roam, may you find the place your heart most desires."

Then he was gone, while she stared into the emptiness and wished she had the guts to admit she didn't know where that place was either.

Chapter 3

Camp was in the midst of being broken down when she peeked around the rock formation and saw the first glimmer of sunrise on the far horizon.

Shadowy figures in camo uniforms hurried across the open space, everyone moving with haste and purpose. Aleka spotted the twins, Kay and May, herding a group of orphaned children toward the passenger truck; from this distance and with the bad light, the pale, painfully thin duo looked like children themselves, though they were close to thirty years old. The tents and stoves and food stash were gone, while the flamethrowers, their only defense against Skaldi, had been loaded onto one of the supply trucks. Laman, Auntie's chief advisor—or errand boy, depending on how you looked at it—was supervising the loading of the fuel, directing the guards as they rolled the heavy barrels up the other supply truck's extendable ramp. Twenty years younger than Auntie at least, with a lean frame and scraggly beard, he spent most of his time jogging after her like a trained coyote, limping slightly on his bad hip. Vicious rumors circulated around camp that Auntie took him to bed when she ran out of ordinary ways to torture him, but for his sake, Aleka refused to believe those stories were true.

She scanned the area, but Auntie herself was nowhere to be seen. Her eyes caught a flash of midnight across the way, and she realized it was Petra, her almost black skin standing out against the pale red dunes as the sunlight spread. That the scout had returned from her tryst was less surprising than that Aleka had detected her at all; usually, Petra was so silent and swift she might have been a hawk's shadow slipping over the sand. It took Aleka a minute to realize that the energy flowing through her body must have heightened her senses too, amplifying her vision and making her attuned to the slightest sound or movement. She felt practically invincible—with the single glaring exception of Auntie. For that challenge, she needed not strength but Petra-like stealth.

She made her way cautiously down the dune to the periphery of camp, keeping close watch for any sign of its leader. Her eyes found Tyris packing medical supplies, and a pang shot through her when she thought about what the young healer could do if she got her hands on Aesir's miracle cure instead of having to patch people up with dirty bandages and sewing needles and whatever herbal cures she and her assistants could wring from the desert. But Aesir was gone, and camp would be gone too in less than an hour from the look of it, so there was nothing to be done.

Sonja, the twelve-year-old Hopi who helped Tyris with her doctoring, looked up as Aleka approached. The girl immediately dropped her eyes and glanced sidelong in the Indian way, no emotion showing on her broad brown face.

"Where you been?" she mumbled.

"Long story. You seen Mouse?"

"Nuh-uh. Why?"

"He's got a date with destiny. In the form of my fists."

38

Sonja's face brightened for a second before lapsing into its usual shuttered expression. "Best make it quick. Auntie's calling everyone together for a powwow before we go."

"She ask about me?"

"She cussed a blue streak."

Despite herself, fear loosened Aleka's stomach. A tongue-lashing from Auntie was nothing new, but the woman had follow-up forms of punishment her victims didn't want to guess at, mostly because the real thing was always worse.

"You maybe might duck her," Sonja was saying. "If you could—"

"Make time go backward," Aleka said.

The crowd broke to let a compact figure through, Laman hobbling behind. Small as she was, Auntie cleared the space around her like a dust devil out on the high desert. Dressed in camouflage pants and a tattered black jacket with frayed gold bands at the cuffs, she wore her iron-gray hair in long, thin braids, beaded at the ends. Her eyes were black, her skin lined and sun-bronzed. Aleka seemed to remember a time when the jacket had been less threadbare and the hair—as black as the jacket—had been shaved almost to the scalp, but that was so long ago, she couldn't be certain if the vision was real or a dream. The only thing she knew for sure was that Auntie was headed straight for her across the open space, her arms held out in what looked like the prelude to a hug but was almost certainly the overture to a lecture.

Aleka didn't foresee the third option: a stinging slap across her face, its sound sharp as a whip in the still desert air.

That got everyone's attention. People who hadn't been looking at her were looking now; the guards, psychopath Araz and the rest of his crew, weren't bothering to hide their evil grins. Aleka felt the power drain from her. It was as if, for the first time in years, she was peering up at Auntie's face instead of down.

"Thoughtless child," the old woman said loud enough for the whole camp to hear. "Selfish, short-sighted, irresponsible. You run and hide when your people need you most."

"I was—"

"I know exactly where you were," Auntie said. "No point making up stories when the truth is as plain as the load in a colicky baby's nappy."

Humiliation made Aleka shrink even further, but she was determined not to fold completely. "What do you want me to do about it? I'm here now."

"*Now* is too late," Auntie shot back. "*When* I needed you *where* I needed you would have been the right choice."

"We haven't even moved out yet—"

"And one of us never will again," Auntie said. "Araz, bring it to me."

A startled look crossed Laman's face. "Asheh, the children—"

"*This* child needs to see the results of her carelessness," Auntie's voice bullied over his. "You heard me, Araz. Bring it here."

The giant guard lumbered over. Everyone else seemed as frozen as Laman; even the littlest ones were silent under the twins' equally silent watch. Araz's thick fingers fumbled with a knotted bag until Auntie snatched it from him and undid the string herself. The bag dropped to the ground as she lifted something from inside and held it before Aleka's eyes.

It was a sheet of brownish material, roughly the size and texture of a crinkled map, but sheer enough that the daylight

40

shone through. Aleka would have thought little of it if not for the stiff brown hairs that clung to its edges, along with the perfect outline of oversized ears. Her stomach lurched and nearly ruined the old woman's moccasins.

"Araz found this while he was looking for you," Auntie said. "Even the old-time Comanches never took a scalp this clean."

"But he was—" Aleka's throat caught on puke and dust. "We were just talking—"

"Right before the Skaldi had their own little chat with him, it would appear. Which means that if I hadn't had to spread my forces thin hunting for *you*, Marcus might still be among the living, not out in the desert wearing some filthy skin-walker's body."

She balled Mouse's remains and threw the crumpled sheet to the ground. Aleka stared at it dizzily, the sand and the skin seeming to blur together as if the wind had picked up what was left of him and hurled it into the heavens.

"Now you know," Auntie said grimly. "Now you see. You think you're the only one who wishes she could get away for a holiday now and again, Miss Aleka? You think we wouldn't all rather play make believe than face the monsters up here? But this boy, he deserved better. I'm just thankful his mother never lived to see what became of her only child, how badly we failed the trust she placed in us. Laman!" she switched gears, rounding on him while he jumped back in alarm. "You're so worried about what we show the children. I'm more concerned about what we *don't* show them, and the romantic notions they get in their heads from those who ought to know better."

Tears pricked Aleka's eyes. "I'm sorry, Auntie. I thought you wouldn't need me yesterday. Petra's the scout…"

From her post across the campground, Petra threw her a dirty look, but Auntie paid no mind.

"I've already dealt with Petra," she said. "Right now, I'm dealing with you. Get in the truck."

She held out her hands for Aleka's climbing gear, and Aleka handed it over. Dropping her eyes so she wouldn't have to face Auntie's furious glare, she started for the passenger truck. She hadn't taken two steps when Auntie called out.

"*My* truck, girl. Where I can keep an eye on you."

Miserably, Aleka changed direction and walked past the silent camp to Auntie's command vehicle. She tried to hold her head up as the guards nudged each other and the younger tunnel rats stared at her open-mouthed, but she felt like a prisoner trying to whistle on her way to face the firing squad.

She climbed into the front seat of Auntie's truck and stared through the windshield at the empty land. She didn't know how much time passed before Auntie squeezed into the cab beside her, holding a satchel full of Aleka's gear. The old woman patted the silver pistol she kept holstered at her side, and Aleka couldn't convince herself the gesture was just for show.

"I shouldn't have to tell you this, but I will," Auntie said, leaning close to bathe Aleka with her foul old-woman's breath. "If I have to chain you like a dog in its kennel to keep my camp safe, don't think I'll hesitate to put the collar around your neck myself."

She sat back and gave Araz the signal to start the engine. The beads at the end of her long gray braids clacked against each other as they jolted across the rocky land and out into the open desert. Aleka stared out the windshield, saying nothing. She thought of Mouse's flesh melting beneath the desert sun, and it seemed to her that the collar had already been tightened around her throat, the stake that held it hammered into the ground.

IT WAS NIGHTTIME when Auntie ordered a stop for food and bathroom breaks, which meant she must have decided to give the twins a rest from tending to the little ones' potty needs. Araz stuffed his belly then sprawled in the driver's seat, snoring with his mouth wide open. Without saying a word to Aleka, Auntie left the truck to order the others around as much as she could for their two-hour layover. She unclasped her holster before she disappeared, but only to hand it to Laman, who took her place outside the door.

"Need a bite to eat?" he asked Aleka.

"I'm fine, thanks."

"How about a walk? Stretch your legs."

"You my bodyguard?"

"Something like that."

He gave her a shy smile as he opened the door for her to climb out. Her legs were stiff from being squeezed between Araz and Auntie for the past fourteen hours, and she stumbled when she touched ground. He caught her until she'd regained her balance against the truck's open door, then ducked his eyes and let her go.

They strolled away from the main body of camp, onto the dunes. Now that she was here in the open air and starlight, she realized how much she'd needed to be free of the cramped cab, with its heavy exhaust smell and disgusting Araz belching and scratching his crotch, not to mention Auntie maintaining the stony silence only she could. Plus, out here the darkness would give her the privacy to ask the things she needed to.

43

"Nice night," Laman said, which was a pretty pathetic ice-breaker even for him. She kept silent until they were far enough outside the circle of trucks that Auntie was just one of many shadows clustered around the small campfire.

"Laman," she asked, "did you ever hear about anyone who knew of a way to get rid of the Skaldi instead of running from them?"

"Not really. Why?"

"I don't know. Just with what happened to … to Mouse, I thought…"

"That wasn't your fault," he said quickly. "Any one of us could have been keeping a better eye on him. That includes me and all the other grownups who let him run wild."

"I know," she said, though she didn't believe him, or even believe that he believed himself. "Still, if there was a way to fight back against them, so we wouldn't have to be on the move all the time…"

He let out a hard breath, ran a hand through his tangled hair. They were too far away for the campfire to illuminate his face, so she watched his profile against the star-filled sky.

"There have always been stories going around the camps," he said. "Mostly from hobos, I guess you'd call them. I wish I could put stock in what they say, but…"

"Auntie doesn't."

He shook his head. "Never has, not in all the time I've known her. She's chosen to stay on the go, and trust me, that's not her natural instinct. If it was just her, I'm convinced she'd stand and fight, but she has all the rest of you to think of."

He seated himself on the dune, probably to take the weight off his hip. She joined him, though her legs felt as jumpy as desert locusts.

"Asheh's been keeping a step ahead of the Skaldi for the better part of two decades, and there's no one more adept at it than her," he said. "She made a vow when they first appeared to protect her people, and she's stuck to it ever since."

"By running."

"Running is only the part you see," he said. "The other part is being careful, being smart. She was one of the first to recognize that the Native people knew this land better than anyone else, and that's why she made alliances with them. It helped that she had some Navajo in her, of course. Did you know her great-grandpa was one of the original code talkers?"

Aleka wasn't sure she remembered what the code talkers were, so she said nothing.

"Anyway," Laman continued, "even with her family history, she had to prove she wasn't just some member of the Wannabe tribe, so she devoted herself to learning their language, adopting their ways. She used to tell stories, long stories she must have learned from her folks years ago, and they'd go on so deep into the night and meander in so many directions no one could guess where they were headed or if they'd ever end. That's how she got her name from the Navajos. *Bizhí na'ashjé'íí.* Auntie Spider."

Aleka laughed. "I haven't heard anyone call her that in forever."

"The little ones still do."

"Does she still tell them stories?"

"Sometimes."

"Laman," she said, "can I ask you something?"

"Ask away."

"Is it true what Auntie says about my mom? That she died when I was born?"

He gave her a quick glance, but her eyes were quicker, and she saw the look of alarm in his.

"Why were you thinking about that?" he asked.

"I don't know," she said. "I just heard some people talking about her, and..."

"Tyris and Petra?"

"Yeah," she said, thankful to him for supplying the names. "And they said ... well, I mean, they weren't entirely sure, but they thought she might still be..."

Laman let out another huge sigh and settled back on his elbows against the dune. He lifted his head to the night breeze, licked his lips. In the light of the stars, she could see his eyes shining.

"Asheh would probably kill me if she knew I was telling you this," he said. "But it never sat right with me the way she decided to handle it. I was your age when I met your mother, and I know how I would've felt if someone had kept something like this from me."

"*You* knew her back then?"

"Sure." When he saw her staring, he laughed. "I haven't always been your auntie's gofer. All of us old people were young once, with lives of our own. Dreams, too. Then the Skaldi came, and all of that changed."

Aleka looked down at her hands. Laman was quiet for a long time before he spoke again.

"Anyway, your mom was like the rest of us, just a normal kid who got thrown into ... abnormal times. Seventeen years old when the Skaldi came, only a year older than me, but she adapted a lot quicker than I did. That was one of the things I admired about her. You know she took the name Diana, but do you know why?"

The sound of her mother's alias, so seldom spoken in camp, thrilled her as always. She'd never been able to convince anyone, and certainly not Auntie, to divulge her mother's real name.

"It was because she was a crack shot with the bow," Laman went on. "Diana the Huntress they called her, after a goddess from the old times. I never saw her shoot, but Asheh did, and she told me your mom once saved Aristodeme's life by shooting a guy right here..."

He bent over to demonstrate, then winced as if he'd moved his bad hip wrong. Aleka waited impatiently for him to continue. Some of the old folks referred to the twins, Kay and May, by their full names, Nausikaa and Aristodeme. Auntie had given them nicknames because she said their real names took too long to say, especially since you always had to say them both at the same time. Typical Auntie, but for once, Aleka didn't disagree.

"But anyway," Laman resumed once he'd found a comfortable position, "the point is, your mom put an arrow in a bad guy's leg when missing her target by even an inch would have meant hitting Aristodeme. She was that good a shot. And she knew she was, or she would have been terrified to even try."

Aleka tried to picture her, this fearless warrior she'd never laid eyes on, not in real life or photographs or even her dreams. She suspected that the things Laman was saying about her mother weren't totally true, that he'd built up his own picture of her in his mind since he'd last seen her, and now he couldn't remember if that picture was the actual her or partly his own. But at least he had something to base the picture on, something real.

"Is that how she died?" she asked. "Fighting?"

"I have no proof one way or another that she *did* die," he said. "All I know is that she went away. Right after you were born."

"Because she didn't want—"

"No," he said firmly. "She would have stayed with you forever if she could have. But she could no longer protect you, and—"

"Was she sick? Was she, I don't know, hurt somehow?"

"She was hurt plenty, but not the way you mean. She was in danger, and she knew you'd be in danger if you stayed with her, so—"

"Auntie took me from her."

"Asheh took nothing from your mother except what she was asked to take," he said. "That meant taking on a responsibility she's never wavered from in sixteen years: to keep you safe, to raise you like you were her own. To run for your life if that's what she needed to do, and to die fighting for you if it ever came to that."

Aleka looked away from his uncommonly fervent gaze. She knew now that he was making things up, not purposely in all likelihood, not in a way he would admit to himself, but in the way adults did when they wanted you to believe them. To believe *in* them. She had one more question, and she doubted he'd answer, but if he didn't, at least she'd know that, too.

"Laman," she said, "why is Auntie so afraid of the Skaldi finding *me*?"

Again, the alarm flared briefly in his eyes.

"I wouldn't say she's more afraid of that than of them finding anybody else," he said. "Except in the sense that she promised your mother she'd keep you safe."

She nodded, having expected no better. He shrugged uncomfortably, which either meant he was conscious of letting her down or he was back to being his old awkward self. Either way, she knew now what she had to do.

"I'm sorry, Laman," she said.

He cocked his head. "For what?"

"For this."

She chopped the side of her hand against his bad hip, right where she knew it would hurt the most. It was a self-defense move she'd learned from one of the Native kids, a boy named Javier who'd been the senior tunnel rat in Auntie's camp until six months ago, when he went off on his own. She'd never trusted herself to try the move before, but looking at Laman now, she could practically see the energy flowing beneath his skin, could tell where the nerves were and where the damage would be the worst. He cried out and doubled over, clutching the limb in pain, which put him in perfect position for her to do one of the other things Javier had taught her: striking him beneath the chin with a sharp upward blow. She was both surprised and relieved when he slumped over, brains rattled. Also the slightest bit guilty, but not enough to wish she hadn't done it to him.

She had no idea how long he would stay unconscious, how soon someone—Auntie or Araz, most likely—would come to check on them. She searched him hurriedly, taking the silver pistol from its holster and a red-handled Swiss army knife from his pants pocket. Unclipping the canteen from his belt and attaching it to her own, she rose to a crouch and dashed back to the command truck. Araz continued to snore; she reached inside the open passenger door and swiped the satchel from where it rested on the floor. Then she ran.

In no time, she'd left the camp behind and was out in the darkness of the desert night. She didn't slow, but sprinted for the row of mesas that stood out faintly as a deeper darkness against the starry sky. If she could make it there before anyone knew she was gone, she could lose herself in a wilderness where no truck could follow her and no search party on foot could track her down. She was confident in her ability to manage the mesas by hand, but the satchel containing her confiscated rope and climbing gear might be useful down the road. Though she preferred not to think about this, she knew that the knife and pistol could be useful too.

The mesas stood in front of her before she had time to realize she wasn't even winded from the run. She had the sensation that she'd been moving much faster than normal, that the darkness was less of an impediment to her feet and eyes than it should have been. She slipped the satchel onto her shoulders and climbed, and as she rose into the night, she thought about where she'd been only a day ago, laid out on her back with the prospect of death a heartbeat away. She'd escaped that fate, and now that she'd been given a second chance, she refused to look back. She knew she could never atone for what had happened to Mouse. She doubted she could make amends to Laman either, who Auntie would absolutely pulverize for letting her get away, and with her prize pistol no less. Her mother might be gone, but maybe, if she could find the man from the tunnels, the daughter of Diana the Huntress could be the one to ensure that what had happened to Mouse never had to happen to anyone again.

She stood at the top of the mesa and looked at the solitary pinpoint of fire at least a mile away. Her heart skipped as headlights came on, and though she knew they couldn't see her

50

from this distance, she ducked and started down the far side of the hill. As she descended, finding her way by the feel of the smooth-rough rock beneath her hands, she thought about what Laman had said, and it seemed to her that she could vaguely remember the stories Auntie used to tell when she was a little girl—stories of the People and the land, of Coyote the trickster, how he got yellow eyes from the gum of a piñon tree and how he tried to steal the moon but was foiled, which is why coyotes howl at the moon all night long. There was another story about a mother who died and whose skeleton came back to haunt her children, but they wouldn't let her in and ran away when she broke down the door. And there was one she was sure Auntie had told many times, about Grandmother Spider who spun the world with her web and saved the People from drowning by weaving a bridge they could stand on while the floodwaters rushed past. The stories came back to her in fragments, along with images of Auntie's face lit by the campfire, her hands gesturing animatedly as if she were weaving the web she was telling about. And then an image appeared that Aleka hadn't remembered until it popped into her head right now: Auntie walking her back to the tent they'd once shared, holding her hand, settling her into her sleeping bag and crooning a lullaby in a language Aleka didn't know. As her boots hit the soft sand and she loped deeper into the measureless night, she wondered where that woman had gone. And where that little girl had gone, too.

Chapter 4

Daybreak found her miles from Auntie's camp, deep in the desert where boundaries blended into delusion.

Last night, once she was far enough from camp for the immediate threat of capture to recede, the first thing she'd done was cut back toward the river that angled northwest through the desert. She took a long drink, filled Laman's canteen, and dug in the satchel, discovering not only her climbing gear but—hallelujah—a cloth-wrapped packet of pemmican bars. She was surprised at how little her belly was grumbling after more than a day without a full meal, but she'd learned this much from Auntie: out in the desert, you didn't take chances. Soon enough, she'd be thankful for whatever she could scrounge from the unforgiving land, and she didn't want to be half dead from hunger and dehydration when it came to that point.

The river was where Auntie would begin the hunt for her, so she stayed by its bank only long enough for another drink before departing and heading south. At roughly fifteen miles an hour driving across dangerous terrain, the trucks would have covered as much as two hundred miles from their last semi-permanent camp, which meant a minimum of a week to return to the area on foot. Taking into account exhaustion, sandstorms, hunting for food and veering off course to replenish her water supply, not to mention hiding from Skaldi if any happened to show up, better make it closer to two. Aesir would be on the move as well, but he hadn't said in which direction; would he stick close to the area where she'd met him, or would he flee like Auntie had, vanishing into the open desert with no signs to tell her where he was? When she thought about it that way, the near impossibility of what she'd risked Auntie's undying wrath to achieve struck her like her own blow to Laman's skull.

But then she calmed herself, counting the assets she had in her favor. Aesir was an old man; he wouldn't move nearly as fast as she did. If the energy juice he'd given her lasted even a few more days, she'd make up far more lost ground than her rough calculation had allowed. Auntie was traveling by truck, she by foot; she'd see the dust plumes of the caravan from miles away, long before anyone could spot her even with binoculars. Petra might be eager to get back in Auntie's good graces by capturing the fugitive, but it was just as likely she'd be surly and uncooperative, leading Auntie on a wild goose chase to pay her back. What did Petra care about pleasing the camp leader? Unless the hunt kept her so busy she couldn't spend her nights with Tyris, she'd be just as happy to let Auntie's meddlesome goddaughter go.

And there was one more thing that made Aleka believe she'd find what she was looking for before anyone found her. It wasn't only the feeling of invincibility that lingered from the day before, giving her confidence that even the supernaturally gifted scout couldn't track her down. It was the last words Aesir had spoken to her, words that now felt like a snippet of prophecy: *Wherever you roam, may you find the place your heart most desires.* Crazy as it seemed, something—if not her heart, then something close—told her that he was the one who held the key to that place, and that she was meant to find him, no matter what.

With that thought in mind, she picked up her pace, moving at an easy jog while the sun was low on the horizon.

The desert spooled past. Sand, cacti, red mesas in the distance that were the only way to tell she wasn't running in place. The heat rose around her before the sun was fully up, and she tied her hair back with a bandana, using a second strip of cloth to shield her face. No wind relieved the stifling air, but Aleka kept her eyes fixed on the flat land ahead, knowing how quickly sandstorms could come up out of nowhere. The other risk—aside from Skaldi—was quicksand, loose and deep enough to sink a truck to the axle as had happened a couple of years ago. But such pockets were rare, and she trusted her instincts to guide her around hidden traps. The thought passed through her mind that sinkholes might be clues to catacombs such as the one where she'd met Aesir, but until she got closer to the place where she'd last seen him, there was no point in checking.

What, she wondered, was he doing now that he'd been driven from his lair? What would he and his army be searching for? She'd overheard Auntie talking to Laman once about missile silos left over from the wars, and she'd gathered from that conversation that Auntie wanted to stay as far away from them as possible. The old woman's exact words, which had struck Aleka as strange even at the time, had been, "Let's not go through that again." So maybe there were secret weapons lying in wait beneath their feet, and maybe that was what Aesir was trying to track down.

And then use those weapons to fight the Skaldi?

It didn't make much sense, but she refused to let herself dwell on it. The man obviously knew what he was doing; he'd cured her of paralysis with a concoction of his own making, and he'd been astute enough to pick up signs of Skaldi that had eluded her. He'd been right about her mother, too; Laman had confirmed that Auntie was lying about her death, which surely meant she was lying about other things as well. It hadn't escaped Aleka's notice that Laman had never said he was present when her mom gave birth to her—but Aesir had, so it sounded like he must have known her even better than Laman did. Could it be that he'd been closer to her than he admitted—that he'd been not only a friend but something more? Who else would be there on the day of her birth if not...

She tried to keep herself from getting carried away. She knew even less about her father than she did about her mom; no one in camp, Auntie included, would so much as say his name. She'd always figured he must have been a drifter, someone who'd gotten her mom pregnant then moved on, possibly without his lover learning who he was. The thought of what that made *her*—a mistake, a castoff, a reject—had gnawed at Aleka's gut for as long as she could remember. But if what Laman said was true, if there was more to the story than Auntie had told her, then maybe it was no accident that Aesir had appeared at just this moment. Maybe he was the one who knew the whole truth everyone else was unwilling or unable to reveal—the truth not only about her mother, but about herself. If so, then it was like he'd said: whatever she might have to face as a member of his army couldn't be any worse than the alternative.

So she ran on through the desert, shrugging off the heat, resisting the lure of her half-full canteen as long as possible.

She couldn't prevent her eyes from nervously roaming the empty land, but she reassured herself that she'd find a way to hide if the roar of engines should meet her ears or spirals of dust should appear over the next dune. She would meet up with Aesir, tell him what she'd decided, study him carefully for signs of what he knew. When the time came, she'd ask. And if they found what he was looking for, what *she* was looking for, she'd never have to run or hide again.

THE FOOD BARS lasted six days at a strict rationing of one bar per twenty-four hours. The canteen ran dry well before nightfall each day, but she pushed herself through the dizziness and nausea until dusk descended and she deemed it safe to head to the river. Even so, she felt like a mule deer creeping to the riverbank with night-vision eyes and super-sensitive ears, then scampering away into the dark. She slept in caves at the foot of mesas or in deep dells in the sand, but exhausted as she was, she couldn't make it through a single night without jerking awake at some sound, or none at all.

Aesir's power drink had abandoned her at first light on day three. She'd felt its boost ebbing the evening before, and she'd tried to increase her pace to eke out a few extra miles before it was gone entirely, but the predictable result of her effort was that she was completely spent when she woke the following day. Her muscles ached from overuse, her skin felt feverish, and there was a sharp pain behind her eyes that throbbed with the beat of her heart. The coming of the sun on that third day brought the bitter knowledge that whatever advantage she'd gained in the first two days would be more than canceled by the weary pace she'd be forced to set from now on.

Still she struggled ahead, walking most of the time, breaking into a jog whenever she could. On day four, she tore the
cloth containing the pemmican bars into strips and shoved
them into the soles of her boots to protect her feet, but that
didn't do much to stop the blisters from growing, spreading,
and bursting. Each day after that passed in a timeless blur of
heat and dust and dejection, with her facecloth seeming more
like a gag than a shield and her body slowly baking under the
merciless sun. She took tiny sips from the canteen as often as
possible, hoping to make it last until nightfall, and nibbled the
few cactus flowers she found in a desperate attempt to stave
off her gnawing hunger. Her eyes were trained on the horizon
for signs of pursuit, even though her brain was too fuzzy to
picture clearly what she was looking for and her limbs felt too
weak to react quickly in case of an Auntie sighting. When she
crawled into whatever hole she could find for the night's sleep,
she fell into a doze almost immediately, retaining consciousness only long enough to remove her boots to give her maimed
feet a chance to heal. All the same, her slumber was too broken
by fever and nightmares to call it sleep; it seemed only the slen-
derest spider's thread stretching from the day before to the
next, and waking felt less like starting anew than resuming a
round of torment that had never ceased.

On the seventh morning, she woke unable to remember
the day before at all. She sat, mechanically squeezed her feet
into the boots, and raked the last few crumbs from Auntie's
satchel into her mouth, chewing without tasting. The terrible
hunger in her gut was no longer an emptiness but a physical
presence, an extra self that seemed on the verge of replacing
the real her with its insatiable demands. Now that her last prepared meal was gone, she'd be forced to subsist on cactus fruit

from here on out, unless she was lucky enough to find a termite mound or an unwary scorpion. She didn't trust herself with Auntie's gun to hunt one of the land's larger animals, and she had nothing to make fire with even if she found a freshly dead carcass. Nor did she feel strong enough to fend off desert scavengers like coyotes or vultures, much less Skaldi; the sole defense she'd possessed when she started out, her speed and climbing ability, had deserted her as well.

She tied her laces with trembling fingers and stood, the headache returning with the stabbing rays of dawn light. On her very first step, she stumbled on feet so callused they couldn't feel the ground beneath them. The sand rushed up to meet her, and her brain told her to throw her hands out, but it was her face that broke the fall. Spitting sand from her mouth, she rolled onto her side and tried to push herself to her feet, only to fall again. Her dreams of a week ago came back to mock her with shrill voices, and every word of reproof seemed to emerge from Auntie's mouth.

Thoughtless child. Selfish, short-sighted, irresponsible. You run and hide when your people need you most.

"I'm sorry, Auntie," she whispered, her tongue too parched and swollen to produce a sound her ears could hear. "I only wanted to make things better."

Her arms wobbled as she got them under her and pushed with all her strength. It wasn't enough, and she would have sloughed to the sand like a Skaldi's shed skin if something hadn't caught her arm and pulled her into an embrace.

Her eyes rose. A vision wobbled and blurred as if it were swimming in desert heat. Then it came into sharp focus, and she gasped when she saw who it was.

"Auntie?" she croaked. "How——?"

58

"There, there, child," the old woman said. "This is no place for you."

"But I—you—"

"We've been searching for you since you left us," Auntie said. "Petra was hot on your trail, but every time she assured us you were close, you gave us the slip." She shook her head, regarding Aleka almost fondly. "You brave, foolish girl."

An arm encircled Aleka's waist, and she leaned against the solid figure of her godmother, whose black jacket felt scratchy against her cheek. With her much-needed assistance, Aleka took another step, and saw them all: Petra, Tyris, the twins, Araz, Sonja, the guards, the other adults, the little ones. Even Laman. Despite the feel of Auntie's strong arm, she was sure it was a mirage, a hallucination, until Laman approached and took the satchel from her hands. Reaching inside, he withdrew the pistol and knife. His cockeyed grin seemed even more bashful than usual as he handed the pistol to its owner and stashed the knife in his pocket.

"That was one heck of a trick you pulled on me," he said. "You'll have to show me how it's done when you're back to yourself again."

Aleka would have cried, but she had no fluid left in her eyes. All she could think of was dropping into the shade of one of the trucks, filling her belly with food and water, and sleeping away an eternity beyond which the past six days would seem nothing but a distant dream. Everything she'd hoped for— finding Aesir, defeating the Skaldi, reuniting with her mom— already felt like a child's fantasy, no more real than Auntie Spider's stories of ghosts and gods and monsters.

Auntie walked her from her nighttime shelter into the open desert. Aleka's vision swam so badly she thought the shadows on the ground were following after her, slinking along contours in the dunes like miniature rivers. At the edge of a rock formation, they stopped, and Aleka looked out over the broad expanse of sun-bleached sand.

"Where are the trucks?" she asked.

"The trucks?" Auntie echoed.

"The trucks. How did you—?"

"There are no trucks," Auntie said. "Just as there are no riders. They have met their doom, and you are the one who abandoned them."

Aleka looked at the old woman's face in time to see it flow like water, turning the dark eyes and deep lines into a mass of squirming blackness. A hole opened where Auntie's mouth had been, and Aleka felt herself being drawn toward it, her body too weak and her mind too numb to resist. It widened until it seemed to blot out the whole world, an inky nebula that emitted the stench of rotting corpses. She tried to pull free, but her hands stuck in the tarry substance that had taken her godmother's place.

Then the blackness fell away, the hole that had formed out of Auntie's mouth emitting a shriek of anger or pain. Aleka looked around wildly as the faces she'd known all her life melted and slid like oil, their bodies pooling on the ground in a single mass. Black tongues burst from the puddle and reached out for her, but when they touched her, they recoiled as if they'd been burned, the whole mass shuddering like a pool of water agitated by a strong wind. Auntie was gone, conjoined with the general blackness, and the weapons Laman had taken lay gleaming on the sand as the entire mass began a slow yet urgent retreat, appendages emerging from its leading edge to drag it across the ground.

Aleka screamed and fell when hands touched her. Darkness flooded her eyes, and she felt consciousness slipping away as surely as her sanity. A voice spoke in her ear, familiar and soothing.

"Drink," it said.

Something was pressed to her lips. Her mouth filled with liquid, and though its taste was as vile as she remembered, she gulped it down greedily, her throat not even consulting her mind as it drew the life-saving fluid into her stomach. Her vision cleared to see the crouched shape of Aesir, his eyes glittering like black coals behind his mask.

She sat up, and found that he wasn't alone. A group of ten or twelve teens stood behind him, their heads swaddled in wrappings but their faces uncovered. Most of them were unfamiliar, but she recognized two former members of Auntie's camp: a very quiet Mexican girl named Dolores who everyone called Didi, and the master of self-defense himself, Javier. He alone wore no head-wrapping, and his hair, much longer than the last time she saw him, was held back by a black and red patterned headband. He reached for Aleka's hand, and though she hesitated to touch him after what had happened to Auntie, his grip was firm as he pulled her to her feet.

She stood leaning against him for an unsteady moment. Then the elixir kicked in, warmth and strength flowing through her limbs. She pushed him away more roughly than she'd meant to, and Aesir took Javier's place by her side.

"Walk with me," the old man said.

He led her in the direction the black being had fled. Aleka scanned the desert, but the creature had vanished, leaving the weapons behind. Moving at its former pace, it couldn't have disappeared so quickly unless it had sunk into the sand.

61

"What was it?" she asked.

"The thing I feared most," he said. "The Skaldi have gained access to the birthing agent. The organism is small and slow at present, but as it amasses energy from those it consumes, it will grow strong, and in time, it will cover the land in darkness."

"But then Auntie..." Aleka reeled, nearly losing her balance. "Everyone in the colony is..."

"They are gone," Aesir said. "The creature must have infiltrated your camp at its previous place of refuge and traveled with it in the form of one or more of its members. Do not blame yourself for leaving them when you did. Had you remained, the creature would have wreaked destruction on them nonetheless, until only you were left."

Aleka crumpled to her knees and bowed her head, but the tears wouldn't fall. Auntie gone, and Laman, and Tyris and Petra, and the twins, and all the children... It seemed impossible that she'd been with them less than a week ago, that she'd lived with them all her life. And the last time she'd seen any of them, the last time she ever would, had been filled with such anger and grief. She raised her head to gaze out over the waste, and it seemed to her it had never looked as blank and empty as it did now.

Aesir's voice came to her out of that emptiness. "We must act with all haste, before the Skaldi achieve their full power. The work for which I have chosen you cannot delay a moment longer."

He returned to the others. Aleka stared at Auntie's pistol and Laman's knife, but at the thought of touching them, she shuddered violently and left them where they lay. All of the teens avoided her eyes except Javier, who threw her a look of sympathy before busying himself with preparing a morning meal. Her stomach felt indifferent to the prospect of food, and she took no joy in the discovery that the blisters that had plagued her for the past four days were gone as if they'd never existed. She couldn't deny that her body felt as strong as it ever had, but her heart was lost to her.

"How did you find me?" she asked Aesir.

"I have tracked you since you left my home," he said. "With this."

He removed a small, handheld device from his robe. A red light flashed in its center. She might have been angry at him, but she felt as if she'd left all her anger behind in the deadly pool that had swallowed her past.

"I was not willing to let you go so easily," he explained. "I believed that, in time, you might reconsider your decision. And as you see, I was right."

"Where'd you put the tracker?"

"It is within you," he said. "You took it into your body when you drank of the elixir."

She accepted this too. What did it matter?

"I have kept much from you," Aesir said, "but I do not beg your pardon. My plans required decisive action, and I could not afford to spend time on persuasion. You are far more important to those plans than you dream, Aleka. The test of which I spoke has been conducted, and it has proved successful."

"The test?" she asked dully.

Behind the mask, she could tell that he smiled.

"When the organism touched you, it was overwhelmed," he said. "You are the one I have been searching for. The one who will help me destroy the Skaldi and reclaim the land."

With that, he left her, and she stared at his black robes until they were lost in the shadows beneath the dunes.

Chapter 5

They ate a quick meal and were on the road before the whole of the sun hung above the horizon.

The food consisted of bread mixed with some kind of meat and fried up in an iron skillet over the fire. Javier offered her a plateful, but she refused. He shrugged and turned to his own meal, his movements as relaxed and fluid as they'd been when he taught her how to knock someone out. She looked away, not wanting to be reminded that the last thing she'd done as a member of Auntie's camp was attack a person who was trying to be nice to her and leave him along with all the others to their deaths.

Plus, she wasn't hungry. As it had the first time, Aesir's drink filled her up, giving her all the energy she needed for the run ahead.

And they did run. She discovered immediately how Aesir had caught up with her so quickly: the ragtag group of teens who constituted his army must have consumed the same elixir she had, and they moved effortlessly across the sand. Old and small as he was, Aesir could never have kept up, so he rode piggyback first on Javier, then, after a few miles, on another of his crew. Crouched there on the runners' backs in his swirling black robe, he looked particularly puny, like one of the ancient, blistered dolls the little kids used to carry. But no one, not even Javier, cracked a smile.

Aleka didn't ask where they were going, didn't care. She noted that they were heading north, but that made no difference to her. She only hoped the new colony she'd joined didn't encounter her old colony's trucks along the way, their supplies scattered and their cargo areas emptied of human bodies.

They ran until noon, not slowing, not talking. No one broke a sweat or struggled for breath, not even when it came turn for Didi, the smallest of the teens, to bear Aesir on her back. When they weren't carrying him, everyone carried something else, whether it was rucksacks or rolled tents or other camping supplies, but there were no complaints from the runners. No one even looked askance at Aleka, who alone among the troop carried nothing except her guilt.

That changed after they finished their midday meal, which Javier once again offered to Aleka and she once again refused with a curt shake of her head. This time, when they got ready to run, Aesir approached her first of all. He said nothing, but she lowered herself to a runner's crouch and allowed him to climb aboard her back. When she stood, she discovered that he was even lighter than she'd imagined, as if he truly were a plastic doll filled with nothing but air and a few handfuls of sand.

They started off, Javier in the lead. Aleka had noticed that the runner who was responsible for Aesir tended to stay several paces to the rear of the pack, so she adjusted her speed and let the others stream past her. When they'd opened a space of ten or fifteen feet ahead of her, she felt Aesir tighten his grip on her shoulders as if to brake her further. It should have made her uneasy to be in such close contact with this strange man, but that part of her must have been dead too, because she obeyed his command without a word.

"You wish to know more of my plans," he said quietly once her pace suited him. "It is right that you should know them now, particularly since they have changed since the events of this morning."

He seemed to expect some kind of response, but all she could muster the energy to do was shrug. That must have been enough for him.

"The despoilers have assembled their forces in a city to the north," he said. "It lies near the shores of what was once a great lake, though the waters have since run low. From this final bastion, they have sent out emissaries to seek the source of their resurrection, and as we now know, they have discovered it and summoned it to their aid."

"Why do they need this stuff so bad right now?" she found herself asking.

"The Skaldi have grown weak," he answered, "as must any organism that depletes its sole food source. Years ago, in the early days of their coming, they must have believed themselves to be gods, immune to the laws of time and necessity that bind all other beings. Or, perhaps, they simply lacked the foresight to imagine their fate should their numbers grow too many and their prey dwindle to near nothing. But then, can any organism truly conceive its end without falling into despair?"

Aleka was in no mood for philosophy, so she remained silent, focusing on the empty land as it flashed by, the equally silent pack of runners just ahead.

"In course of time, some among the creatures' ranks have grown wise, or as wise as their nature allows," Aesir continued after a moment. "They have come to understand what awaits them should they continue indefinitely as they have done for the past sixteen years. The oldest among them, it may be, have grown immeasurably weary, and this is why they now seek a new path."

"Weary?" Aleka said with an involuntary laugh. "When they get tired, they just take another body and move on."

"Ah, but think of the burden such a life entails," Aesir said. "Never to know one's true form, always to rely on the life-force of another to retain a semblance of one's own. The Skaldi exhaust the bodies they consume within weeks or even days, which means that those who remain from the earliest times have run through a course of hundreds of lives, shedding each one just before it failed, acquiring another shell to cover their emptiness despite the knowledge that it, too, would desert them long before it felt truly their own. Such an existence barely merits the name, and it must be one of utter wretched-ness."

"You sound like you feel sorry for them."

Aesir shifted his hold as if in response to the anger in her voice. "Not sorry, Aleka. Sympathetic."

"What's the difference?"

"To sympathize with one's enemy is to know its mind," he answered. "To plumb its deepest desires, and in so doing to anticipate its acts. I have devoted long years to studying the despoilers, ever since I lost my home and all that mattered to me. I know what it is they want, and so I know what must be done to prevent them from obtaining it."

"But you said they already had."

"I said that they have gained access to the birthing agent," he replied. "But I said as well that the organism is weak as of yet, and that it will require time to grow strong. If we move with all speed, if we arrive at the Skaldi fortress ahead of this new being from which they hope to secure their rebirth, we may yet be able to thwart their plans."

"All speed," she repeated, another unintentional laugh leaving her lips. "Which is why we keep stopping to refuel?"

"The others cannot run as you do," Aesir said in an even quieter voice than was usual for him. "They require sustenance of another kind, while you are powered by the elixir alone."

He fell silent. Aleka wished she could stop herself from asking, but within a few strides, the words burst from her mouth. "What's so different about me?"

"Everything," he said. "Strong as the elixir has made my company, none of them could have withstood the organism that absorbed the members of your camp. And yet, when it attacked you, it was thwarted—rebuffed by a power so great it chose to leave other living beings behind rather than risk further damage. You are one of a kind, Aleka, and within you lies the key to our salvation."

"Bullshit," she said.

For the first time since she'd met him, a sound left his mouth that might have been a laugh. "You doubt the power you have felt in your own blood? My elixir fortifies the cells of the human body, enabling any who partake of it to endure injury, hunger, and fatigue. In you, however, the serum has met a cellular structure uniquely designed to maximize its effects."

"Stop talking in riddles," Aleka said in a voice that grated to her own ears. "Just tell me what's so different about me."

"You are part-Skaldi."

She stumbled as if the power of the man's elixir had deserted her. When the momentary spell passed, she felt her body trembling not with weakness but with a whirl of feelings she could barely tell from each other: anger, disbelief, fear. She stopped, letting the others pull ahead, and turned to look at the man who crouched on her back. From this close, his eyes gazed at her so intently they seemed to pierce her soul.

"That's impossible," she said.

"If you knew your history, you would know it to be the truth," he answered calmly. "Yet all you need do is search your own heart to know that it is the *only* truth, the one you have been seeking all your life. It is why you have always felt restless and isolated, as if you did not belong among those who took you in as their own. It is why you have never known your mother, and why you were taken from her only days after you were born. It is the reason your past has been kept from you, as well as your present and future—the reason the Indian watches you so closely, for she fears not only what you are, but what you may yet become. It is the one truth about you that can never be changed, and that will rule your destiny to the end of your days."

"My mother," she said. "Are you telling me she was Skaldi?"

"Not your mother," he said. "Your father. A product of the early Skaldi experiments, a man once human but infused with the creatures' genes. From their union you were born, a child equally of the human and Skaldi races."

He slid from her back just as her knees gave out and she sank to the ground. Her stomach felt unbearably tight, as if she were about to disgorge the drink that Aesir had given her this morning. Everything inside her rebelled against the thought that she was linked to the fiend that had turned Mouse into a scrap of wrinkled skin, the creatures that had reduced her people to black tar slithering across the endless desert. Even worse

70

was the voice that whispered in her ear that Aesir was right: that those people had never been *her* people, that Auntie had stolen her from her mother to prevent her from learning the truth of who she was. The truth that she was half-monster, and that her life from now until the end of time was doomed to be every bit as wretched as theirs.

She looked up at Aesir as he stood there in his wind-whipped cloak, arms folded across his chest. The others had run so far ahead that they were nothing but black specks against the desert glare. Aesir seemed unconcerned about their departure, and his dark eyes showed neither cruelty nor mercy when Aleka rose to face him.

"Now you know," he said. "This is why the Skaldi cannot defeat you, and why I need you in order to carry my plan into effect. The power that enables them to consume living hosts is one of energy absorption, but you possess the same power, strengthened by the drink I have given you. When they seek to assimilate the cells of your body, they are countered by a force every bit as deadly as their own—an outburst of cellular energy akin to fire. It has panicked them to discover one of their own lineage who can stand against them, an adversary who can breach their fortress and end the scourge they have visited upon the land."

"A weapon," Aleka said. "That's what you want me for. That's what I am to you."

"That is what the human race needs you to be," he said. "Denying what you are will not alter your fate, though it will ensure the destruction of all who remain."

He turned from her and raised a hand. The others halted, their silhouettes just barely visible at the crest of a distant dune. Aesir threw her one last look devoid of pity or understanding

71

before he started toward them, his cloak whipping as he labored across the waste. She didn't move while he joined his troops, didn't move while one of them—they were much too far away to tell who—bent to let him clamber aboard their back. She watched as the runners started up again, watched until they dropped below the level of the dune and were lost to sight.

Did he worry that she would head back the way she'd come, leaving him and his legions to face the Skaldi on their own while she searched for the ruins of her camp? Did he fear that she would lose herself in the desert, letting her body be picked to pieces by fire ants or burned to a crisp by the sun? Maybe she would lie down on the sand to test the truth of his words—wait for some random Skaldi to show itself and see if it would burst into flame at her touch. At least then she could die sure in the knowledge of who she was, what she was.

She waited for hours, squinting in the direction where they'd vanished, until the sun started its descent and she was sure he wasn't coming back for her. Then she rose, composed her face, and followed their tracks in the dunes, sand stinging her eyes as she covered ground with greater speed than she'd ever known.

Chapter 6

She woke before sunrise with an ache in her gut as deep as the sand and as wide as the desert waste.

She looked around, wondering how she'd gotten here, wrapped in a blanket in the hollow of a hill. She remembered running after Aesir and his crew, scanning the land but finding no trace of them, losing the trail of their footprints as dusk descended but continuing blindly into a clouded night devoid of stars. The elixir that had buoyed her for three full days the first time she'd tasted it had petered out long before she threw herself headlong onto the sand, unable to take another step. Her legs were shaking, her lungs burning, but those were minor annoyances next to the gnawing hunger inside her, an imperishable emptiness as if she'd never tasted a morsel of food in her entire life. She'd lain in the dark hugging her stomach, trying to puke up Aesir's formula, but nothing would come. At last, she must have fallen into a sleep without dreams, without memory, a sleep that might have lasted for weeks if the hunger that consumed her was any indication.

Aleka stood on shaking legs. When she did, she saw shadowy shapes bundled at the base of the hill and recognized the members of Aesir's army, though their leader's small form and swirling robes were nowhere to be seen. Maybe they'd found her last night and set up camp while she slept; maybe she'd crawled to this spot in a delirious state. Or maybe everything she thought she remembered—her colony gone, her life turned to something she no longer recognized—was a terrible nightmare, and she was still caught in its grip.

Then a distinct memory from last night came to her, a flash of black robes and a warm rush down her bone-dry throat as she'd taken another sip from Aesir's flask. Whatever else might be true, she knew that was no dream; she could still taste the fluid on her tongue, still recall how wonderfully it had filled her empty body. But now its power was gone, and she felt as weak as a desert shadow that would be scattered like dust when the sun rose above the dunes.

She stumbled to where the others lay, tore open one of their backpacks and rummaged inside. No sooner did the smell of smoked deer meat penetrate her senses than she doubled over and threw up, a thin stream of bile that burned her throat but did nothing to relieve the sickness in her gut. She wiped her chin with the back of her hand and tried to empty her mind of the thoughts that came to her: tearing off pieces of meat with her teeth, chewing the sticky, salty stuff, swallowing it down. All of these familiar motions struck her as grotesque, the kind of things that wild animals did. They couldn't satisfy her hunger; there was only one thing that could, and there was only one person who could supply it. If he didn't show up soon, she didn't know what she'd do.

She glanced up the hill and saw a figure in dark robes seated at the crest. Her heart beating in her throat, she left the others and trudged in ankle-deep sand to where he waited.

When she reached the top, she found that the figure wasn't the one she sought. It was Javier, wrapped in a cloak that looked like Aesir's from a distance but that she now saw was a lighter shade than his, more brown than black. He sat Indian-style, his head tilted upward and his eyes closed in the pose of meditation she'd seen Aesir adopt in the tunnels. On his lap, he held a large sheet of paper like the mostly useless maps Laman and Auntie used to pore over. The only difference was that Javier's sheet was completely blank, a map of the empty land that stretched out before them.

At the sound of her approach, he opened his eyes. He didn't seem fazed to see her, and she wondered if Aesir had told the others what she was.

"I'm trying to catch the sunrise," he said.

She tried not to show her annoyance at finding him instead of the man with the flask. "What for?"

He didn't answer, but reached into a pocket of his robe and took out a small leather case with a mostly functional zipper. When he opened it, she saw a collection of black and gray sticks like the burnt remains of a campfire, all of them arranged in a neat row from lightest to darkest. His hand hovered over the row before selecting one in the middle range, then he zipped the case closed and tucked it into his robe. He held the stick lightly over the paper and returned his attention to the horizon where the sun would soon rise.

"You're drawing a picture?" Aleka asked.

He nodded.

"Of what?"

"The land," he said. "I got a good look at it before we camped last night, and I thought this would be the best place to capture it."

She followed his eyes, but saw nothing worth taking the time to capture. "What do you want to do that for?"

"No reason," he said. "It's just something I do."

She laughed, not very kindly. "Do you know where Aesir is?"

"He's around," he said. "But you won't see him until sunrise. Might as well wait with me."

With the hand that wasn't holding the charcoal, he patted the ground beside him. She looked over her shoulder, hoping to catch sight of the camp leader, but all she saw were the sleeping bodies of his runners. Taking a deep breath to ease her jitters, she sat. It wouldn't be long before the sun rose. She could wait here for a few minutes until Aesir appeared with his magic flask.

Javier had closed his eyes again and sat motionless, his hand poised over the paper, his breath coming easily. Minutes passed in silence, adding to Aleka's edginess. "When did you start drawing?" she asked.

"I've been doing it all my life," he said, eyes still closed. "Except there wasn't much time for it in Auntie's camp, so I put it aside."

He volunteered no more information, and Aleka couldn't think of anything else to say—nothing he wouldn't consider completely rude, anyway. Drawing pictures while running for your life from Skaldi? What was the point of that? At least the self-defense lessons had come in handy. When the minutes stretched on without the sun making an appearance and the hunger in her body began to feel like a second self trying to eat its way out of her skin, she decided to forego politeness. "Aesir lets you waste your time with this? He never told you where we're headed?"

"He told us."

"And I suppose he told you about me, too?"

"Only that you're important to the mission."

"You want to know why?"

He shrugged. "Your call."

His nonchalance infuriated her, and she felt like grabbing the paper from his hands and tearing it to pieces. She would have done it too, except her hands shook too badly to trust them.

"He told me that I'm one of them," she said. "That I'm half-Skaldi. You sure you want me sitting right beside you while you draw your pretty picture?"

He opened his eyes, but not to look at her. Instead, his gaze was fixed straight ahead, his body leaning forward as his hand dropped to the paper. Aleka flushed with anger and was about to say something to him when the first rays of the sun shot out from behind the distant horizon.

At the appearance of the light, Javier's hand began to move in broad, sure strokes across the page. He never looked down, only at the vacant land before him, but as Aleka watched, the paper filled with swaths of pigment, from light gray to almost black. It seemed like nothing at first, a child's scrawl in the dust, and another cruel laugh found its way to her lips. Then, all at once, she saw the pattern, the order, the landscape emerging under his hand. When she looked up from the page to the empty waste in front of her, she was shocked to see that it *wasn't* empty, that it had shape and contour and dark and light, just like the picture in Javier's lap. It was as if he wasn't drawing what he saw but the reverse—as if his drawing had created what was there, or at least, she'd never seen what was there until his drawing showed it to her.

When he was done, he set the almost-spent charcoal stick down and rested the drawing in his lap. His eyes closed; she was surprised to see that his face was sweating though the day wasn't yet warm. She was even more surprised when he lifted the drawing with charcoal-smudged fingers and released it, letting the wind carry it out over the land it so perfectly mirrored.

"Why—?" she asked, and felt her throat rasp as if it were filled with sand.

He opened his eyes and looked at her. "No place to keep it. At least, not where it wouldn't get ruined. I figure it's best to return it to where it came from." He tilted his head toward the campsite. "Looks like Aesir's up. Better get to him before anyone else does."

She stood unsteadily and walked down the hill toward the small robed figure. Her mouth was dry, her heart pounding; she felt that she was floating above the earth, twisting in the air like Javier's drawing. His final words made her wonder if he knew how badly she was craving the elixir, and that thought filled her with shame. But she could almost taste the fluid on her tongue, and nothing else mattered more than that. She approached Aesir, who said not a word as he reached inside his robe and unstoppered his flask.

THEY RAN THE entire length of the day, and this time, none of the others carried Aesir for a single minute. Aleka had no sooner quaffed the elixir and felt the energy flow through her starved limbs than she crouched to receive her passenger, then rose ready to obey his command. Once the others had eaten a quick bite and packed their bags, she sprinted up the hill and out into the desert, moving at a pace much faster than anyone on Aesir's team could match.

She could no longer lie to herself about what was happening to her, what had already happened. She'd known people in Auntie's camp who'd indulged day after day in mescaline or opium; she'd seen them when they were on a high, gibbering fervidly about the nonsense from their hallucinations. Auntie hadn't stood for anyone in that condition staying in her camp for long; they either cleaned themselves up, or she sent them on their way. With very few exceptions, heading off alone was the choice they made.

So she knew what Aesir's drink had done to her. She knew because, though she'd downed it only a few times, she felt utterly empty without it, wracked by hunger that seemed to come not from her stomach but from her entire body. None of the other runners seemed to need the stuff the way she did, which must have meant the elixir wasn't addictive to fully human beings; so far as she'd observed, they got by exclusively on food and water, the mere sight of which made her queasy. In her case, she knew she'd lost her will in the matter when, on the second consecutive day under the drug's influence, she had to stop twice after the morning dose to swallow another sip from Aesir's flask, her legs shaking too badly each time to continue without it. If Auntie had been able to see her, a junkie careening through the desert with her dealer crouched on her back like a giant bloodsucking bat, she would have cursed her goddaughter as she had the others, either that or killed her with her own bare hands rather than watch Diana's child sink so low.

But Auntie was dead, and Aesir's drink was all she had left. For the three or four hours it lasted, it made her feel unstoppable, as if she could run forever without tiring. More, it made her forget everything about her past life: Mouse's death, the destruction of Auntie's camp, the defeat of her dreams. It even, for those few blissful hours, made her forget what she was— not only a monster but a slave, and a willing slave at that. A slave who, she had to admit to herself, would do almost anything to receive the one pleasure that remained to her.

She wondered, during the brief spells of lucidity that settled on her as the drug wore off and the hunger and shakes returned, what Aesir might force her to do to earn a sip from his flask. She had no qualms about the main task he had set for her: confronting the Skaldi in their lair, fighting them in some way he hadn't specified, likely giving her life in the effort. She almost welcomed that—an end to it all, to grief and guilt and the knowledge of what she'd become. But if he should ask for more, if he should demand her body the way he now controlled her soul, what then? There was enough of her left to quail at the thought—not because she was afraid of him asking but because she knew how readily she would comply if he did. In her most desperate hour, when she woke the second night bathed in sweat and found him stooping over her to pour the drink down her tightly clenched throat, she wished he *would* ask so she could get this final humiliation over with and not have to wonder about the depths of her depravity any longer.

But he didn't ask. And, repulsed as she was by her own filthy thoughts, she couldn't bring herself to ask the question for him.

Her only consolation was that the others, with the possible exception of Javier, didn't seem to know what the drug had done to her. Running well behind her during the day and sleeping in a huddle separate from her at night, they didn't see Aesir reaching into his robe on a regular basis or her falling apart physically and emotionally before he put the flask to her lips.

The Indians among his company, roughly half the teens including Javier, minded their own business the way their people generally did; the rest of them, including Didi, appeared simply uninterested in the new addition to Aesir's troop. Considering she didn't know most of them, she wondered why she even cared; the drug had taken over every other aspect of her life, so why should a bunch of strangers' opinions matter?

Except, in the case of Javier, she found that his opinion *did* matter. The two of them had never been close when he was a member of Auntie's camp, but they'd been social enough to explore the tunnels together a time or two, and of course there'd been the afternoon when he showed her how to defend herself against an attacker. Did he view her as an addict plain and simple, one of those sad, skeletal drifters who followed the camps around, letting anyone take advantage of them so long as there was the chance of a score at the end? Or did he attribute the closeness that had developed between her and Aesir to something else, something that was none of his business and that made no difference to him anyway?

She didn't know. She only knew that, during the in-between times when her body was starving for relief but her brain was mostly her own, she found herself watching him guardedly but keenly: the smooth lope of his stride, the quick humor in his eyes that took the place of a genuine smile. She didn't know what it was about him that both troubled and fascinated her; she certainly had no desire for a protector, much less a friend. But she never had time to sort her feelings out, because they arose only when her body's pangs were the worst, and when those times came, the old man was quick to fulfill her need. That done, she sprang forward like a rocket, and everything else fell behind her as if it had never existed.

81

A third day passed, identical to the second. Aleka couldn't guess how much ground they'd covered in those three days; when the drug was racing through her veins, she had very little sense of time or distance. They might be closing in on the city Aesir had spoken about for all she knew, but the red-brown dunes and red-hot sky looked no different than they had the day her colony died. It struck her in one of her rare moments of insight that the only time she'd seen the land as a genuine place, with its own unique features and its own meaningful life, was when she'd seen it through the contrasting tints of Javier's drawing. But though he drew another picture at dawn on the third day, waking before the other runners and finding the spot he judged best for the morning's artwork, she was too busy hunting for Aesir and his flask to see what Javier had created before he let the wind snatch it away.

Aesir forced them to run deep into that third night, and—to Aleka's dismay—he refused to give her an extra dose of the drug even though her stomach roiled with nausea and her legs felt too wobbly to carry the two of them. Was he testing her today for some unknown reason, seeing how far he could push her before she collapsed? Or was he growing worried that the Skaldi birthing agent would reach the finish line before his army? They hadn't seen the creature that had destroyed her colony since the first day, but Aleka had no doubt it was out there, huge and black as the sickness in her gut when Aesir finally called a halt and she sprawled along with the others on the dark desert floor.

Hiding her dependence from her companions was no longer an option, as Aesir immediately produced the flask and she drank sloppily in full sight of everyone, fluid dribbling down her face like bloody drool. For the first time since she'd tasted it in the tunnels, the immediate energy surge didn't come, and the pressure of her hunger built behind her eyeballs until she thought her head would explode.

"More," she gasped.

"More of the elixir will do you no good," he responded. "Your body has already been taxed to the limits of its endurance."

"Why…"

"Why?"

Why are you doing this to me? she'd meant to ask, but she feared rousing his anger if she questioned his motives. Her body was already so weak, she didn't think it could survive if he denied her what it needed. She shuddered violently at his next words.

"You must sleep now," he said. "When you wake, I believe you will find that a great change has come about."

She tried to muster the strength to scream at him, but no words came. She felt squeezed, caved-in, hollow. He stood, moving away from her to congregate with the others. All of them turned from her with obvious disgust on their faces, all except Javier, who lingered on the edge of the group, his brow lowered in concern. She was so far beyond control, she wanted to scream at him too, but found that her body could do nothing but convulse helplessly on the ground. She saw his hesitation, but at last, ignoring the others, he approached and knelt beside her.

"Take this," he said.

The darkness made it impossible for her to see what was in his hand, but she lashed out at him, assuming he was offering food or water. Not what she could hold down, not what she needed. Her arm, spastic as a newborn's, caught only air.

"Come on," he said, and trapped her flailing hand in both of his. He pressed something into her palm, then folded her fingers over it. She would have thrown it at him, but her fist tightened reflexively, nails digging into her own flesh.

Javier stood, letting a hand trail from her shoulder. The touch of his skin against hers made her shake with a feeling of wintry cold that only the oldest members of her colony had spoken of. She moaned and squeezed her eyes shut, and Javier's voice came to her out of the blood-red miasma that descended over her sight.

"This isn't you, Aleka," he said. "You're stronger than that."

His footsteps crunched away across the sand. The fist that held the object he'd given her jerked to her mouth, where she bit into her own knuckles in a spasm she couldn't stop. She tasted dirt, chalk, something ashy and unclean. It gagged her, and she would have spat it out, but her teeth clamped shut when she tried. She felt herself spinning into a freezing, fiery sleep, and her last thought was that when she woke, she would rise from this place and seek vengeance against the world that had betrayed her.

Chapter 7

The night was filled with wailing voices that cried out to her in a million tongues.

"Aleka! Come to us!"

She opened her eyes to see shadows dancing around her, insubstantial as flames. They swung their arms and leaped high into the air; when they landed, they bent down like coyotes or javelinas and trotted along on all fours. They were naked and fur-covered, and as she watched them undergo the transformation from human to animal and back again, she knew what they were: witches, skinwalkers, impure spirits only the most powerful of healers could dispel. Demons of the Navajo nighttime that Auntie had warned her about but that Aleka had never truly believed in until now.

Their circle drew tight, and she felt herself suffocating in bodies that stank of sweat and fur. Hands that were more like paws ran over her arms, her face, her lips. Laughter erupted from their throats, carrying a smell so rotten she would have vomited if there'd been anything left inside her. She couldn't resist when they pulled her to her feet, pushing and prodding until she took her place in line. The next moment, she found herself whirling around the circle, grunting and moaning like the rest of them at the unbearable weight of the flesh she wore.

"See!" their voices howled in her ears. "He comes! The master!"

The dance stopped. A hulking shape separated itself from the circle and limped forward on mismatched feet, one human, one hooved. It stood before her, sweat steaming in the night air, bristles on its back erect. Clawed hands reached inside its mouth and peeled the flesh back like a hood. When the thing shook the final shreds of the skin covering free, a naked figure stepped forth, glistening with blood like a baby emerging from its mother's womb.

Her scream tore her from sleep. She lay shaking violently, soaked in sweat like the witches from her dream. The emptiness inside her was as acute as a rat gnawing a hole through her stomach. She glanced around her in the darkness, but all she saw were the bodies of Aesir's soldiers, huddled in their blankets at a safe remove from where she lay. It didn't take long to figure out why they'd given her distance; her shirt was slick with vomit, and the smell of her own piss rose around her. Aesir had been wrong when he'd suggested that she would wake free of the drug's hold. She needed it now more than ever, and the one who kept it was nowhere to be found.

She sat up, her skin itching as it had in the dream. She felt as wild as an animal, heedless of anything except the terrible hunger in her belly. Images came to her of plunging her face into raw flesh, her mouth full of blood and viscera as she wolfed the chunks down whole. The thought should have sickened her, but she was beyond being aggrieved at the thing she'd become. She was a predator, and predators thought only of their prey.

She nosed the air for the scent of her meal, but though the runners lay within easy reach, none of them tempted her.

Something else was calling out to her—something primal, hot and pulsing with life. She glided past sleeping bodies to the edge of the camp, looked around furtively. Eyes sharp in the moonless night, she saw the thing she was seeking.

Javier slept alone at the top of the gully, where he must have bedded down to get an early start on his daily sketch. A low, anticipatory growl escaped her at the thought of catching him by himself. Dropping to all fours, she crept silently up the hill. As she neared, the thought came to her that she mustn't allow him to see her like this, that she must pretend to be the human being she once was, not the cunning predator she'd become. It took an effort of will to lift herself onto two feet; the restricting skin she wore stretched uncomfortably to fit her former shape. When her hands left the ground, she realized she was still gripping the thing Javier had given her last night, and she cast it aside, where she saw that it was nothing more than one of his used charcoal-sticks. She would have laughed at that, but it was hard to remember how to laugh, and the sound that came from her was more like a dog's bark.

She took an ungainly step forward. How best to approach him so he wouldn't suspect? What did humans say or do when they came into contact with each other? She tried to recall, but the blur of her hunger made it impossible to concentrate on anything except the promise of the coming feast. He'd given her the charcoal-stick last night to ... what? To comfort her? To remind her of the drawing he'd made? That must mean he pitied her, that he saw her as weak and needy, not as the powerful being she was. If she played her part well, he might let her come close to him—and then she could strike.

Her plan decided, she fell to the ground with a soft moan and lay in the dust, clutching her stomach. His eyes opened at once, and a look of concern chased all sleepiness away. She smiled to herself when she felt the warmth of his hand pressed against her icy skin.

"Aleka," he said. "What's wrong? Are you—?"

She groaned and rolled over, exposing the spot where she'd befouled her shirt. Whether he could smell her pissed pants was of no concern to her, as long as the stink wasn't so bad that he'd refuse to let her near. When he edged closer, she satisfied herself with the conclusion that either his human senses were inadequate to smelling it, or he was as stupidly compassionate as she'd hoped.

"I'm sick," she whimpered. "I can't stand it, Javier. You have to help me."

"You're going through withdrawal," he said. "I don't know what that crap is that Aesir keeps making you drink, but…"

She was mildly surprised to learn that he hadn't been given the elixir, but her mind was quick to turn the discovery to her advantage. "It's a bad drug, Javier. He got me hooked on it so he could … so he could…"

She curled into herself and sobbed. The sliminess of the fluid on her cheeks gave her a slightly sick feeling, but the re-alization that she could produce tears when she felt no sorrow thrilled her. She cried even harder, and was rewarded when Javier reached for her and gathered her in his arms.

"I'll help you through this," he said. "You've just got to fight it. To tell yourself there's more to live for than that."

She pulled closer, so close she could detect his beating heart against her cheek. "It feels like…"

"Like you'll die without it," he said. "That's just the drug talking. It gets so big, it seems like it's all you can hear. You need to find your own voice, remember what it was like to be yourself."

"I hate myself," she whispered.

"No, you don't," he said. "That's the drug talking too. You've got to talk back, let it know you're the stronger one."

He pulled her against him, not seeming to notice the stickiness or stench. Her mind spun with excitement that she could fool him so easily, that she could say all the things humans were supposed to say and make him believe they were what she really felt. In truth, she felt nothing except the aching emptiness inside her, along with the fever-hot anticipation of consuming his flesh. If not for that, she might have strung him along forever, enjoying every false word that fell from her lips, every purblind gesture of understanding he offered in return. She'd known some old Indians back in Auntie's camp who talked like he did, the ones who'd been sober for years and babbled on about inner peace and God and the daily struggle to find the light. She wondered if Javier's people had been like that, and if that's where he'd learned to parrot the mantra so well.

No matter. She had him where she wanted him, his body wrapped so tightly around hers he'd never be able to extricate himself when the moment came. Still, she couldn't deny herself the pleasure of fooling him one last time as she held the threads of his life in her hands.

"Javier," she said. "I never told you this, but … I always loved you. It killed me when you went away."

He stiffened. She waited for him to say that it was only the drug talking, but he didn't. After a moment, he pulled her close again, his hand stroking her matted hair.

"That's all right," he said. "I'm here now."

"Stay with me," she whispered. "Forever."

She lifted her face from his chest to look into his eyes. He looked back with a softness he'd never shown before, and she pulled herself upward to bring her mouth within inches of his. A shiver passed through her at the thought of what was about to happen: the opening, the kiss, the taste of his soul on her tongue. It would be the first time she glutted herself on another's life, but it wouldn't be the last. Once she'd savored the Skaldi's feast, she knew she could never have enough of it.

His mouth neared; she could feel its heat, sense the sweetness inside. Before she could lay her burning lips on his, he placed a hand on her mouth to stop her.

"Aleka," he said, "this isn't the time. You don't know what you're doing."

"Yes, I do," she said. "I need you, Javier. You have no idea how much I need you."

"You need to sleep. And eat and drink and get better. You don't need this."

Gently but firmly, he pushed her away. Rage swelled in her as he untangled her arms from his and stood, leaving her huddled at his feet.

"Fool!" she hissed. "You are mine now, whether you wish it or not!"

She rose to a crouch. Her body shuddered, and she felt it beginning: the skin peeling back from her forehead to her chest, the emptiness inside her expanding to encompass the world. Javier's eyes widened, and he took a step backward. It was then that she pounced, moving with lightning speed as his clumsy human skin stumbled to evade her.

"Aleka!" he cried. "What—?"

She collided with him and brought him down, trapping his wrists with her sharp claws, snaking the coils that had become of her legs around his waist. He was strong, but she was far stronger, an elemental being driven by pure bloodlust. She snapped at his mouth, felt fangs strike teeth. He turned his head away, but she flowed over him, drawing him into the emptiness of her skin. Ecstasy overwhelmed her as he became hers—

Searing pain made her shriek and let go. The burning sensation radiated from the point where her shoulder had been, and though she knew she had no body except what she'd stolen from this boy, she shrank into a ball as the pain spread. Looking down at herself, she was enraged to find that her scar had closed, restoring her to human shape, a cringing creature of blood and bone. She willed the scar to open once more, to grant her the Skaldi's world-devouring power, but the pain made it impossible to focus, and she slid to the ground as limp and helpless as the pathetic thing she'd been when she awoke.

The boy was on his feet, moving not away but toward her. He stopped short when a bright light danced in the air between them.

"Back!" a voice spoke in an urgent whisper. "Don't let her come close to you!"

He retreated, fear constricting his features. "What did you do to her?"

"What all your fine speeches couldn't do. Now help me with this."

The brightness drew nearer. She shied from it, growling and gnashing her teeth, hissing in animal dread. When it was mere inches away, she swatted at it, only to release a howl of pain. The injured fingers flew to her mouth, and while she was occupied with sucking them to reduce the burning agony, the boy caught her in his arms and bore her to the ground.

She struggled wildly against him, only to discover that she was trapped; every time she thought she'd gained the advantage, the dancing light swooped closer, making her cower from its heat. Fury coursed through her at the thought of how this boy had tricked her, he and whoever the other voice belonged to. If she'd been able to wait a little longer, to let the power of the Skaldi take deeper root inside her, her scar would have opened as wide as the night sky, and they would never have been able to restrain her. As it was, she was still half-human and vulnerable, and she cursed them, cursed herself, cursed the world for denying her the eternal life that had so nearly been hers.

Something tightened around her—not human arms but bonds, rope. Her scream was cut off by a gag that sank deeply into the tender skin of her mouth. She whipped her head back and forth, but stopped, paralyzed, when the bright light moved directly in front of her eyes and held its position there.

"Where is he?" the voice spoke.

She snarled against the gag, but the voice wasn't speaking to her.

"Where is who?" the boy asked.

"The leader. The one you call Aesir."

"He never stays around at night. I don't know where he goes."

"I can make a pretty good guess. Into the tunnels, where he can brew his next batch of poison for the coming day."

The light drew so close, her skin sweated like melting wax. She whimpered, but didn't dare move.

"What's the matter with her?" the boy asked.

The other one laughed humorlessly. "Let's just say she's not herself."

The light withdrew a fraction of an inch, and she realized at last what the bright torment was: a flame, flickering at the end of a stick held by someone she couldn't see through its painful glare. A flame that could shrivel her to a mound of ash to be scattered by the night wind.

The person holding the flame spoke. "You're Apache?"

"How'd you know?"

"Lucky guess. Can you run?"

"I can run."

"Then let's go. Try to keep up."

"I need to get my supplies," he said. "And I've got to tell the others."

"The others are gone," the voice responded. "Lost forever to the darkness. As this one will be too, if we wait much longer. Bring her, and I'll do what I can to burn the filth from her blood."

The boy hesitated a moment, then bent down and scooped her into his arms. The flame moved away to avoid burning him as he straightened, and its light shone briefly on the one who held it. There was a flash of white like a halo before the figure fell into shadow.

"Who—?" she tried to ask, but the gag muzzled her.

"Who are *you*, girl?" the shadowy figure answered. "That's the only thing that matters."

The figure signaled, then vanished into the night. The boy followed, the pinpoint of light twinkling far ahead of them as if the one who held it were moving at great speed. She tried to keep sight of it, but the hypnotic movement made her eyelids heavy. She gave herself up to her body's all-too-human weakness at last, and let forgetful sleep fold her in its veil.

Chapter 8

Sunlight stabbed her like a lance.

She opened her eyes, then was forced to shut them as the white-hot globe flooded her vision. She lay spread-eagled on sun-heated sand, but when she tried to rise, pain cut into her wrists and ankles. She lifted her eyelids in cautious slits and found that she was held down by ropes tied to wooden stakes. Even more terrifying, long branches topped with flame were planted in the sand all around her. If she managed to free herself from her bonds, she'd be penned in by a circle of fire.

She hissed helplessly, turning her head against the sun's assault, which seemed hot enough to burn her to nothing all by itself. She tried to reconstruct how she'd gotten here, but the past slipped away, fading into void like the tatters of an interrupted dream. The only thing she could remember was all-consuming hunger, the need to fill her empty frame, the supreme moment when she'd been preparing to feast on…

Javier.

The memory cut into her, sharp as the sun's rays. She recalled fighting with him last night, trying to ensnare him, to *become* him in a way that now seemed impossible. Shame filled her at the recollection of the things she'd said and done, though at the time it had felt as if something other than herself were speaking the words, dictating her actions. Something inside her, something she'd needed so badly she'd been willing to do anything to get it...

Then she remembered what the thing was, and a sob rose to her throat.

It was still there, the hunger awakening inside her body with the memory of it. It felt no less urgent than it had the night before, no less controlling. The only difference was that she couldn't bear to think what it had done to her, what it had made her do, and she longed for anything that might help her escape its power.

Voices floated to her. Two voices, only one of which she recognized: Javier's. The other seemed to emerge from her broken memories of last night—a deep voice, probably an adult's, though she was unsure if it was a man's or a woman's. She tried to locate the speakers, but they were behind her, and she couldn't turn her head far enough to see them.

"What did she tell you?" the unfamiliar voice said.

Javier mumbled a reply.

"Did she tell you she has Skaldi genes? Did she tell you that much, at least?"

"She might have mentioned it."

"Did you believe her?"

There was a long pause before he replied. "She was out of her mind when she told me. Flying high on some kind of drug. I didn't know what to believe."

"Well, believe this."

"But that's crazy!" Javier protested. "You're trying to tell me people can be Skaldi?"

"Skaldi can be people," the voice said. "So why not the other way around? The original Skaldi *were* people, if you must

95

know. There was a separation early in our shared history, a divide that turned us into what we are now: mortal enemies, each vying for the other's destruction. But the seeds of our unity remain within us to this day, and it wouldn't take much to bring the two back together. Maybe, in time, that will happen, and we'll stop wondering who's human and who's not. What you saw last night was the result of someone trying to force the issue before either side was ready for it."

"Aesir."

"As he now calls himself."

"Do you know who he is?"

"I have my suspicions. They don't matter much at the moment. What matters is how we're going to undo the damage he's done."

Silence descended on them once again. There was the sound of a rock skittering across the sand, as if Javier had kicked it in frustration. "You said something last night about burning it out. Did you mean…?"

"Yes."

"But that'll kill her."

"It's entirely possible. I'm hoping it kills the thing inside her first."

Footsteps squeaked against the sand. Javier called, "Wait!" There was the noise of people scuffling, a yelp of pain, the thump of a body hitting the ground.

"Who the hell *are* you?" Javier cried out.

"Why is everyone so concerned about who *I* am?" the other person answered. "If you care about *her*, you'll get out of my way and let me do what I have to."

A shadow fell upon the sand where she lay. She stared straight up, but the speaker's face was invisible against the sun's corona. Javier appeared a moment later, limping as if he'd been injured when he fell; she sickened with mortification at the thought of her crazed behavior from last night. She was trying to form words to apologize to him when the first figure took another step closer, and she gasped at the sight.

For a second, she thought she was seeing a ghost. The person was tall and thin, with white hair that descended in such thick waves it seemed to wrap its owner in a shroud. Beneath the tousled mass peered an ancient visage covered in wrinkles as deep as scars from long-ago fires. The eyes below the whitened brows, though, were bright blue, not at all dulled as were most old people's, and they stared from the wasted face like twin headlights fixing a culprit in their beams.

The wraith pulled one of the torches from the sand and squatted inside the circle. From this close, it was apparent that the face belonged to a woman, but a woman as lined and weathered as a piñon tree split by lightning. A gnarled hand reached out from the sleeve of her camouflage jacket, gripping the prisoner's chin so she couldn't look away.

"Listen to me," the old woman said in a deep, measured voice. "What is your name?"

"I…" She struggled to make sense of the question. "The Skaldi have no name."

"That's not an answer," the old woman said, stern as a teacher. "So I'll ask you again: what is your name?"

She tried to turn her face from the fierce stare, but the hand held firm. "I … I don't know."

"Better," the old woman said as she let go. "Now listen carefully, because I'm only going to tell you this once."

She sat Indian-style, the wild white hair falling all the way to the ground as if it were a dress, and began to talk.

"The Skaldi aren't truly alive," she said, "which is why they hate and envy us so. It drives them to madness that they can do nothing more than mimic what comes naturally to us. Their existence is marked by peaks of rapture and depths of torment soothed only by brief moments of repose, and their keenest wish is to become like us forever, to know the comfort of living a single life and laying it down at the end fully aware that it was theirs alone."

She paused. Javier stood close behind her, a look of wariness and doubt in his eyes.

"There are three stages of Skaldi existence," the woman continued. "Three distinct phases they're compelled to pass through time and again to avoid dissolution. Immediately after consuming a human host, they enter the satiation phase, a period of bodily vigor as they draw on the stolen energy from human cells to power their own. But this physical reprieve is accompanied by emotional turmoil: anger and self-loathing at the need to live such a life, fear of discovery, guilt at destroying another."

"Guilt?" Javier said with a laugh. "Skaldi feel guilt?"

The old woman ignored him. "In the second stage, that of acclimation, the Skaldi live out their borrowed life for as long as they can: weeks in most cases, a month if they're lucky. It's during this time that they feel most at peace with themselves; anger, fear, and guilt diminish as they forget what they are, how they came to acquire the life they're living, and convince themselves they *are* the one they replaced. Human beings have always wondered how the Skaldi can be such perfect mimics, and this must be the answer: they're able to deceive others because, during this phase of their existence, they're able to deceive even themselves."

The old woman transfixed her audience of one with a piercing blue stare. A memory surfaced of Mouse, with his injured leg and the weird reflection on his face. The whole time they were exploring the tunnels, could he have been Skaldi, living Mouse's life with no knowledge that it wasn't truly his?

"Acclimation doesn't last long," the woman's voice broke into her thoughts. "There's a final phase to come, and it's what the creatures dread the most: the starvation phase. It starts as soon as the physical body begins to break down, and it grows to the point where the hunger to consume a new body erases the Skaldi's identity as a human being, turning it into a mindless, murderous beast. No such thing as guilt or remorse is possible for a Skaldi in the last stages of the starvation phase; it will do anything, risk anything, destroy anything to obtain its prey. I've often thought that the amnesia that settles over them during this phase is a defense mechanism. Without forgetting what they are and what they're doing, I don't know if they'd be able to do it again and again and again."

She gazed knowingly at her rapt listener, and for once, a hint of compassion was visible in her eyes. There was no way to know how the old woman had learned these things, but there was no doubt that they were true: the crushing memory of last night was almost too much to bear, and it would have been a godsend to be able to expunge the memory entirely, to flee from shame and self-recrimination into eternal forgetfulness. Javier was shaking his head violently, and he seemed about to speak when she cut him off.

"It's true, Javier," she said. "Last night, I would have killed you if I could have. I wanted to do it. I was dying to. But my scar must have ... failed. I'm sorry," she whispered, and tears began to fall. "I'm so sorry."

She squeezed her eyes closed so she wouldn't have to see him, but the tears fell even faster. A gentle touch on her stomach was followed by the old woman's equally soft words.

"Girl," she said, "you're not scarred. You're human, every bit as human as you were last night. No Skaldi would apologize for what it had done, much less weep for its intended victim. Look at yourself now, in the pure light of day. See yourself as you are, not as his poison made you believe you were."

She was reluctant to open her eyes, but under the pressure of that voice, she did. She gazed down at her stomach where the old woman had unbuttoned her uniform top, and was amazed to find no trace of the gaping hole she'd felt last night, no scar, no line, nothing but tanned skin and smooth muscle and her unexceptional belly button. She flushed at Javier's stare, and the old woman carefully redid the buttons. When she looked up, the woman smiled, showing a full set of straight white teeth behind her withered lips.

"You see?" she said.

"It was there. I swear it was. I wouldn't have attacked Javier if I…"

"It was here," the old woman said, laying two fingers on her captive's forehead. "It was a powerful suggestion brought on by your body's need, but it was never a part of you. He's done his best to claim you for his own, but you don't belong to him yet."

She stood abruptly, pushing herself erect on long legs. Taking up the torch she'd thrown to the ground, she knelt, the flame dancing as dangerously close to her prisoner as it had the night before.

"This will hurt," the woman said. "I can't pretend it won't. It will hurt your body, and the thing inside you will make the pain worse in an effort to stop you from expelling it. Even with the ropes, you'll probably try to get away. But I need you to listen to my voice and make every effort to do as I tell you. I can't fight this thing alone, and in the end, only you can triumph over it."

She withdrew a knife from a sheath at her belt and, before either of them could react, slashed it across the back of her prisoner's hand. Javier cried out, but he stayed outside the ring of torches, watching the blood seep from the deep cut. Much as it hurt, the sight of her own bright red blood made her chest swell with relief. *Skaldi don't bleed*, she thought, and her heart raced with the hope that what the old woman had said might be true.

Then the woman laid the torch against her hand, and she screamed.

The fire touched her for less than a second, not long enough for her skin to redden or blister. But it felt the way it had last night: as if the flame were her deadliest enemy, as if it would burn her to nothing, or already had. She struggled against her bonds, twisting and tugging, but they held fast. When the old woman moved the torch toward her again, she couldn't help the hiss that burst from between her teeth.

"Steady," the woman said. "Look at my eyes, and try to remember who you are."

The torch came down again, and pain consumed her once more. The moment of contact lasted no longer than the first time, but the torment was far worse, as if she were engulfed in flames that would never die. She snapped her teeth at the torch, but the old woman moved it out of reach. Trembling, she tried to obey the woman's commands, to focus on her bright blue eyes, but the pain was too great.

"Javier!" she screamed. "Stop her! She's lying—she's trying to kill me!"

"Get away from her!" Javier yelled, and threw himself at the squatting figure.

Her reaction was too fast to follow. The hand that bore the torch lashed out, striking a sharp blow against Javier's temple. He fell without a sound, and the woman shoved his body aside as if it were a pile of bones.

She turned back to her victim, a rabid blue light in her eyes. There could no longer be any doubt that this woman was the true despoiler, the one who had come to kill them all and take control of the land forever.

"Stay away from me, you human bitch!" she shrieked, but the old woman just shook her head.

"Don't listen to it," she said slowly and distinctly. "It's trying to deceive you, to convince you that your only salvation lies in clinging to the rot in your blood. Its power over you is strong, but not as strong as you are."

The torch came down again. She writhed against her bonds, screaming in anguish as the wound began to smoke and sizzle. Again the torch descended, and again she screamed, cursing her tormentor. The screams seemed to come not from her mouth but from something deep inside her, something that had taken her voice to use for its own.

At last, after what seemed an eternity of pain, the torch retreated and she lay there, panting and trembling, the smell of scorched flesh filling her nostrils. The woman's eyes, blue as flame, burned into her soul.

"Now," the woman said, "what is your name?"

She struggled, gasped, heaved words from her throat. "The Skaldi have no name."

The torch was before her eyes again, so quickly she hadn't seen the woman retrieve it. "Once more: what is your name?"

"Devil!" she screeched. "Killer!"

The ancient face shifted in a sardonic smile. "I asked you your name, not mine. Tell me now!"

The torch was about to descend. She pulled with all her strength, and the stakes erupted from the ground just as a single word poured from her lips: "Aleka!"

She fell back, exhausted. Her eyes closed, and she saw nothing but red: flames, blood, the hot desert sun. Then a cool, dry hand touched her forehead, and the old woman's voice came to her, softer than ever before. "I told you, Aleka. You did it."

Aleka opened her eyes. The woman held her wounded hand, from which blood still flowed. Something else leaked from the cut as well, something much darker than her natural blood, and it moved not with the pull of gravity but with the volition of a living thing as it crawled down her arm onto the desert sand. It pooled on the ground beside her, so much of it Aleka thought her entire body would be drained. When the discharge stopped flowing and her blood ran clear again, the dark fluid began to move away, its shape curling and lashing like a sidewinder's as it aimed for the single opening in the ring of torches.

It hadn't gotten far when a white mist appeared from the old woman's hand, freezing it in its tracks. A thin scream issued from the sticky mass, which writhed as if trying to free itself from filmy strands that clung to it like a spider web. Its struggles didn't last long; in less than a minute, all motion ceased, and it rested on the ground completely coated in a glistening, misty shell.

The old woman held her hand out to Aleka, revealing a small capsule clutched in her palm, a few last wisps of the smoky stuff curling from its nozzle. She stashed it in her breast pocket, then reached out to cradle Aleka in her arms. The close contact was unexpected, but Aleka clung to her in an effort to stop herself from trembling.

"Hush, now," the old woman said, stroking Aleka's sweaty hair. "It's over."

"What … what was that thing?"

"The evil Aesir planted inside you," the woman said. "A seed of the Skaldi germ plasma, which had colonized your body to such an extent it had nearly destroyed your cells' ability to function on their own. If you'd taken another dose or two, it would have consumed you utterly, and you would have become one of them: a starved, pitiful creature that spent the rest of its days stealing the lives of others to stave off its own demise."

Aleka shuddered at the image the old woman drew. "But why would anyone want to do that to me?"

"If you mean to *you* specifically, I don't know the answer," the woman said. "All I know is that you weren't the first, and unless we stop this thing that calls itself Aesir, you won't be the last. Those who travel with him are proof of his potion's ability to consume the living and bend them to his will."

"But not Javier." Aleka glanced at his prone form, and was grateful to see that though his eyes remained closed, his chest rose and fell in the semblance of natural sleep. "He's still human."

"I'd say he's more human than most," the woman answered. "From what I've seen, he's passionately, foolishly committed to doing right by others."

104

Aleka looked at Javier's peaceful face, and the memory of the night before came back to her with renewed force. How could she ever earn his forgiveness after what she'd done?

"In any event, I can't imagine how someone like him got mixed up with Aesir," the woman continued. "But that can wait. For the time being, let me tend to you."

She left Aleka and returned holding a medical kit with tape, gauze, and some sort of salve she spread on Aleka's cut and burns. It soothed the worst of the pain, and Aleka rose to stretch her limbs. The old woman watched her for a moment before asking, "Are you hungry?"

Aleka looked at her in alarm. "For...?"

"Not for that. Your body has been without food for as long as the plasma was inside you, supplanting your needs with its own, and you're going to need to regain your strength."

She produced a ration bar from her pocket. Aleka took it warily, fearful that when she brought it to her mouth, the thing that had been housed inside her would reject it as it had rejected all food before. But she was ravenously hungry, so she turned away from the old woman and sank her teeth into the bar. As soon as she felt the juices flow to her mouth, she realized that the woman was right about this too: what she felt was natural hunger, her empty stomach protesting against the near-famine of the past ten days. A bodily hunger, not a starvation of the soul.

She gobbled down three bars and polished them off with a long swig of water. She would have eaten more if the woman's look hadn't conveyed that she'd had enough.

"You should rest while you can," the woman said. "As soon as this one's steady enough on his feet, we're going to have to get moving."

She pulled the branches from the ground and extinguished their flames in the sand. She was walking back to the spot where she'd gotten the medical kit when Aleka held out a hand to her. "Wait."

The woman stopped.

"Please," Aleka said. "You've done so much for me, and I ... I don't even know who to thank."

The old woman drew a deep sigh.

"Daughter of the desert, why do you need to hear from my lips what your heart already tells you?" she asked. "Rest now, and be ready to run."

Chapter 9

Aleka raced after her mother, trying to match the woman's long, graceful strides.

At least, Aleka *thought* the woman was her mother. She carried no bow or arrows, nothing but the staff with which she'd burned the organism from Aleka's blood and a bulging backpack as soiled and tattered as her uniform, but who but her own mother would know so much about her? Who but her mother would care so much what happened to a lost tunnel rat that she'd tracked her down in the middle of the desert, risking an encounter with Aesir to free her?

And yet, every time Aleka glanced at the woman's wild white hair and the deep grooves carved into her face, she doubted. From what Laman had told her, her mother was no older than eighteen when she gave birth, which would make her thirty-four now. The apparition who was pacing her and Javier—outpacing them, actually—had to be almost double that age. There was no way she could be the right person, unless...

A disguise, the answer came to her. Laman had said her mother was in danger, which was why she'd left Aleka with Auntie. She must have grown her hair out for the past sixteen years, let it bleach white in the sun, and prematurely aged her skin—Aleka didn't want to think how—in order to turn herself into a shriveled old crone. Looking at her, none of her enemies would believe she was the thirty-something-year-old they were trying to hunt down.

Unless, that is, they saw her run.

It wasn't only how long she ran without stopping, how she forced Aleka and Javier to exert themselves to the utmost to keep up with her. It was that she didn't seem affected by the distance at all: she maintained a steady pace, her head held high, her eyes focused straight ahead while her arms and legs cut the air with superhuman ease. Aesir's crew had run fast, and so had Aleka when she was one of them, but that was because of their leader's potions and spells—or, in Javier's case, because of the legendary running ability he'd inherited from his people. The Huntress ran like someone who'd trained her body for years to do this one thing, and who hadn't stopped doing it in all the time she'd lived in the western desert.

They paused for water and a meal at high noon. While Aleka and Javier collapsed in exhaustion, the woman stood with her hands on her hips, breathing deeply but without the appearance of being the slightest bit winded. When Aleka's legs had stopped feeling like jelly and she'd made another dent in the forced famine of the previous days, the woman pulled her to her feet, then set off again at a brisk jog. With the exception of the days when she'd run under the influence of Aesir's drug, Aleka had been hesitant to continue during the hottest part of the afternoon, but that didn't seem to make any difference to her new guide. Maybe, Aleka thought as she fastened a scarf around her head to block the worst of the sun's rays, there was a simple explanation for the Huntress's wrinkled skin. If she'd been out running at this hour every day for the past sixteen years, she was lucky she hadn't withered away completely like a drought-starved desert flower.

When night fell, Aleka discovered something else: the Huntress had been taking it easy on her two young companions during the daytime hours. With the sun down, she ran even faster, her feet churning the sand to a dusty cloud in the moonlight. She hadn't said a word about where they were going, but Aleka assumed that she was trying to put as much distance between themselves and Aesir as possible, so she quieted her questions and pushed herself even harder than before. Weary as she was, what kept her going was the elation at having her own body back, without anyone or anything else pulling the strings. The pain she felt was all too real, but it belonged to her alone.

She never knew what made the woman decide they'd run far enough, but when she did, the decision was made all at once, as she held up a hand and came to a dead stop. The moon had dipped behind a row of mesas; maybe she'd decided the cover of darkness was adequate, or maybe she was tired too. Not that she looked it. She put her hands on her hips and drew a single long breath, then she was all business.

"Rest," she said to Aleka and Javier, and the word had no sooner left her mouth than the two of them fell to the sand as if their bodies had been emptied of bones. Aleka threw her arms over her head and lay there gasping, staring into the infinite expanse of the night sky, with its swirling bands of stars like strings of lanterns.

The woman squatted beside her and laid a hand on her forehead. "How are you feeling?"

"Drained," she confessed.

"As well you should be," the woman said. "Look."

109

She opened her hand, its wrinkled palm damp with Aleka's sweat. There was something strange about the sheen of fluid in the starlight; it looked greasy, less like water than oil. Aleka ran a finger over her own forehead and held the digit close to her face, but she couldn't tell clearly what was wrong until the woman lit the torch-staff and moved it close to Aleka's hand.

In the torchlight, she saw that her finger was tipped in a reddish color much darker than blood. When the woman waved the torch over it, the dark fluid started to move—not to drip but to twitch this way and that as if trying to escape the flame. Aleka shook her finger violently, but the stuff wouldn't come free. The woman planted the staff in the sand and gripped Aleka's shoulders.

"Hold still," she said.

Her hand went to her jacket pocket, returning with the capsule she'd used before. She sprayed cool mist against Aleka's finger, and the living fluid turned to a solid bead of dark red that dropped to the ground like spent ammunition from a pellet gun. The woman next rolled up Aleka's sleeves and pant legs and sprayed the exposed skin, then told her to close her eyes while she sprayed her face. The tickle of the toxin trying to escape felt like miniature bugs crawling over her skin, but she held perfectly still until each droplet had curled up and fallen as a tiny carcass to the sand.

"I wasn't sure we got it all," the woman explained when she was done. "It's one of the reasons I pushed you so hard."

"Where'd it come from?" Aleka asked, suppressing a shudder.

"Pores, tear ducts, any small opening in your body. I'd suggest you take a good long piss, in case any of it collected in your bladder."

She rose to unpack supplies from her bag. Aleka had needed to pee for most of their run, but now the thought of peeing bloody tar made her sick.

"Will I ever be free of it?" she asked.

"You're mostly free of it now," the woman said. "Free of the longing, anyway. There's not enough of it to mount an attack on your body, though it'll keep trying to colonize your cells as long as the tiniest trace remains. Skaldi genetic material is aggressive, as I'm sure Aesir told you. And he stuffed you as full as a Thanksgiving turkey."

"A what?"

"Not important." She tossed a piece of canvas on the sand, then unrolled it to reveal ropes and metal stakes. "Go pee. We can talk before bedtime."

Aleka rose and scanned the desert, seeking a place distant enough for privacy. When her eyes fell on Javier, her cheeks warmed, though she wasn't sure why; his arm was flung over his face, and he seemed to be asleep. Still, she snuck away quickly and didn't stop moving until she was sure the darkness shielded her. She'd already shown him more of her body than she'd ever dreamed she would, and she wasn't about to let him see her with her pants down.

When she returned to the campsite, the woman had the shelter up, a rickety thing consisting of a small piece of canvas, a few frayed ropes, and some sticks she must have collected on the spot. She was crouched over another pile of sticks she'd placed across each other in a shallow hole, and was using a plastic firestarter to coax out a flame. Aleka stood beside her, uncertain. "Do you need me to do anything?"

"Not at the moment." She got down on her hands and knees, lowering herself close to the fire pit to breathe on the flames. When the larger sticks caught, she hopped up quickly, and Aleka was struck again by how impossibly lithe she was for someone who looked as old as she did. The woman scrounged in her pack for more supplies and came out with long strips of dried meat that made Aleka's stomach growl.

"Prairie dog jerky," the woman said with a hint of pride in her voice. "Tasty and nutritious, and they're easy to catch once you figure out how their lairs are constructed. The trick is to set a fire at the front door and wait for them at the back with a really big stick."

"Could you," Aleka asked, feeling tongue-tied and stupid, "could you show me how?"

"Some other time. For now, eat."

She handed Aleka a strip of the jerky. Aleka bit into it, finding it stringy but flavorful, salty enough to satisfy her hunger without making her thirsty. She munched in silence while the woman hunkered down beside the fire, her eyes fixed on the crackling flames.

"You're not eating anything?" Aleka asked.

"Not hungry."

"But you…" *You must have run thirty miles*, she was about to say, but the woman's piercing eyes stopped her.

"I come from the school of 'save it for a rainy day,'" she said, whatever that meant. When Aleka didn't respond, she shrugged. "You'll thank me later."

They sat in silence by the fire, which emitted the sweet smell of piñon. When Aleka was done with her first jerky strip, the woman wordlessly handed her a second. Aleka gnawed, glancing at her companion from time to time while trying not to look like she was staring. Nonetheless, every time she stole a peek, she became more and more convinced that minus the wrinkles and scars, the face she was seeing was not only that of a much younger woman, but the same face that looked back at her from the mirrors of the trucks or from still water.

When Aleka was done, finishing off her meal with another long pull at the offered canteen, the woman rose and packed everything away, then produced a bedroll from her seemingly bottomless bag. Aleka assumed it was for her guide's own use, but the woman spread it out and patted it with a hand. "Time for bed."

The way she said that made Aleka's mouth curl. *No bedtime story?* "I thought you said we could talk."

"I did, didn't I?" She pulled her knees up to her chin, wrapping her arms around her long legs. "So talk."

Aleka was taken aback. "About what?"

"Anything. The stars, the desert, the coyotes that are going to start singing right about … now." A chorus of yips sounded in the night the moment she said that. "The price of rice in China. Is that what you want to talk about?"

She stared at Aleka, who had no idea what she'd done to offend. The woman was even worse than Auntie at saying things Aleka didn't understand, expressions from before the wars that probably hadn't made any sense back then and certainly didn't make any difference now. "I just wanted to talk."

The woman held her in the beam of her eyes a moment longer, then released another dramatic sigh. The next second, she sprang from the ground, shaking out her legs and pacing in front of the fire. She stopped just as suddenly as she'd begun and looked down at Aleka before returning to her seat.

"Listen," she said. "I know there are many things you want to ask, and I know I haven't exactly been forthcoming. Stop," she said, though Aleka hadn't made a sound. "We'll get to that. But there's something you need to understand: I've been by myself for almost as long as I can remember, and it's not easy to drop everything and settle down for a heart-to-heart. Especially now. It feels as if I've been running across this desert for a hundred years, and now I have only a few days to fix everything I've failed to. Can you understand that?"

"It's how I feel every day."

The woman's face softened, and her eyes sparkled in the firelight. For a moment, she looked far younger than she had since they'd met. Then the softness was gone, leaving behind a face that seemed older and wearier than ever before.

"First things first: the man who calls himself Aesir," she said. "I still don't know his true name, not with certainty. Nor do I know what he wants from you. But if he was taking you to the city by the lake, you must play some important part in his grand scheme."

"He said the Skaldi were there. That he was going to use me as some kind of a … weapon against them."

The woman rubbed her chin. "Interesting. But, as usual, only half truthful. They're there, all right, but if you'd remained with him, you'd have been no more of a threat to them than that ground squirrel you just chowed down on."

"He said they were dying."

"Again, correct. What he didn't say is that he's trying to bring them back."

Aleka had no response to that. Somehow, it seemed she'd known all along, even on that first day when he'd found her in the tunnels. Known that he was the one who'd engineered her fall, her injury, and everything that followed, from her first sip of his elixir to the last moment she'd been held helpless in its grasp.

"Who is he?" she asked.

Another sigh. "I told you I don't know."

"You also said you can guess. You said the same thing to Javier this morning."

"So you were listening after all?" the woman asked. "Good. If we're going to spend the rest of this ride together, the one thing you're going to have to be is a good listener."

She poked the fire with a stick. It flared brightly, showing something Aleka had never expected to see on the ravaged face: the tracks of two tears, one from each eye. Then she blinked and averted her gaze, and Aleka wasn't sure the tears had been there after all.

"In answer to your question," the woman said, "I believe he's the chief of the scientists who created the germ plasma. He's grown old in the time since, which makes it hard to know precisely, but that's my best guess."

"You knew him?"

"If he's who I think he is, yes. Before you were born, and before he became what he is today. A very different time, but as it happens, not far from where we are now."

"And you knew ... you knew my father too?"

The woman's eyes shifted to Aleka's. "What's that got to do with anything?"

"Aesir told me," she began, her voice catching as the woman's thin lips hardened into a frown, "he told me my father was ... one of the people they experimented on."

Aleka recoiled when the woman let out a harsh, ugly laugh. She threw her stick into the fire, a shower of sparks revealing the furious gleam in her eyes.

"He was really on a roll, wasn't he?" she said. "But that was always his way of operating: reveal just enough to earn your trust, while withholding the things you needed to know to resist his advances."

"But was it true?" Aleka pressed. "What he said about my father?"

The woman didn't answer. She studied Aleka's face in the firelight, as if the question required careful consideration or an assurance of Aleka's talent for listening. Then she shook her head, let out a short laugh, and reached inside her pack. Her hands came out cupping a small object, which she set gently on the ground at Aleka's feet.

It was a glass jar, dark green in color and filled to the midpoint with what appeared to be fine grains of black sand. Aleka stared at it, unable to tell if the campfire was reflected on its shiny surface or if the jar itself was a lantern filled with a miniature flame.

"Your father," the woman said.

Aleka's eyes jerked to her face. "What about him?"

"Your father," the woman repeated, inclining her head toward the jar but saying nothing more.

"You mean…"

"Yes. What's left of him, in any event." Her fingers reached out to stroke the jar, then she picked it up and placed it in Aleka's unwilling hands. "Don't flinch, girl. We all come to this sooner or later. To him, it just happened a lot sooner than it should have."

Aleka gazed at the jar that held her father's ashes. She found her hands trembling, and they didn't stop until the woman reached out and placed a hand on hers. Their fingers wove together, and when Aleka looked at the woman's face, the tears she'd glimpsed a few minutes ago shone like stars in the deep furrows of her cheeks.

116

"Mother," Aleka said, almost too softly for her own ears to hear.

"Don't call me that," the woman said. "It's not safe."

"But you are … you are my mother, aren't you?"

The woman let go of Aleka's hand and stood, facing away from the campfire with her arms wrapped around her middle. "Would it make any difference if I were?"

Yes, Aleka wanted to answer. *It would make all the difference in the world.* But the woman had turned back to her, and the intensity of her eyes made the words die in Aleka's throat. "What should I call you, then?"

The woman unloosed her deepest sigh yet. "A friend. One who has no name anymore, but who's here with you now. Why do you need to call me anything, when you know I won't leave you again?"

She held out a hand for the jar, and Aleka reluctantly parted with it. The woman stared at it for a long time before returning it to her pack. Then she sat once more, this time beside Aleka. Her hands held a thick piece of paper, folded over many times and so frayed and filthy it looked like one of Auntie's less-than-accurate maps. She spread it on the ground and gestured for Aleka to lean close. When Aleka did, she was surprised to find the wrinkled cheek pressed against her own.

"His name was Kareem," her mother whispered in her ear. "Now that you know where his life ended, I need to take you to the place where it began."

117

Chapter 10

The Huntress crouched beside her daughter at the peak of a ten foot high ridge of rock, peering out at the desert landscape.

The woman pointed a skinny finger. "There."

"Where?"

"I told you it's well hidden. Come on."

Keeping low, she led Aleka to ground level, where Javier waited. The three of them crept to the corner of the outcropping; when the Huntress froze, the other two followed suit. They'd been copying her motions since morning, when Javier woke up and Aleka's mother gave him the same lecture about being a good listener she'd given her daughter. It was awkward and a little weird, as if she thought the two of them were toddlers, but Javier had modeled what she asked for, taking the lesson in but saying nothing. The Huntress hadn't probed him about Aesir or anything else, which Aleka figured meant she trusted him. Then she'd taken out her knife and reached for his hand, and Aleka wasn't so sure anymore.

"I hate to do this," the woman had said, "but believe me, it's not anything I haven't done to myself plenty of times."

Javier's eyes had widened, but he didn't flinch when she slashed his hand like she'd done with Aleka's the day before.

She'd then lit her torch-staff and repeated the procedure from yesterday, holding it briefly against his skin to see if anything other than blood would flow from the wound. Aleka had almost objected when her mother lowered the torch a second time, but Javier said nothing, only confronted the woman with a level, defiant stare. When she was satisfied that his blood was just blood, she'd splashed water on the burns, bandaged him up, and packed her bag for the road.

"You're clean," she said. "He never put anything in you in the first place."

Javier nodded, but kept silent.

"It's odd," the woman mused. "I got a single injection of Skaldi genes sixteen years ago, and we all know what Aesir did to you," she added with a glance at Aleka. "Why he decided to leave this one alone…" She'd stared at Javier, then shrugged. "In any event, he won't be able to track us now."

The way they'd run after that final conversation, at top speed and without so much as a break for lunch, it seemed her mother wasn't taking any chances. But then, the Huntress moved so swiftly, Aleka doubted Aesir could catch up to them even if they still had his tracker in their blood.

Moving steadily eastward, they'd reached their destination before night fell. Or at least, they'd reached it according to her mother. Even now that they were supposedly within range of the underground base, Aleka couldn't see anything except sand dunes turned deeper red than usual by the light of the setting sun.

"Now, listen," her mother said in a whisper. "This place has been abandoned for years. It's where your father was … made, I guess is the word for it. And yes, it's also the place you were born," she said crossly to the question her daughter hadn't asked. "But we're not here for a trip down memory lane. My memories of this place aren't all that pleasant, with one possible exception."

She scowled when she said that, which made Aleka wonder if the exception was giving birth to her or if that was one of the unpleasant memories.

"I've been inside only once in the sixteen years since then," her mother continued. "I met no resistance, but we still have to be extremely careful. If any part of the organism remains, it's not going to roll out the red carpet for us."

Aleka ignored yet another old-time saying that made no sense. "How do we get inside?"

"Through the hole it dug," her mother said. "How else?"

She glared in that disconcerting way that made her young-woman's eyes bug out of her old-woman's face. This time, though, Aleka glared right back. She'd been a good listener for the past two days while her mother tied her down like a criminal, burned her, and ran her ragged between lectures. Now she needed answers.

"Look," she said. "If we're going in there, it's only fair to tell us what to expect."

Her mother snorted. "You think the Skaldi care about fair? You think Aesir does?"

"I think I do."

Her mother looked away, grumbling. When she turned back, she wore the softer expression that made her appear almost her true age.

"I guess I can't complain," she said. "You come by it honestly."

Aleka rolled her eyes at yet another adage from a past she'd never know.

"All right," her mother said. "There's a weapon inside that base with the power to neutralize the germ plasma. It's the same as this." She held out the capsule she'd used to freeze the bloody gunk from yesterday. "When they mature, Skaldi can be killed by fire, but in their larval form, volatile energy only feeds them. Helps them grow. If we're going to take on Aesir, we're going to need a much larger supply of this cryogenic gas than the single cartridge I was able to sneak off the base sixteen years ago. This one's almost spent as it is."

She shook it, and the canister made a sound as if a ball bearing were rattling around inside.

"Aesir told me the plasma can be burned," Aleka said. "That's how he knew I had Skaldi genes."

"He was trying to confuse you," her mother said. "I saw with my own two eyes what happens when the organism's exposed to fire, and believe me, it's not pretty."

"But if fire doesn't affect it," Javier spoke up for the first time since morning, "why do you use a torch to burn it out?"

He asked the question mildly enough, but the Huntress frowned.

"Fire can incinerate the host," she said. "And then the plasma would be up a creek without a paddle, wouldn't it?"

Aleka had pretty much given up on deciphering her mother's endless stock of whimsical sayings. She wasn't sure she understood the woman's explanation—the germ plasma in the form of Auntie had reacted as if it had been burned when she touched it—but it was obvious this was no time to argue. "So we go in there and get some more of these cylinders…"

"And then we run right back outside and save the world," her mother said. "You think it's going to be as easy as that, Princess?"

121

Aleka was shocked by the sudden change in her tone. "I never thought it would be easy."

"You never thought about it at all," her mother snapped. "It never occurred to you that something this potent would be kept in a locked containment vault, and that we don't have the tools we need to force our way inside. Or that we might not be able to reach the vault at all, what with the damage the base sustained sixteen years ago. And then there are the creepy-crawlies we might meet along the way, without a hope of fighting them off." Her eyes shifted away from her daughter's, and her mouth worked silently before she spoke again. "Plus there's one more thing."

Aleka waited silently for her to say what it was, but the woman continued to look elsewhere, muttering under her breath as if arguing with herself. Finally, she let out air and turned back to her daughter. Her eyes had lost their fierceness, and Aleka thought she appeared almost apologetic. Or almost fearful, which was far worse.

"The last time I was here was two months ago," she said. "I'd been checking the place over the years, walking the perimeter, trying to determine if anything had escaped. There's a missile line deep belowground that extends for hundreds of miles, so obviously I couldn't cover that, but each time I returned, I found no evidence of a breach in the immediate area above the base."

She looked out over the blood-red sand, and Aleka could have sworn she shivered.

"Then two months ago, I got the strongest feeling that I had to come back. Less than a year had passed since my last inspection, but I sensed—no, I *knew*—that something was wrong. Maybe it was the tracker that was still in my blood at the time that told me the situation had changed, but whatever it was, I knew there was danger."

Aleka and Javier opened their mouths to speak at the same time, but the woman cut them off with an impatient motion of her hand.

"So I came back," she said. "And found that it had broken free. Straight through tons of concrete. It must have been drilling for the past sixteen years, advancing an inch a day at most. Which meant not only that it was much more resilient than I could have imagined, but that when it finally broke through, it was hungrier than ever. And angrier." This time, her shiver was unmistakable. "I stayed long enough to gather information on its history and habits, then I hightailed it out of there and went hunting for your godmother's colony. I barely slept. The only time I took breaks was when I was working on burning the stuff out of me."

She flourished her hands, showing thick, ugly scars. Aleka wondered whether the marks on her face were from the same source.

"I searched for well over a month before I found them," her mother continued. "I told Arachne what I'd discovered at the base, and she assured me she'd break camp immediately. Then I was off again to search for where the creature had gone. I'd no sooner started out than she sent a truck back to tell me you'd disappeared in the middle of the night."

Guilt descended on Aleka when she realized it was her mother's warning that had made Auntie so urgent to move out on the day Mouse died. She debated whether to tell her mother what had happened to Auntie and the rest of the colony shortly after their last meeting, but she didn't get a chance to, because the woman kept talking.

123

"So I changed my tactics, looking for you instead of the creature, and of course I found you in the company of Aesir himself. Some might call that coincidence, but it's been years since I believed in the concept. You," she said to Javier, "when did you join up with him?"

"About six weeks ago," he said.

"And the others?"

"They were already there," he said. "Didi and everyone else. I was the last to join before Aleka."

The Huntress turned to her daughter, and beneath the scars and wrinkles, her face wore an expression of sibylline knowledge. She nodded as she saw the light go on in Aleka's eyes.

"Yes," she said. "It had been cooped up in there for your entire life, but the instant it got free, it came looking for you. Not for anyone else—for *you*. Unless I miss my guess, that's why it was so persistent in making its escape. The day after you were born, it tried to assimilate you, but fortunately, I was around to foil its plans. It tried again just days ago, and it came a lot closer to succeeding than the first time. At this point, I think we have to assume that it's going to keep on trying until it either conquers you at last or we destroy it utterly. And I don't think we can count on me always being the one to stop it."

She looked away as if she couldn't bear to see the stunned expressions on her young companions' faces. It was Aleka who found her voice first, though her words were faint. "You lied to me. You told me you didn't know what Aesir wants with me."

"And I still don't. I only know he wants you very badly, more than he's ever wanted anything before."

"But you said I was free of the germ plasma."

"I said you were free of the longing for it. I never said it was free of the longing for you."

Aleka closed her eyes and leaned her head against the sun-warmed stone barrier. She wanted to hate her mother—for abandoning her at birth, for torturing her yesterday, for talking in a language so confusing you could hear what you wanted while she was saying the exact opposite, and most of all, for bringing her here to confront all over again the demons she thought she'd defeated—but she found herself too weary to do more than ask, "Why is this happening to me?"

"Because of who you are," her mother answered. "Because, through no fault of your own, this is where you find yourself. So now you have a choice to make: run from your past and hope for a miracle, or go in there with me and prepare for a fight. I'll be fighting right beside you as long as I'm able. That much of a promise I can make."

"And if I can't fight anymore?" Aleka asked. "If it wins?"

"Then I'll kill you with my own hands," the woman said in a voice that shocked Aleka with its harshness. "The same way I killed your father."

Aleka opened her eyes to see her mother's furious, grief-stricken face. She would have retreated from that look, but the wrinkled hands clutched her shoulders and pulled her so close their foreheads touched, the blue eyes staring directly into hers with terrifying intensity.

"Kareem Reza was overtaken by the Skaldi genes inside him," her mother said. "But I didn't know that when we met. Neither did he. I loved him, and you were the result."

Aleka tried to pull away, but her mother's grip was unyielding.

"Don't be squeamish," she said. "If you're lucky, you'll have half of what your father and I had, and if you're even luckier, it'll last. But he was Skaldi. I promised him I wouldn't let him live that way, and when it got to the point where he couldn't control it and I saw how much he was suffering, I had to put an end to it. I'll do the same to you if I must. I watched your father become everything I hate, everything we both hated. I won't let that happen to the child we made."

She pulled her daughter against her, and Aleka felt the taut muscles and sharp bones of her mother's frame. She hugged back, wishing she could have known her father, wishing there were a picture of him that she could keep. But it was like the drawings Javier had released to the wind: they were gone, and all that remained were the words of the woman who held her. The woman who held *him* in her memory, and would never let him go.

This is what she meant when she said she wouldn't leave me, Aleka thought. *She'll kill me first*, and there was a strange comfort in that promise.

The hug ended as abruptly as it had begun, and Aleka stumbled forward when her mother's arms left her. Javier caught her, using the opportunity to whisper in her ear: "I don't trust her."

"But I do," Aleka surprised herself by saying. "If you don't, maybe you'd better leave."

Javier let her arm go. Aleka's mother gave her an approving glance, and the two of them slipped around the side of the stone ridge. A moment later, Javier followed.

The three of them skidded down sand to the desert floor. There was nothing to hide them here, not even a cactus or a sage bush to crouch behind. A hundred yards away, a dune shaped like a pyramid rose out of the desert, its peak tipped red by the sun. Aleka's mother headed for it at an easy trot, her shadow stretching long across the sand and her white hair flying. Without slowing down, she leaped onto the dune and climbed to the top.

Aleka set a foot on the dune. When she did, she realized there was rock beneath it—not a natural formation like the other ridge but something built by human hands. The giveaway in this case was the flash of metal that showed beneath the sand—barely a few inches, but enough to tell that there had once been a doorway embedded in the rock. Now it seemed as if the structure had collapsed from whatever its original height had been, covering most of the door with slabs of broken stone. The desert wind had completed the disguise by burying the windbreak beneath a foot of sand.

"This was the main entrance to the base," her mother confirmed. "Until your godmother blew it to smithereens. You probably didn't know she had a history in explosives." Her teeth gleamed briefly. "Her handiwork kept the base sealed for sixteen years. No one in, nothing out, not until two months ago."

Dropping nimbly to the ground, she led Aleka and Javier to the spot where the sand was piled deepest. When Aleka appraised the carefully sculpted dune, she revised her original theory: the dune was a product of human design as well, not of the desert's whims. Probably her mother had crafted it this way to conceal what lay beneath.

"Help me out," the Huntress said. "I want to be in before dark."

They fell to their knees and began digging in the deep, soft sand. It wasn't easy, because the dune kept shifting to fill what they removed, but eventually, they reached the base of a stone wall, where they found an irregular opening just broad enough for a person—a skinny person—to wiggle through. Aleka's mother smoothed sand away, showing her daughter a separate seam in the stone where the organism had emerged.

"It forced its way through solid rock like water doing the work of centuries," she said. "It must have destabilized the wall in the process, which opened this larger hole for Aesir to get out. Unfortunately for us, he's always been a shrimp." She measured Aleka and Javier with her eyes. "I'm afraid your friend is going to have to wait outside. He can guard our supplies while we're gone."

"You're allowed to use my name," he said. "It's Javier."

"Diana," she said with a crooked grin. "Pleased to make your acquaintance."

She dug the glass jar out of her backpack, tucked it inside her jacket, and dropped the pack at Javier's feet. Then she poked her staff into the larger hole and let go. The clatter of its landing came a second later. Without a moment's hesitation, she crouched low and plunged headfirst into the hole. Her feet kicked once before she disappeared.

Aleka gave Javier an apologetic look. "She really does like you."

"That's not exactly the vibe I'm getting," he said. "You tell her we're just friends?"

Aleka felt warmth spreading across her cheeks, so she clambered after her mother before he could see.

She found herself in a trapezoidal chute made of rough, jagged concrete, barely wide enough for her shoulders and hips. The air was much cooler here than outside, and the space was completely dark until the click of her mother's firestarter heralded a warm yellow light at the end of the tunnel, no more than ten feet away. Aleka had never been in this tight of a spot in all her years of climbing, but she overcame the feeling of claustrophobia and inched deeper inside, using mostly the muscles of her shoulders and stomach to advance. Her hands were useless—it was too tight to extend her arms—so she continued to edge forward with a wormlike motion until she saw a wrinkled face surrounded by ghostly white hair that seemed to float out of the darkness.

"Careful," her mother said, an echo to her voice. "There's a drop."

She set her lighted staff on the floor and held her hands out. For a moment, when Aleka's legs came free, all of her weight rested in her mother's arms, but that didn't seem to trouble her as she swung her daughter to the ground and set her on her feet as easily as if she were a child. Then she stooped and retrieved the torch so Aleka could look around.

They weren't in a cave as she'd expected, but in a more or less square room whose floor was piled high with blackened stone. A solitary concrete pillar seemed to be all that held up what was left of the roof; elsewhere, the ceiling tilted at a sharp angle before vanishing into the rubble. Protruding from the pile was a single large, dark object that reflected the light of the torch. When they came close, Aleka saw that it was the hood of a black vehicle the size of a small truck, though it was twisted and scorched by fire. It seemed that Auntie's explosion had spread outward from this point, the parts of the floor that were visible darkened like a single ripple in a black pond.

"No sign of them," her mother said.

"Who?" Aleka asked, then lowered her voice to a whisper when it echoed eerily in the underground room.

"The scientists who made the Skaldi. They're either buried under all this debris, or..."

She squatted and ran her fingers over the black, then dabbed at them with her tongue before standing.

"Just dust and ash," she said. "That could be good news for us."

"You told me Aesir was the head scientist. How could he be alive if he was here when Auntie's explosion went off?"

"I said that's who he *might* be. There's always a possibility I'm wrong."

"That doesn't help," Aleka said in frustration. She was starting to feel as if her mother's story changed every time she asked.

"I'm afraid it's the best I can do," the woman said. "You have to understand, we're dealing with things from the way past that have just now reemerged in the present, and I don't know what to expect. That's why I'm choosing to expect the unexpected." She held out a hand. "Stay close. If there's plasma left, it could be hiding anywhere."

"Then how are we supposed to—"

Her words were lost in a crash that came from behind them. They spun, Aleka raising useless fists, her mother wielding the torch and the near-empty canister as if it were a gun. Aleka breathed a sigh of relief when she found that it was only Javier, who'd landed on his face when he fell from the hole. He shook his head woozily and was pushing himself from the floor when the ceiling above him shifted and a slab of rock started to fall.

Aleka cried out. Before she could move, a white flash threw itself at Javier and tackled him, the two of them rolling across the floor.

The ceiling poured down a second later. Aleka lost sight of Javier and her mother as rocks tumbled and crashed, followed by a flood of desert sand. When the avalanche stopped, the entrance overhead was completely blocked by a mountain of sand and stone.

Aleka ran the few steps to where Javier and her mother lay on their backs, coughing on the dusty air. The torch had fallen clear of the cave-in, and its glow revealed bloody cuts all over Javier's arms where he'd forced his way through the narrow opening. Her mother's furrowed brow had received a fresh gash, and her legs were buried in sand at the edge of the pile. When Aleka knelt to free her, she found that a chunk of falling rock had trapped her mother's right knee, twisting it at a worrisome angle. Aleka shoved the stone off and tried to help her mother to her feet, but she shook her daughter away and brought her face so close to Javier's it looked as if she were going to bite.

"There's a reason I asked you to be a good listener," she breathed. "I need that a lot more than I need another dead Romeo."

Chapter 11

Javier stood as soon as Aleka's mother was done reprimanding him, but she lay on her back, breathing heavily and staring upward at where the ceiling had been.

Aleka inspected her injuries more closely. The cut on her forehead was deeper than she'd thought, blood following the lines of her face like a river flowing through dry land. The leg hadn't been crushed or mutilated that Aleka could tell, but her mother held it rigidly extended as if she feared to bend it. When Aleka tried to roll up the leg of her pants to check the damage, her mother winced and swatted her hands away. Aleka had grown so accustomed to the woman's uncanny speed and strength, she'd practically stopped seeing the scars and white hair that had troubled her before. Now, stretched out on the floor with her eyes squeezed shut and blood dripping down her face, the Huntress looked not like the woman in her mid-thirties that she was but like the frail, ancient being whose appearance she'd assumed.

After a long time, she drew a deep breath and opened her eyes. Their blue was undiminished, but she seemed to be having trouble focusing on Aleka's face.

"Concussion," she announced, gritting her teeth. "Give me a minute."

She closed her eyes again. Aleka gently mopped some of the blood from her forehead with a sleeve, but it wouldn't stop flowing. She looked beseechingly at Javier, who dug in his pockets and produced a wadded strip of cloth.

"It's not clean," he said, but Aleka took it from him anyway.

As carefully as she could, she lifted her mother's head to loop the cloth around it and tie the bandage in place. When she checked to make sure the knot was secure but not too tight, she saw that the cloth was covered in dark smudges. They were quickly effaced by the blood that soaked through.

"For your drawings?" she asked Javier.

"Yeah."

"You take them everywhere you go?"

He swallowed, his eyes darting around the room. "Aleka, I never meant to—"

"The damage is done now," she said. "Just let her rest."

They did, for another few minutes. Then Javier cleared his throat. "She shouldn't go to sleep," he said. "Not if she has a concussion."

At that, her mother's eyes opened. They stared at Javier with such undisguised malice he physically shrank away.

"Someone help me up," she said.

Javier knelt beside her, but she shoved his hand from her arm. "Wrong someone," she said.

Aleka got an arm around her mother's back and helped her to her feet. Or one of her feet; the moment her right foot touched the ground, she bit her lip to keep from crying out. Javier took a step toward them, but the Huntress's eyes lashed out at him like a striking snake. When he backed away, the woman turned to Aleka with an embarrassed grunt.

"Everyone has to learn sometime or other that their parents aren't invulnerable," she said. "Now let me see if I can put any weight on—"

Her words were cut off by a sharp intake of air. She shook her head, the wild white hair scratching Aleka's cheek like thorn bushes.

"No good," she said. "I tore something in there, probably my ACL. Maybe the meniscus too." She grimaced. "Runners know."

She signaled for Aleka to lower her to the ground, where she sat with the leg held straight out. She reached inside her jacket—checking for the jar, Aleka knew—and that seemed to relax her a little. "Get your boyfriend over here," she said.

"He's not my…"

Her mother's look was sharp enough to shut her up.

Javier came forward slowly, looking as if he was the one whose legs weren't working properly. Aleka's mother gestured impatiently for him to sit.

"Listen," she said. "*Really* listen this time. I don't blame you. Or maybe I do. But that's irrelevant. What matters is that the two of you are going to have to leave me while you get the gas."

"I can carry you."

She shook her head, then put a hand to her temple as if to stop the room from spinning. "The big ones are heavy. Nothing will happen to me here that couldn't happen just as easily somewhere else. Aleka."

Aleka kneeled and took her hand.

"I'm sorry about this," her mother said. "I told you I'd be there to fight for you, and I meant it when I said it. It's just this old body of mine—"

She clenched her teeth in a sudden spasm of pain.

"The two of you have to do exactly as I say," she continued when she got her breath back. "Collect the canisters. I'll tell you where to find them. Once you've done that, you can hunt for the rail line. It was blocked the last time I checked, but maybe you can force a passage through."

"Where does it go?" Aleka asked.

"Out of here is all I care about at the moment," her mother said. "With any luck, it'll reach all the way to the city, and if any of the cars are still working, it'll be a much quicker ride than the overland route. But it's deep belowground, and if either of you is ... taken before you arrive, you have to promise me you'll end it right then and there."

Twisting awkwardly, she reached into her pants pocket and brought out a nearly empty bottle of lighter fluid and her firestarter, then shoved them into Aleka's hands. The starter's operation was simple, but she went over it twice and made Aleka show that she could produce a flame before she seemed satisfied.

"Now, you," she said to Javier. "The artist."

She took the thickly folded map from her jacket and handed it to him. He spread it out face down, then found a lump of charred stone from the debris in the room. Following her spoken directions, he drew a map of the base that was much more than a simple floor plan: it had the appearance of depth and shade and contour, and yet, like that day Aleka had watched him draw the dawn, he produced it all in deft, confident strokes, scooping grime from the ground and spreading it with his fingers when his improvised charcoal stick ran out. By the time he was done, he'd created a detailed portrait of a place he'd never seen, a multi-level labyrinth as complicated as the inside of a termite mound. Aleka's mother insisted he hold it up for her inspection, but when he did, she whistled appreciatively.

"You're even better than I thought," she said. "I guess the listening thing comes and goes."

He averted his eyes and mumbled a nearly inaudible "thanks," then picked up the torch and stood. Aleka was about to join him when her mother gripped her arm and pulled her close.

"Be careful," she whispered fervently in her ear. "Stick to the path, and don't be tempted to go exploring. If all goes well, it should take you a couple of hours. I think I can hold out until—Jesus!"

Something about the way she'd changed position had set off the pain again. She cursed silently for a minute, then lifted her eyes to Aleka's.

"I wish you could have seen me when I was your age," she said. "I set school records in track. I know that doesn't mean anything to you. By the time you came along, school was another word for survival, and track was something the Skaldi left in the sand. But I could really run then. I ran for miles and miles through tunnels like these back east, and I was bleeding from a gut wound the whole time. I was trying to save your father, but it turned out I was too late. I was—"

"Mom," Aleka said. "Please stop."

"Don't call me that," her mother said breathlessly. "And stop wasting time. Get out of here."

Aleka tried to rise, but her mother clutched her arm as if she were dangling from the edge of a bottomless pit.

"I never should have left you," she said. "I was just a girl when you were born, not even eighteen years old, and I was scared, and I didn't know what to do, so I ran. Sixteen years—I missed out on sixteen years of your life. And then when I came back, I was useless to you, just a broken-down old woman whose own body betrayed her at the first opportunity. I used to be able to *run*, and now—"

"Mom," Aleka said. "Stop."

She put her arms around her mother's bony frame and pulled her into an embrace. Her mother gasped, which Aleka thought was from the pain, but then she realized the woman was crying, deep and hard. Aleka held her and stroked her hair, and a little song came to her from somewhere she couldn't remember—probably something Auntie used to sing to her—so she hummed it softly in her mother's ear. Maybe her mother knew the song too, because she gave one more big gulping sob and then quieted, her head bobbing up and down against Aleka's shoulder as if to keep time with the tune. Aleka pulled away, looking at her mother's face, where blood mingled with the tears. She bent to kiss a wrinkled cheek, and the aged face smiled.

"That's the way I kissed you when I said goodbye," she whispered.

"It's not goodbye," Aleka said. "It's just..."

Her mother touched her face. "Whatever it is, it's enough. Now go."

She lay back, breathing deeply but without apparent discomfort. Her eyes closed, and Aleka was about to remind her not to fall asleep, but she knew it wouldn't matter. The Huntress might demand attention from everyone else, but she wasn't such a good listener herself. That thought produced both a smile and a tear, but she brushed them both away when Javier took her arm.

"Come on," he said.

They crossed the room, Javier raising the torch high as they threaded their way around debris. Aleka almost stopped when she realized the ceiling might be unstable and could fall where her mother lay, but Javier's hand was insistent. At the far end of the room was an empty doorframe; the explosion from sixteen years ago must have blown the door off its hinges. Javier shined the torch into the dark tunnel beyond, then released Aleka's arm to consult his map.

"This way," he said.

"Javier," Aleka's mother called out.

Aleka looked back, but the only thing she could see distinctly was ghostly white hair glowing in the darkness of the room.

"Take care of her," her mother called.

"I will," he said.

"We'll be back soon," Aleka reassured her. She thought she saw her mother blow her a kiss, but she was too far away to be certain. Javier took her hand and pulled her into the corridor, and when Aleka glanced back, the darkness had swallowed all sign of her.

THEY MOVED AS quickly as they could, following the twists and turns in Javier's hand-drawn map. The tunnels were clear of debris, but Aleka felt jumpy the whole time, the shadows from the torch making her think something dark was crouched in the corners, waiting to spring out at them. Neither of them said a word, Javier focusing on the path ahead and Aleka letting his hand guide her. After his initial scan of the map, he didn't pause to check it again, so he must have memorized it. Aleka couldn't stop thinking that if he hadn't insisted on forcing his way into the room, they wouldn't have needed a map in the first place, because her mother would have been right by her side.

Why didn't you listen to her? she almost asked him more than once. *Why couldn't you trust her?* But the words refused to leave her mouth, probably because she didn't want to hear his answer.

"Quiet," he whispered, though Aleka couldn't remember making any noise, unless he was telling her heart to stop pounding.

He'd come to a stop. Aleka focused her attention on the corridor and saw that something blocked the path fifty feet ahead of them, shadowy mounds that loomed out of the deeper darkness. They looked more or less the same as the piles of debris in the room where they'd left her mother, and she wondered if there'd been another cave-in here. If so, she wasn't sure what they'd do; her mother might know a way around the impasse, but Javier had only the map in his hands and in his head.

He was studying the first of those maps now, holding the light close and scrutinizing it much longer than before. Aleka peeked over his shoulder and tried to make sense of his drawing, but she'd been paying too little attention for too long to know which part of it corresponded to the area where they were standing. Her years of experience as a climber were useless; every time her eyes switched from the map to the tunnel, the darkness seemed to blur and flow as if it were another charcoal sketch smudged by giant fingers.

"What is it?" she asked in a tight whisper.

"Nothing," he said. "Just we should be there by now. This should be the storage room."

139

"Are you sure?"

"I was extra careful with the scale," he said. "I could be off by a little, but not by that much."

He lifted the torch again, trying to illuminate the darkness ahead. This time, Aleka was sure she saw something flowing across the walls and ceiling, but then she told herself it was only the movement of the light, not the dark.

"Is there any way we missed it?" she asked.

"Unlikely."

"Then this must be it."

She took a step forward, but he gripped her wrist to hold her back. Annoyance compounded by anxiety rose in her, and she pulled free.

"This isn't the time to be all cautious," she said. "She's waiting for us."

He was about to say something else, but he must have decided better of it. Tucking the map in his pocket and taking her hand again, he held the torch high and matched her steps toward the darkness.

Individual shapes emerged as the torchlight fell on them. Most were unexceptional, shoulder-high piles of shattered concrete that were obviously the result of structural damage to the tunnel's ceiling or walls. In the center of the piles, however, a twisted black column of some unknown material stretched from floor to ceiling like a frozen waterfall. Glints of light made this larger shape seem to be in motion, but Aleka was convinced by now that that was nothing but an optical illusion. Still, her eyes didn't know what to make of it, especially when it seemed to glow white as if it were trapped in cobwebs or— she couldn't keep the thought from entering her mind—in strands of her mother's hair. Only when they stood in front of it, with Javier's torch practically touching the dark pillar, did she realize what it was.

A torrent of darkness had spilled from the ceiling and splashed against the floor, forming a broad puddle before freezing in place, every wave and droplet coated in a shiny film like a chrysalis. The source of the film was immediately evident: a canister shaped like the one her mother had used but as large as a propane tank lay on the floor beside where the black gunk had cascaded, its valve wide open. Leaning closer to the pillar, Aleka saw that the germ plasma had been in the process of forming human figures when the gas solidified it; arms and legs jutted from the central mass, while faces were buried deeper inside, many of them with mouths open as if they were screaming or drowning in the deluge. When Javier held the torch as high as his arm could reach, Aleka saw that the ceiling was gone, torn down by the germ plasma that had poured into the room. He waved the torch at the area behind the frozen shower, and the rest of the room jumped out of the shadows: wire shelves lined with the larger-size canisters, and at the far end, a metal-plated door with a wheel in the center to lock it. Except the walls of the room had collapsed along with the ceiling to form the piles of concrete that surrounded the Skaldi germ plasma, and the door stood by itself, a lonely sentinel guarding nothing.

"The plasma must have tried to get in," she said to Javier. "It must have broken down the whole room, but the gas was waiting for it."

"Yeah," he said, letting out a breath. "I guess that stuff really works."

Aleka walked past the leering faces and contorted limbs of the Skaldi, and found a wheeled cart beside the shelves. When she tried to roll it into position, she discovered that one of its wheels was mired in the black puddle. A sharp tug made it come loose, the fossilized plasma breaking apart like embers from a long-dead fire.

"Help me with these," she said.

"How many should we take?"

She lifted the first heavy tank and set it on the cart. "As many as it'll hold."

He joined her, and together, they quickly filled the cart. Aleka wished they could carry more canisters in their arms; powerful as the gas was, her mother had made it sound as if they might be facing a huge mass of the plasma once they reached the city. But one of them needed to keep their hands free to help her mother, so despite the longing look she threw at the tens of canisters still occupying the shelves when their cart was full, she knew they had to go.

"All right," she said to Javier, who was gripping two more tanks, one under each arm. "That's it."

"I can take these."

"Not if you have to carry her."

"I was thinking…"

"We don't have time to discuss this," she reminded him. "Let's go."

He tried to balance the tanks on top of the others in the cart, but then, with a reluctant sigh, he replaced them on the shelf. Hefting the torch once more, he lighted the path for Aleka to steer around the hideous monument and weave through the piles of fallen concrete.

She gave the cart a shove. Weighted down by its contents, it moved sluggishly, one of its wheels spinning in a circle and another turning sideways. Shadows from Javier's torch flowed past her boots, tricking her eyes again. She paused to shake the illusion from her head, but when she returned her attention to the cart, she found that it wouldn't move at all.

"The cart—" she started to say, only to realize her feet were stuck in place, too.

"Aleka!"

She spun to find him waving his torch at the pillar of Skaldi, which was frozen no more. Inky figures stretched against the goo as if it were a birthing sac, while the whole column whipped violently back and forth like a funnel cloud. Droplets had escaped from the edges of the puddle and were racing across the floor to join with the smaller pool that ensnared her boots. She watched in horror as something emerged from the center of the pool, a snaky shape that unfolded into a human form.

Its head rose from its chest, and she saw that it wore a face almost like her own.

"The fire!" she screamed at Javier. "You're feeding it!"

He turned to her, panic in his eyes. With nothing to douse the flame, he threw the torch as far down the corridor as he could, where it lay smoking amidst the fallen concrete. In the semidarkness that followed, Aleka saw the Skaldi's shadowy arms reach out for her, the face it had stolen from her teenage mother beginning to split.

Before it could touch her, she grabbed a canister from the cart and opened the valve wide.

A powerful jet of gas exploded from the spout, hitting the Skaldi where its face had been. It toppled to the floor while the rest of the plasma tried to retreat, but Aleka aimed the spray at the ground and stopped the liquid in its tracks. Pushing Javier out of the way, she directed the nozzle upward at the looming black pillar. The darkness and mist blinded her, and the only way she knew she was hitting her target was because of the unearthly moans that sounded all around her. It was as if the germ plasma held an entire army of Skaldi, all of them releasing their death wails at once.

The canister sputtered, emitting a last weak puff of gas. She threw it aside and was groping for another when hands clutched her shoulders. Without thinking, she lashed out and struck something solid and warm.

Javier's face appeared from the swirling mist. "It's dead!" he shouted. "We have to get out of here!"

Aleka looked dazedly at him. The moaning of the Skaldi echoed in her mind, but she realized that the actual creatures had gone silent. The pillar stood frozen again, wreathed in a second coating of smoky white, faces caught in expressions of anguish and horror. The black flesh seemed to have dripped from their skulls, distorting their features, but she recognized them nonetheless.

Auntie. Laman. The twins. Her mother. All of them younger versions of themselves, except for one.

Herself.

"It's not dead," she choked out. "It never dies."

"It's dead enough," he said.

He pulled her to her feet, grabbed a new canister to replace the one she'd emptied, and shoved the cart until its wheels came free of the petrified plasma. Together, they set off at a run, pushing the wobbly cart in front of them, Javier stopping only for an instant to retrieve the fallen torch.

They flew through the tunnels as fast as their burden would allow. Javier didn't glance at the map, and Aleka followed where he led, barely registering the endless hallways, the sharp turns, the intersections that appeared in a flash of torch-light then vanished as they plunged ahead. Even the flowing shadows on the walls passed her by without notice. All she could think of was that they'd be back soon, and her mother would be waiting for them.

Javier reached a door that was partly ajar and tried to pull it the rest of the way open, but it was stuck. He was wrestling with the cart, angling it in an attempt to squeeze it through the narrow opening, when Aleka finally came out of her trance. They'd walked down so many corridors to get to the containment vault, she'd lost track of their direction, but she didn't remember passing through any doors.

"Wait," she said. "We didn't come this way."

Javier hesitated with the cart balanced against him. "We're going another way."

"There's a shortcut?"

He rested the cart against the doorframe and took out the map. With a grimy finger, he traced the path they'd followed since leaving the containment vault, and Aleka saw that they were moving away from the room where they'd left her mother. Aghast, she snatched the map from his hands.

"What are you doing?" she said. "She's waiting for us!"

"No," he said. "She's not."

For a moment, she was too stunned to speak. "She's not?"

"She never meant to come with us," Javier said. "If she had, she'd have told us to carry her to the vault, load the cart, then take her the rest of the way to the rail line. It makes no sense to double back. She wanted us to go on alone."

"But—"

"It's why she gave us her firestarter," he said. "Why she had me draw the whole base. She was telling us to leave her."

145

"She never said that!"

"She didn't need to." His eyes met hers, and they blazed with guilt in his blackened, sweat-streaked face. "She told me to take care of you, Aleka. That was her way of saying good-bye."

Aleka released a single choked sob, then wheeled and was tearing back the way they'd come when Javier caught her around the waist and lifted her from the ground. She grabbed his wrists to try to free herself, but she knew at once that it was no use; his grip was as strong as steel, and she wondered momentarily if the Skaldi germ plasma had taken his body and was using him to trick her. But his skin was warm against hers, his pulse hammering in his veins. He wasn't Skaldi; he was a human being with strength and conviction on his side, while she was nothing but a fool whose heart had failed her at the realization that he was right. In less than a minute, she stopped fighting, and he set her back down.

"Why?" she cried. "Why did she do it?"

"Because she wanted you to live, and she knew she'd jeopardize that. But she also knew that, even if she was with us, she wouldn't have been able to bring herself to kill you if she had to."

He held the flaming torch before Aleka's eyes. Its heat drew sweat from her flesh, and she wished he would hold it against her until her body caught fire, consuming her as her father had been consumed, letting her melt into nothing rather than drag out this mockery of a life.

"You did this," she said to him in a voice shaking with anger. "If you'd listened to her, she'd still be with me."

"That's right," he said. "And it's why I'm listening to her last wishes now."

146

He lowered the torch, then went back to struggling with the cart. Aleka studied him, hating the businesslike way he was treating this, as if it were a logical puzzle he'd worked out to his satisfaction. She tried to convince herself there was a way to return, to save the woman who'd given her life not once but twice, but she could almost hear Auntie's voice shooting down her elaborate schemes, berating her for dreaming she could escape harsh reality. Or maybe it was her mother's voice she heard, telling her to be strong, reminding her that sometimes, to save the thing you love the most, you have to let it go.

She did say goodbye, she told herself. *She said it the only way she knew how, and I was the one who refused to listen.*

After a moment, she joined Javier, lifting the back wheels of the cart so they could wiggle it through the opening. It seemed heavier than anything she'd ever carried, and her feet were leaden as they took the first step into the darkened hallway beyond.

Chapter 12

Twice orphaned, Aleka followed Javier without caring where he was leading her.

He didn't seem the slightest bit lost. Map in hand, he turned at the intersections it told him to, chose the correct branch when tunnels bifurcated. Each time she helped him lift the cart over debris or steer it through a half-open doorway, she glanced listlessly at his drawing, but the combination of weak light and defeated will made it blur into illegibility, a faded landscape of gray and black through which her body floated like a wraith's.

No matter where her feet went, her mind was on her mother, alone in the room where they'd left her without food or water or the ability to run. If there were Skaldi elsewhere in the complex, if the parasite that had demolished the containment vault was only one of many such monsters haunting the hallways, they'd find her in time, possibly before she had a chance to starve. Was that better, to die in a single instant of soul-draining agony than to linger for days while hunger consumed her body and wracked her mind?

But she already knew the answer to that. She'd lived through starving times in Auntie's camp, months-long stretches of drought when the adults walked around dazed and hollow-eyed while the children took to chewing hunks of desert clay to keep the hunger pangs from tormenting them all night. Those times had been nearly unendurable, and yet they were nothing next to the torture Aleka had felt during the starvation phase of Skaldi existence. As a human being, you could only starve once. As Skaldi, you starved again and again and again, and there was no end to the cycle short of crumbling into dust. The thought of her mother being forced to endure such hell—and all to give her daughter a second chance at life—opened a jagged scar in her heart that she knew would never close.

Javier had unlatched a bolted door and Aleka had helped him lower the cart down a stairwell, pausing to rest at a landing then taking a switchback to the next lower level, when he consulted his map and announced, "This is it."

Aleka looked around them. They stood in a gloomy compartment at the bottom of the stairwell, the light of the torch reflecting off a closed metal door. Black streaks that looked suspiciously like claw-marks covered the cement stairs and floor. "This is what?"

"The rail line," he said. "We're here."

He pointed to the map, his finger resting on a tube-like shape that snaked off the edge of the page. She might have marveled at how he'd produced the illusion that the tube lay deep beneath the other levels, but she couldn't muster any enthusiasm either for his artistry or their arrival.

"It's cold," she said, hugging her shoulders and feeling goosebumps up and down her arms.

"Probably because we're so deep underground." He inspected the torch, which was sputtering badly. "Help me out with this."

He set the torch on the floor and extinguished the meager flame with his boot, then held out a hand toward her. Aleka remembered that her mother had given her the fire-starting kit, so she took the items from her pocket and handed them to him. The instructions for using the firestarter were fresh in her mind, but even that simple task felt like it would take more energy than she could muster.

"We need rags or something," Javier said.

"I'm sure there were some in her pack," she said. "Which is now in the middle of the desert."

He let that pass without reaction. "I might have a few pieces left."

He hunted in his pockets, but came up with nothing except a miniscule strip of cloth. Aleka tried not to think of the bloody bandage wrapped around her mother's head, but it seemed that one way or another, everything led back to her.

"Try these," she said.

She sat and unlaced her boots. The bandages she'd wrapped around her feet more than a week ago stank of dried sweat and blood, but she handed them over, and he accepted them silently. He tied the lengths of cloth around the end of the staff, squirted a few drops of lighter fluid on them, and relit the torch. When it burst into flame, he returned the kit to her.

"We have to be careful," he said. "We're pretty low on fuel."

"Something else I'm sure she had in her pack."

"Look," he said, "I told you I was sorry."

"That doesn't change anything."

"Which is why I'm not going to tell you again. We're all sorry about a lot of things. Me, you, your mom, everyone. It's not a contest. It's called life."

He pulled the door open, waving the torch in front of him as if to ward off Skaldi. Aleka was about to remind him that fire would only feed the creatures, but what was the point? He turned to her, his face expressionless.

"Good news," he said. "The lights are on."

She glanced through the doorway. What he called the lights—and what he counted as "on"—were matters of opinion; a few weak bulbs glowed at a distance of twenty or more feet from where they stood, just enough to see that there was a step down from the doorway to the floor of the tunnel. Carefully, they lifted the cart and, with Javier walking backward, negotiated it through the door. When they set it down, Aleka saw that the lights were embedded at floor level, tracing the path of the tunnel as it receded into distance and darkness in both directions.

"Which way?" she asked.

He gestured. "West. But it's not like we can walk the whole way pushing this thing. She said something about cars…"

He looked around, but there was nothing to be seen except the metal rail that ran along the floor of the tunnel. After a minute's inspection, he handed the torch to Aleka and took hold of the cart's handle.

"All right, so we head west," he said. "And hope we catch some luck along the way."

"Because we've had so much of that."

"Better than standing here waiting for the Skaldi to show up."

"You've got an answer to everything, don't you?"

"I've got a job to do," he said. "You're welcome to join me if you want."

Without another glance at her, he started down the tunnel, pushing the cart in front of him. Aleka steamed in silence for a minute before following.

The going was much easier here than it had been in the corridors above. The way was smooth and straight, and though the lights didn't provide enough illumination to see clearly, they did mark the direction of the tunnel. After a minute or two, Javier took the torch back from Aleka and doused it to save on fuel. She would have preferred to be able to see Skaldi coming at them, but she kept quiet. They were well armed with the only weapon that worked against the creatures, and if they didn't find a car to carry them, they wouldn't make it to the city alive anyway.

They'd walked for no more than ten minutes when the floor lights came to an abrupt stop and Javier took the fire-starter back to relight the torch. When it blazed again and Aleka saw what lay in front of them, she let out a laugh.

Their path was blocked by a massive cave-in. A few pieces of broken concrete were piled at the base of the obstruction, but other than that, it looked less like the ceiling had collapsed than like the entire tunnel had folded in on itself the way desert flowers did at night. Javier rapped the cement with his knuckles, but there was no reverberation to suggest how thick the wall might be.

"End of the line," Aleka said.

"Not necessarily." He laid his ear close to the wall and tapped in a few other spots. Aleka couldn't hear any difference, but he seemed satisfied with the results. "Your mom said the rail line was blocked the last time she was here. She wouldn't have told us to come this way if she didn't think there was a chance of breaking through."

He wheeled the cart closer and braced the torch against it to give him light. Then he began assailing the roadblock at the point he must have deemed weakest, using his fists and fingers to scrape against the cement. He kept at it for long minutes, the scratching sounds making Aleka's goosebumps reappear. When he paused to catch his breath, she saw that there was nothing to mark his efforts but a few indentations in the wall no larger than tooth-marks.

"Forget it, Javier," she said. "You'd have just as much luck digging a hole through the floor."

He didn't relent. If anything, he attacked the wall even more wildly, clawing against it like a mountain climber trying to scale a sheer rock face with his fingernails alone. When that didn't work, he lifted one of the gas canisters from the cart and slammed it against the wall, denting the canister badly but producing no change in the barricade.

"You're going to break that thing," she said.

He didn't listen. The canister came down again, hitting the wall so hard it flew from his hands and rolled to a stop in front of her.

"My hero," she said.

He spun to face her, and she jumped back involuntarily. His eyes were filled with such a baleful light she wondered again if the germ plasma had infected him in the containment vault.

"I'm no hero," he said in a rasping voice. "But I'm no quitter either. You think it's going to save your mom if we give up? Or were you planning to let her and everyone else die just to prove I did wrong?"

He turned back to the wall and resumed his assault with bare hands. There was no apparent change in the obstacle, but the torch began to sputter again, filling the tunnel with so much smoke she could only see his shadowy outline. A prolonged coughing spell bent him double, but when he was able to stand up straight, he went back to pummeling the wall as if there'd been no interruption. Aleka thought she heard a noise from behind her, but when she turned, she saw nothing in the dim illumination of the floor lights. She looked back to find Javier wrapped in a smoky corona, no longer hitting the wall with his fists but standing with his palms against it as if he could push it over. His arms and shoulders tensed, and the crazy thought passed through her mind that the wall was actually going to come crashing down. Then his body slumped, and he slid to the floor with the wall at his back, head bowed and long hair hiding his face.

Aleka took a step toward him. He was panting heavily, and beneath a coating of chalky dust, his hands were marred with bleeding cuts. Behind him, red smudges showed on the gray concrete like childish copies of his drawings.

She came closer and crouched beside him. When he spoke, his breath shuddered like he was crying.

"I didn't want to believe it," he said. "I didn't want to admit those bastards had won."

She sat while he turned his head toward the wall. Delicately, she reached for his hand and held it in both of hers. The blood felt tacky from all the dust mingled with it.

"It was never going to work," she said.

He glanced at her, eyes wary beneath his long hair. As if he really were a child who was in for another scolding.

"I was so excited when she found me," Aleka said. "I must have been living my whole life in mourning without knowing it, and then she was there, and I didn't question anything else.

154

It was like I was a little girl again, and I believed in magic, the way the kids in camp believe grown-ups can work miracles. Keep them safe. Make the nightmares go away. Stop the Skaldi from coming for them in the dark."

She removed one of her hands from his and brushed hair from his forehead. His eyes focused on hers, and this time, there was no distrust in them.

"But the truth is, she never had much of a plan," Aleka said. "The Skaldi were always going to win, and I think she knew that. But she never said it, and so I let myself not think about it, because she was there, and she made me feel ... I don't know. Complete. Content. Whole."

"And I took that from you."

"No," she said. "I got to be with her, to learn that she was real and not some dream I'd made up. I must have known all along that it wouldn't last forever, but that doesn't make it any less real."

His eyes never left hers. "You were lucky."

"Yes," she said. "I guess I was."

He inched closer. The intensity of his gaze made her think he was going to try to kiss her, and that made her wonder whether she would let him if he tried. She'd never thought of him that way, mostly because she'd never thought of anyone that way. He was cute and strong, and he could be helpful like he was on the day he taught her how to fight dirty, but she'd spent the past sixteen years looking away from where she was, ignoring the things right in front of her while her eyes strayed to some far horizon. He'd been a shadow in her life for as long as she could remember; everyone had. Now that her vista had shrunk to this wall two feet in front of her nose, maybe a first kiss—and a last one—wouldn't be such a bad idea.

155

"I never told you why I left camp," he said.

She was surprised by the direction of his thought, but she went with it. "You just kind of … vanished one day."

"I didn't have a choice. Arachne would have killed me if I'd stuck around."

"She…" Aleka realized that she was even closer to his face than to the wall, and she pulled back a tiny bit. "Why would she do that?"

"Because I was running drugs. She knew for a long time it was someone in camp, but then she caught me with a whole pile of the stuff. She gave me a choice: leave, or face the music. I laughed in her face when she said that. I figured it was just old-woman talk."

He reached out a bloody hand. Aleka froze, but all he did was lay a finger lightly against her throat.

"Next thing I knew, that old woman had me flat on my back with a knife right about here," he said. "I didn't stick around long after that. She gave me a canteen and enough food to last a few days, and I was gone."

His hand left a tingling sensation when it withdrew. Aleka had trouble picturing the small, gray-haired woman taking down someone as strong as Javier, but then again, if she was the one who'd taught Aleka's mother to fight, anything was possible.

"I drifted around for months after that," Javier continued his story. "Living aboveground some of the time, mostly exploring the tunnels like I used to. I'd never been into the crap I sold, so I didn't have any bad habits to break. But I remembered the people I'd sold to, the ones who would come to my tent in the middle of the night begging for a fix, and it was like they were still with me. Men, women, old folks—I think

Arachne knew they would come back to haunt me in my dreams. I think she knew that the worst thing she'd done to me wasn't pushing me out, it was making me carry around all the people I'd wronged and couldn't apologize to."

"Is that when you met Aesir?"

"Yeah," he said. "He showed up one day when I was in the tunnels, told me his plans, made me an offer. Gave me a purpose. Didi and the others were already with him, and sometimes it seemed to me like they were on some kind of drug, but I was never tempted to get back into the business. I'd found an old drawing kit after I left camp, and I started sketching again like I used to when I was younger, which helped me get my head straight. That plus believing I was going to work with Aesir to destroy the Skaldi. The way I saw it, those bastards were the ones who'd made us what we are, some of us dealers and the rest of us junkies. I didn't care what happened to me as long as I could do my part to help everyone else get clean and sober."

"You helped me," she said.

"That was your mom. All I did was get in her way."

"No," she said. "Javier, I can't explain, but ... you stayed by my side. You never gave up on me. Even when I'd given up on myself."

He grinned. "You trying to make me out to be some kind of hero?"

"I don't need a hero," she said. "Not anymore."

She'd drawn closer to him again, as if the flow of his words had exerted a magnetic pull. A minute ago, she'd been asking herself whether to seal their death with a kiss, but now she felt an urgency to do it, as if kissing him would be a way to deny the Skaldi their victory at the very end. A way to show them that no matter what they could kill, there were some things they couldn't.

His face neared. She was closing her eyes in anticipation of the moment their lips would meet when she realized he was standing, not leaning toward her. She flushed, but hoped he couldn't tell with the bad light and the grit that caked her cheeks.

"We should get back to your mom," he said. "Maybe she was wrong and we can break out that way. Or at least be with her when the time comes."

She accepted his hand. Her heart warred over the lost kiss, but really, what did she expect? The last time she'd come on to him, she'd been trying to kill him. And anyway, she decided he was right. She could spend these final moments hiding in the dark kissing a boy she barely knew, but it was much better to spend them with the woman who'd given her the life she was about to lose.

Javier retrieved the torch and used the few remaining drops of lighter fluid to restart it. He took one last look at the cave-in, where the marks he'd made were as insignificant as the heart-enclosed initials people from before the wars used to carve in the strata of the Grand Canyon. He lingered for a long moment, until Aleka tugged his arm.

"Javier, we—"

"Wait," he said. "Do you hear that?"

She listened. Expecting to hear the Skaldi's moans, it took her longer than it should have to realize what was happening. But she was a veteran of the underworld; she knew the warning signs of collapse when she heard them. And felt them, the tunnel vibrating as if the ground were about to split in two.

"Run!" she said, grabbing his hand.

They turned to flee, but they'd taken only a half-dozen steps when they collided with a barrier as solid as the wall and were thrown to the ground. Javier's torch spun free of his grip, and he seemed too dazed to retrieve it. Aleka could see something moving just beyond the torch's glow, but when she scrambled to stand, a black shape like a huge clawed hand closed on her ankles, pinning her to the ground. She cried out for Javier, who'd no sooner regained his feet than another shape whipped out of the darkness and flung him against the wall twenty feet away, where he crumpled to the floor and lay without moving.

Aleka looked up as the thing stepped into the light of the fallen torch. It was every bit as dark as the tunnel it had emerged from, and except for the hand that held her, it was as formless as night, a mass of plasma that stood and moved without visible limbs. The organism shifted and flowed, sometimes extending snaky pseudopods, sometimes producing a bubble that might have become a head before it popped and was sucked back into the rippling body. Streams of darkness dripped from the central mass and slithered across the floor, only to rise as recognizably human forms: Didi and the other runners, all of them staring at Aleka as if pleading for help. She would have reached out to them, but the shape that belonged to Didi dissolved into a viscous tentacle that wrapped around Aleka's chest, draining her of the will to speak even if she'd been able to draw breath.

The creature came closer, and Aleka watched it dwindle in size until it assumed the diminutive shape of Aesir, his eyes afire behind the opening in his black head-cloth. The cloth unwound itself, revealing the features of a man Aleka didn't recognize, dark-haired and beady-eyed but at least twenty years younger than she'd assumed Aesir to be. The stranger's hands flew to his neck as if he were strangling, and a deluge of black vomit that couldn't possibly have been contained within his small body forced its way from his mouth, spilling to the floor until there was nothing left of him except a hollow shell like a spider's empty egg sac. The black fluid spread in a sticky pool at Aleka's feet before coalescing into an enormous form that towered above her: a man at least eight feet tall, dark-eyed and grim-faced and dressed in an immaculate uniform of nighttime blue. He was there for only a second before the fluid bled from his body, shrinking him to the size of a ten-year-old boy who stood before her with long brown hair and a smirk frozen on his face.

The boy took a step toward her, coming close enough to bend down and caress her cheek with a daintily shaped hand. He half-turned as another figure emerged from the darkness of the tunnel.

It was a woman, long-legged and with wild white hair that surrounded a visage as scarred as the desert. She moved stiffly, dragging her right leg, and the stink of a corpse that had rotted for days in the sun came with her.

"Faithless daughter," the shade of the Huntress said. "You should never have deserted me."

Chapter 13

The boy who'd emerged from the germ plasma gestured with petite hands, and the puppet-shape of Aleka's mother moved at his will.

She hobbled like a broken doll, her right leg bending unnaturally when she put weight on it. Based on that, Aleka was convinced that her mother hadn't been fused with the shapeshifting organism that had consumed Didi and the other runners; it seemed that the Skaldi had taken over her actual body, damaged though it was. But Aesir—or the boy who lay beneath Aesir's false covering—held her on a leash as surely as the rest.

When he'd made her go through her paces, the boy waved his hands again, and she stalked directly toward her daughter, leaning down until their foreheads touched. From this close, Aleka saw spirals of darkness swirling through her mother's irises, all but obliterating their original blue. When her wrinkled lips parted, the stench of rottenness was so overpowering Aleka felt as if she'd been lowered into her own mother's grave.

"We were fools to think we could defeat him," the Huntress spoke in a voice of bitterness and self-loathing. "He's been playing games with me from the start, disguising himself so completely I had no idea who he was. He allowed me to run off with you so he could trap us in this place, where he can carry us to the city by the lake and force me to witness his triumph before the end."

Her lips drew back in an expression of intolerable pain. With a sound of wet tissue tearing, her stolen body opened, the Skaldi's scar splitting her down the center. Aleka caught a glimpse of moist gray insides, smelled the suffocating stench of decay. She felt herself being drawn into the cavity, and she struggled to free herself from the coils of plasma that held her. But before the edges of the scar could close, her mother screamed, collapsing to the floor as though every sinew in her body had been cut. A new smell wafted through the tunnel, the acrid scent of singed flesh.

The Huntress lay shaking violently like someone dying of fever. Her scar had closed and her face had returned almost to normal, except where dark red blotches of burned skin marred her wrinkled cheeks. She panted heavily, each gust of breath bathing Aleka's face with the smell of putrescence. When she gazed up at the boy, her blackened eyes beseeched him the way a child would its parent.

"Please…" she said.

"Surprised?" he taunted in a high-pitched voice, his thin lips curling. "Try again."

Once more his hands gestured, and the body of the Huntress was pulled upright as if by invisible strings. This time, the Skaldi that had taken her mother's shape squeezed its mouth shut in an apparent attempt to keep the scar from opening, but the boy spread his hands, and her face and chest were peeled back with the precision of a scalpel. Moving jerkily, the figure advanced on Aleka, but it had no sooner touched her than it shrieked and fell backward to flail on the ground. This time, the scent of seared flesh was so strong it overwhelmed the odor of rot, and patches of exposed skin smoked like the carcass of an animal over a campfire.

The Skaldi raised its head blindly. Aleka averted her gaze, but not in time to prevent the image of her mother's empty eye-sockets and blackened cheeks from being seared into her memory.

"You might wonder about all the theatrics," the boy said in an offhand way. "But I thought the famed Diana would enjoy a demonstration of what her little girl's capable of." He prodded the broken creature with a toe. "Now, aren't you the proud parent?"

With the irresistible power he exerted over her mother's body, the boy made her flip onto her stomach and crawl like an insect toward Aleka. Bony hands clutched her daughter's uniform and pulled her close, until the two were face to face again. Aleka shut her eyes to escape the vision of her mother's skull-like countenance, and so she only heard the woman scream and fling herself away once again. When Aleka dared to open her eyes, she saw a crumpled form smoldering on the floor at the boy's feet, its hair gone and its naked pate tattooed with angry black burns.

"That was fun," the boy said, sweeping his arm sideways and making the miserable creature crawl back into the darkness of the tunnel. "But let's move like we've got a purpose, as my dad used to say."

Ignoring both Aleka and her mother, he strolled toward the cave-in, where Javier lay unmoving against the stone. The boy beckoned with a hand, and another of the teen runners sloughed into a pool of inky fluid that ran along the ground toward Aleka's unconscious companion. When it reached him, the plasma solidified into a tentacle, wrapping around Javier's ankle and depositing him roughly beside the rail. She saw that he was breathing shallowly, but the blood dripping from his nose made her worry about internal injury. She tried to reach out toward him, only to have the Didi-tentacle cinch tight, pulling her arms against her sides.

The second tentacle had returned to the cave-in, where it reared from the floor and stood swaying back and forth like a snake sizing up its prey. Apparently having determined how best to attack the obstruction, it metamorphosed into long, ropy fingers that sank into the concrete as if it were putty. Even so, the blockage was as sturdy as Javier had discovered, and long minutes of scooping and digging failed to break through to the other side. When a groan from the ceiling heralded a second cave-in that effaced the small area the fingers had cleared, the boy stamped his foot and shouted childish obscenities at his servant.

"You worthless piece of shit!" he ranted. "I'm not paying you by the hour! Faster!"

At the sound of his voice, all of the runners except for the one that held Aleka melted into black sludge and joined the first. They rose from the floor not as human figures but as hundreds of appendages that plunged into the cave-in with such abandon the tunnel filled with choking dust. The cloud swirled around the small figure of the boy, cloaking everything but his reddened, screaming face. When the cacophony of flying stone and violent curses had faded past a final echo, his rigid posture relaxed and his face assumed the semblance of a smile.

Smoke hung in the air, but the obstruction was gone, the dim floor lights vanishing to a distant pinpoint of darkness. Aleka and Javier's cart had been tipped over and the canisters spilled onto the floor, along with large slabs of cement that had been hurled in every direction. Some had landed just short of the boy who'd ordered their removal; he must have had such control over these extra appendages that they'd known exactly where to deposit the rubble without risking his safety. When he snapped his fingers and the wretched creature that had been the Huntress scuttled out of the dark to cower at his feet, Aleka knew that the Skaldi inhabiting her mother's body had spoken the truth: they'd been fools to think they could defeat this demon, whose power seemed as limitless as his capacity for evil.

"Go," he said to the pseudopods that waited patiently like well-behaved children, and they turned into black bird-shapes that flew shrieking down the newly opened tunnel. As soon as the flapping sound of their wings faded, the boy turned to Aleka.

"Vampire bats," he said. "Very common down here."

Aleka shuddered, wondering if any more of the foul creatures were roosting overhead.

"They'll take a while to return," the boy said in a conversational tone. "Which gives us plenty of time to get acquainted. *Really* acquainted, I mean. Now that we have nothing to hide."

He sat, showing his teeth in a disturbing combination of smile and snarl. A wave of his hand made the Didi-thing release Aleka, its body slithering away to curl around his arm while she sat up and faced the boy. His fingers idly drummed against his knees, and as they did, the thing that had been her mother writhed on the floor. Aleka couldn't believe there was enough of the woman left to feel pain, but it looked like her body, or maybe her soul, was being tortured beyond endurance.

"Stop that," she said.

The boy's eyes lit maliciously. "You mean this?"

165

He closed a fist, and the Skaldi contorted impossibly, its head leering between crablike legs. Aleka needed to summon all her willpower to keep her voice from quavering.

"You've made your point," she said. "Now *stop*."

The boy's face reddened. Then, emitting a careless laugh, he made a sweeping motion with his hand, and the Skaldi untangled itself, dropping to the floor like a pile of rags.

"Have it your way," the boy said. "Though it's only fair to note that she made me look like a fool the first time we met, so this is basically payback. Trust me, if the shoe was on the other foot, she'd give as good as she gets."

His tongue protruded to lick thin lips. In the second before it shot back inside his mouth, Aleka was sure it was forked like a rattler's.

"To give you some background, this all started the year I met your mom," he said. "The same year you were born. I know I don't show my age, but appearances can be deceiving."

His features rippled like nighttime water, and the face of the middle-aged man with beady eyes replaced the childish countenance. Another ripple, and the grim-faced giant was there, his craggy visage completely incongruous on the child-size body. One more ripple, and she caught a fleeting hint of Mouse's sharp nose and large ears before the self-satisfied look of the boy returned.

"That's just a sample," he said. "You've already met the old geezer. I'll admit he was a bit of a challenge after these mindless things"—he lifted the arm that held the Didi-creature—"but I'm pleased with the results: just mysterious enough to be tempting, not so obvious as to make you overly mistrustful. More courtly in manner than suits my usual style, but he served my purposes, don't you agree?"

"So Aesir was … part of you?" Aleka asked. "Like the rest of them?"

"He was one of the people who used to work at this base," the boy answered. "A guard or something. Possibly one of the first to become infected by the germ plasma, before he passed it on to the scientists who'd created the stuff. I was banking on your mom not recognizing my hand behind the old gent, and it seems my gamble paid off."

He examined his fingernails idly. For a moment, they grew long like the fingers that had removed the cave-in, then they shrank to child-size again.

"Do you know what Aesir means?" he asked.

Aleka shook her head.

"It's a collective," the boy said. "The name for a group of gods that people used to worship eons ago—a pantheon, to use the term from those days. In their time, the Aesir were said to be all-powerful, rulers of the earth and sky. But there were also legends that spoke of their end, a catastrophe that those who worshipped them called the Twilight of the Gods. A day when all the powers of the underworld would be unleashed and the lords of creation would topple from their thrones, never to rise again."

He looked at her expectantly, but most of what he'd said made no sense to her. The only gods she'd ever heard of were the animal-spirits Auntie and Mouse talked about, and no one said anything about them ruling the earth and sky, much less succumbing to the powers of the underworld. When it became obvious he wasn't going to get the reaction he was looking for, the child shrugged.

"No biggie," he said. "It's not like I believe any of that crap either. People make their own gods, which means the gods they make are as weak as their creators. The Skaldi happen to be the latest iteration, but like all their predecessors, they were born with a fatal flaw—an Achilles heel, as it were. They were doomed to wither away like the gods of old, and there was nothing anyone could do to avert their fate." He looked at her eagerly, the snake-like tongue emerging once more. "Until I had a better idea."

"Which was what?"

"Which was going to change the course of history, that's what. It came to me sixteen years ago, but it wasn't until recently that it came of age. It was born inside the body of this old bag"—his hand flicked carelessly toward the inert shape of her mother—"and now that it's matured, I'm going to use it to make sure the gods really *do* live forever, with a power that outlasts the fools who dreamed them up."

His voice had grown heated and his face flushed. Aleka would have asked him to explain, but he went on without her needing to.

"You've probably already figured out that the power inside you doesn't destroy the germ plasma," he said. "That was the old man's little white lie, necessary to get you on board. The truth is a lot more complicated, but the basics of it derive from the fact that you bridge two species, correcting for the shortcomings of each. In its embryonic form, the germ plasma is capable of consuming enormous amounts of energy from available hosts, but once the engorged cells replicate the bodies they've drained to form mature Skaldi, they break down quickly and are forced to colonize new bodies over and over again to avoid dissolution. Human beings, on the other hand, consume relatively insignificant amounts of energy, but their cells are designed to keep that process going for sixty, seventy, even a hundred years. Putting the two together, we've got what I theorized back before you were born: a perfect fusion of humankind and Skaldi-kind, capable of unlimited energy absorption *and* retention. Much stronger and more durable than the old-time Skaldi, and capable of feeding a guy like me the fuel to do *this*."

Faster than thought, his small shape reared in a massive wave that shadowed the tunnel. Hundreds of faces bulged from the fluid the way they had from the plasma that she and Javier had encountered in the containment vault, only this time, every one of the faces belonged to the boy. The many faces merged into a single face large enough to swallow Aleka whole, but then it vanished as quickly as it had come, and all that was left was the demon-child, hands on knees, grinning as before.

"Like I said," he commented. "Food of the gods."

Despite herself, Aleka was shaken. She tried to keep her voice level when she asked him, "But my mom bled the germ plasma from me. She told me it was gone."

"And mother always knows best, right?" the boy scoffed. "Except this time, her knowledge was based on partial data. I made sure of that before I dispatched the old man to track you down." He shook his head in mock mournfulness. "From the information I left behind, she concluded—correctly, as it turns out—that expelling the plasma from your blood saved you from becoming just another washed-out Skaldi wandering the desert in search of its next meal. What she didn't know was that once your Skaldi genes were switched on, they'd *stay* on, plasma or no plasma. With each moment you've existed in that heightened state of activation, you've pulled exponentially greater reserves of energy from the world around you, and

169

grown increasingly powerful in turn. You've become a living, breathing embodiment of the germ plasma, a human analogue to its limitless potential. *You're* the new god, Aleka. You're the one we've been waiting for, and we've prepared a whole city—hell, a whole planet—for you to command. All you need to do in return, and this seems like a minor thing to ask, is to help me produce more of your kind, more gods to rule by their mother's side."

He paused, his eyes roving over her, his tongue sliding out to lick his lips. Aleka gagged at the lurid anticipation in his childish gaze. She didn't fully understand what this creature was, but she knew he would never allow anyone else to rule alongside him. He would use her to fulfill his desires, but *he* would be the one to lord it over all of creation.

"What if I refuse?" she asked.

"Don't be cute," he said. "I've been extremely understanding given the circumstances, but there are limits to my patience."

"I could kill myself."

"With what?" he said glibly. "You're a *god*, Aleka, don't you get it? An inexhaustible source of power that can no more extinguish itself than the sun can. Go ahead, try. Show me how easy it is to escape what you are."

The dark coil that used to be Didi unwound itself from his arm, slithering across the floor to where Javier lay. It fished around in his pocket, emerging with her mother's firestarter and dropping it in Aleka's lap. She didn't wonder how the boy had known it was there; she no longer believed there was anything he didn't know. She faced him, wishing her eyes could burn as hot as the flame. Wondering if, based on what he'd said, they actually could.

"I dare you," he said.

"I know you do," she answered.

She took up the firestarter and flicked it until a flame caught. Every instinct in her body rebelled against what she was about to do, but she turned her head away and shakily moved her other hand into the flame.

"Believe me now?" the boy asked.

Aleka stared at her hand, its flesh as healthy and whole as if the fire had never touched it. For a moment, she thought she must have been shaking so badly she'd missed the flame. But when she tried again, there was no doubt about what her eyes showed her: the flame sparked, briefly encircled her hand in tongues of orange and blue, then was snuffed out. Her hand felt warm as if she'd held it over a campfire on a chilly desert night, but the fire that should have burned her even worse than her mother's torch from two days ago had left no permanent mark on her skin.

She was trying to process what she'd seen, what she *was*, when the boy startled her by clapping joyfully and jumping to his feet.

"They're here," he said.

Black figures separated from the darkness. They were human in form, but faceless and slit down the middle by the scars characteristic of their species. As they lumbered forward, Aleka saw that they were dragging some kind of mechanism along the rail behind them, a pair of connected platforms with metal handgrips and wheels. The cars came to a squealing halt, and the creatures melted back into black muck and dribbled across the floor until they were sucked into the boy's body.

"All aboard!" he called out, pumping his fist several times as if he were checking a rope to make sure it was tied tight.

Aleka rose and took a wooden step toward him. She had reached the rail line when she stopped.

"What about Javier?" she asked.

"Oh, geez!" the boy said, smacking his forehead. "I must be getting forgetful in my old age. Your boyfriend's already served his primary purpose—I needed human prey to test how well the plasma was working on your physiology—but by all means, let's bring him along. If he wakes up, he can watch the show. If he doesn't, well, it never hurts to have some collateral around in case you become ... uncooperative."

Aleka glared at him. The idea of the boy using Javier as some kind of hostage made her sick, but at the same time, she couldn't leave him here. "And my mom?"

"Afraid not," he gibed. "She's already jumped through all the hoops I needed her to. She'll crumble to dust a few days from now, and that loose end will be tied up as neat as can be." He performed an elaborate, mocking bow. "Any time you're ready, milady."

Aleka bent down to check on Javier, who lay on his back beside the rail, surrounded by spilled gas canisters. When she turned to the boy, his face was fixed in a leer as if he'd been studying her butt. He was about to say something when she opened the nozzle of the canister she'd retrieved and pointed it directly at him.

His mouth froze in a perfect *o* of astonishment. His body disappeared under a dense, smoky film; she was so close to him and pouring so much gas at his small form, he had no time to struggle as it hardened into a shell. When it was done, she pushed against where his chest would have been, and he fell backward, the frozen shape shattering into a million fragments that sparkled on the ground like obsidian.

172

Aleka was kneeling beside her mother when something tapped her on the shoulder, and she spun to face it.

The boy was there, his body restored to its normal size, his eyes shining with delight. The black fragments were gone. In the few seconds her back had been turned, the plasma had resurrected itself and resumed its accustomed shape.

"Nice try," he said. "But I told you the plasma feeds on energy, and you're simply oozing with it."

"I got that part," she said. "I guess it doesn't make you any smarter, though."

Before the boy could stop her, she flicked the firestarter and set her mother's body ablaze.

The boy cried out, but the body of the Huntress was little more than a dried husk, and it caught fire at once. For a second, Aleka thought the few scraps of flesh on her mother's cheeks wrinkled in gratitude, but then her head burst into flame as well, and the look was gone.

"I love you, Mom," Aleka said.

A tentacle shot out to shove her aside, but there was nothing left for it to vent its rage on except burning ash.

Tears from the smoke filled Aleka's eyes. She rose calmly to face the boy, who for once seemed unable to summon a retort. His cheeks were infused with blood or whatever else ran beneath his false skin, and his eyes bulged like a rabid coyote's. Aleka dropped the dead firestarter at his feet.

"Javier stays with me," she said. "If you lay a single finger on him, you can forget about all your little plans."

The boy gaped at her. Gradually, his face returned to its pale hue, and his voice recovered its carefree tone.

"Okay by me," he said. "The two of you being an 'item,' there's someone in the city who might want to meet him."

JOSHUA DAVID BELLIN

"Who?"

The boy's face spread in a gleeful smirk.

"An old friend of the family," he said. "The leader of the Skaldi from back in the day, who's got it in his head that we're going to help him and his kind live forever." He reached up to chuck Aleka under the chin. "I was never much for following orders, though. How about you?"

Chapter 14

The cars flew down the track, Aleka holding a handgrip in one tightly clenched fist and Javier in the other.

He hadn't woken up, but he was breathing normally and his nosebleed had stopped. Her deepest fear was that he'd suffered brain damage and would never regain consciousness—or if he did, it would be as a person completely different from the one she'd just started to know. But she had no way to determine when or if he might revive, so all she could do was cling to him as the cars careened into the darkness.

She was amazed by their speed. In Auntie's trucks, the best they'd managed was twenty or twenty-five miles an hour, and that was only when they were fleeing an imminent Skaldi attack and the terrain permitted it. On the missile line, it felt as if they were moving at a rate two or three times that, the rattle of the wheels roaring in her ears and her eyes stinging beneath her streaming hair. Even when they reached a curve, they didn't slow down but whipped around it with a metallic screech and a feeling in her gut like they were about to tip over as the wheels lost contact with the track. At those moments, Aleka forgot her own safety and clutched Javier with both hands to keep him from tumbling out, his head flopping against her chest with the motion of the cars.

"Nice catch," the boy said after one particularly miraculous save. He lolled on the second car behind them, while the rest of the Skaldi organism snaked along the ground beside the track, moving as fast as the cars. Aleka gulped a breath to holler a question at the boy.

"How long until we get there?"

"No need to shout," he said. "Sit back, enjoy the scenery."

"How long?" she repeated.

"Weeks if we'd taken the overland route," he replied. "At this rate, I'd guess only a matter of hours." He shrugged, the movement of his shoulders snaky enough to remind her that beneath his visible body, he was a mass of shifting protoplasm. "Why? What's the rush?"

"Just trying to figure out how long I'm going to have to wait to kill you."

He laughed at that. "Good luck, kid. To kill me, you'd have to kill yourself. And we've already gone over the likelihood of that happening, haven't we?"

"I'm still working on it," she said, and turned away from him as the color suffused his pale face and he swallowed down whatever he was going to say.

They rushed on through the darkness, the occasional light flickering in the periphery of her vision like a random star that had fallen to earth. She didn't know how many hours passed this way; she'd long since lost track of whether it was day or night outside. She felt sleep coming on, her body and brain exhausted from everything that had happened in the past two days, but she forced herself to stay awake by counting the lights that flashed by, focusing on the feel of Javier's body against hers. She wondered idly what was moving the cars, whether the power source that ran this base was still operational or whether the Skaldi plasma that raced beside the rail was some-how propelling the vehicles as well. And if it was—if the boy was right and the germ plasma was feeding off of her, growing stronger and stronger as it did—then was *she* the one driving them toward the city? Was she the one responsible for every-thing that had happened since she'd left camp—not only to her and Javier but to her mother, Auntie, Laman, and everyone else?

I never meant for any harm to come to them, she told herself as the cars took another hairpin turn and her hands reflexively gripped Javier's chest and pulled him close. *All I wanted was to be free.*

It's too late for that, a voice that sounded like hers answered. *You're on this ride as long as it lasts, and the only thing you have to figure out is what to do when you get to the end.*

What can *I do?* she asked. *How am I supposed to fight something if I'm the one who gives it strength?*

The voice that answered this time didn't sound like her own. It spoke in words she knew she'd heard before, but they came to her as though they'd emerged from the belly of a deep, dark dream.

Its power over you is strong, but not as strong as you are, the voice said. *He's done his best to claim you for his own, but you don't belong to him yet.*

How do you know that? she asked.

I don't, the voice answered. *I only know it's all you have.*

"We're here!" the boy cried out, and Aleka shook herself fully awake to realize they'd come to a stop.

The boy leaped from his car and stood beside the rail, his hand held out to assist Aleka to disembark. She ignored him, checking Javier to see if he'd woken up, but he was still out cold. The spot where they'd stopped didn't look like anyplace special; it was simply the junction of multiple tunnels, each of them plunging into darkness except for one where a faint light glimmered in the distance.

"Where's the city?" she asked the boy.

"Up above, about twenty miles from here," he said. "We've reached the closest access point to the surface, so this is where we get off."

"I'm not going anywhere without Javier."

"Faithful to the end, huh? Well, I'm not lugging his carcass around, so either you do it yourself or you can leave him here to rot."

"Or your friends can carry him."

She pointed at the creatures that had formed out of the germ plasma, their bodies roughly humanoid but their faces blurred like mud pies under children's fingers. The thought of relinquishing Javier to these creatures made her queasy, but she was determined not to leave him. She didn't understand why—guilt, loyalty, the desire to have one companion beside her when she confronted her fate in the city—but that was the way it was.

The boy looked back and forth between Aleka and his minions. He seemed torn, if a being with as many bodies as he possessed could be torn. Even more than that, he seemed anxious to complete their journey, and Aleka suspected he wouldn't want to risk further delay.

"You do realize he's not going to make it, don't you?" the boy said at last.

"Then there's no harm in him coming along."

"Fine," he said. "But I'm warning you, no more favors after this one."

She let that pass without comment, and yielded Javier's unresisting body to the two dark creatures that came forward. Having made sure they were handling him gently, she climbed from the car and followed the boy down the single tunnel where the light gleamed.

When they reached the source of illumination, she found that it wasn't from the floor lights. Instead, the tunnel ended in a circular room with no ceiling, a vertical shaft intersecting the horizontal rail line. High above, a weak beam descended, suggestive of faraway sunlight. Aleka craned her neck, but she couldn't make out the exit. Still, after all the hours under-ground, she felt her spirits lift at the thought of returning to the surface, even if that meant heading immediately for the city and whatever awaited her there.

The boy walked to the perimeter of the shaft and gripped a metal ladder affixed to the wall. He shook it as if to test its strength, then turned to Aleka.

"If I recall correctly, you were quite the spelunker back in the day," he said. "That's how you met your friendly neighbor-hood pusher, isn't it?"

She said nothing as she joined him at the ladder.

"Did the old coot mention that he used a nerve block to paralyze you?" the boy asked. "Probably not; he's gotten kind of scatter-brained of late."

He grinned, but Aleka was finding it easier and easier to ignore his taunts. Setting her hand on the ladder, she looked over her shoulder at him and his creatures.

"I can climb just fine now," she said. "So don't even think of making them drop Javier, or the whole deal's off."

The boy sputtered with barely restrained rage. "You think *you* can threaten *me?*"

179

"I think you don't want to find out," she said as she started up the ladder.

She heard the boy cursing behind her, but she didn't stop. It occurred to her that he must possess—or believe he possessed—some additional leverage to hold over her once they reached the city; with his apparent willingness to abandon Javier, he must have discarded his plan to use her companion as a means of keeping her in line. For now, he seemed unwilling to antagonize her, but a knot of mingled dread and impatience formed in her stomach at the thought of what he might be withholding.

She climbed steadily, the metal rungs cold beneath her hands. Tired as she was, the motions came back to her automatically from a lifetime of exploring, and she had no fear that she might fall. The light grew stronger until she had to squint and finally turn her head away, but almost immediately afterward, the air freshened and the sun beat down directly on her, and she knew she'd exited.

She crawled away from the access shaft and waited an anxious moment for the others to appear. The boy came first, and then, almost long enough for her to believe he'd betrayed her, his creatures crawled from the hole, still bearing Javier's unconscious body. Satisfied, she stood and looked out over the place where they'd emerged.

The sight made her draw in an involuntary breath. The sun stood just past its meridian, and the light gleamed bronze and orange off a vast western plain that lay hundreds of yards in the distance. Or no, not a plain—a body of water, larger by far than any of the pools that formed in sheetrock during the rainy season. The expanse was so huge Aleka thought at first she was looking at the ocean, that still more distant mystery some of the old people in camp talked about. But that was hundreds, maybe thousands of miles away, much too far to reach by walking, too far to risk the fuel for driving. The people who reminisced about it must have known they'd never see it again, because they always referred to it as more of a fantasy than a reality. If they could only make it there, they said, they would find a paradise of endless white beaches and pure blue water, a place no monster could sully and no beating heart could resist.

"The Great Salt Lake," the boy said, glancing at the fiery waters to their west. "So called because of its mineral composition. You can't drink it, but I've heard you can float in it. What's left of it, anyway. It used to be ten times this size, but it's shriveled like everything else around here, and one of these days, it'll be completely gone."

"I thought you were some kind of god," Aleka said. "Shouldn't you be able to bring it back?"

"Gods don't cling to the past, sweetheart," he answered. "Once you've given me what I need, we won't have to worry about this hunk of rock anymore, because we'll be headed for the stars."

Aleka stared at him, unsure whether he was serious or just boasting. Did he honestly believe he could not only rule the world, but the galaxy as well?

"No one's that powerful," she managed to say.

"Just you wait," he replied, and with a jerk of his head, he started toward the east.

Aleka followed, the creatures that bore Javier coming behind. There were mountains in that direction, soaring ranges much taller and steeper than the buttes she'd climbed since childhood. Their color was gray, shading to almost white on the highest peaks, which made her wonder if they might be topped by snow, something else she'd heard the old folks talk about. The ground that lay between her and the mountains, however, was the same red-brown of the basin where the salt lake rested, the same red-brown, probably, that girdled the globe. Dust stirred with every step they took, and the air had the stifling, odorless quality she knew so well, the stale patina that told her little had grown here for many years. A stiff breeze blew at their backs, but even that wasn't enough to lend the desert atmosphere any degree of freshness. She wondered if they'd find food or drinkable water in the city. The boy might call her a god, but she remained human enough that her throat felt caked with dust and her vision grew blurry as she stared into the heat mirages that danced across the plain.

How could the Skaldi have survived so long in this wasteland? If they'd congregated in the city, how had they kept themselves from starving once the human population was gone? The boy had said that the leader of the Skaldi was counting on them to revive its kin. But even if the devious child wasn't planning to double-cross the one who'd preceded him, what reason did the leader have to believe that she could help him and those of his kind when, at the moment, she felt half-dead herself?

The sun was about to set and her legs felt on the point of giving out when the boy paused at the crest of a steep hill. The wind blew even more strongly at this elevation, drying the sweat on her back. Nonetheless, her nose detected a whiff of decay emanating from below. She joined the boy at the edge of the hill, her eyes taking in yet another sight they'd never seen before.

The city.

Or what remained of it. The mountains stood directly behind the valley in which the city lay, their towering ridges forming a stark contrast with the devastation of collapsed buildings and shattered streets. Yet even in ruin, Aleka found this city—one of the last cities on earth, it must be—even more awe-inspiring than she'd pictured from old people's tales. It spread before her like an endless, long-abandoned campsite, piles of wreckage spilling across the valley and blending into the dusk beyond the point her eyes could see. Most everything had toppled to the ground, but some of the needle-thin buildings still stood, impossible as that appeared given their precarious height and the damage they'd sustained. The tallest of them all, made entirely of glass that reflected the dying sunlight, seemed to rise even higher than the mountains, a motionless leviathan upholding the purple dome of the sky. It was as wounded as the rest, with its top sheared off at a sharp angle and a chunk taken out of its side as if by some Salt Lake behemoth's bite, but as soon as Aleka saw it, she knew it was the place they were headed.

"Home base," the boy confirmed when he saw her staring at it. "The head honcho's waiting for us there."

She took a deep breath to speak, then regretted it when the stink from below collected in her mouth and throat. "Right now?"

"The Skaldi don't sleep," he said. "And hunger has made them buggy. They've been waiting weeks for us to show up."

"Maybe *they* don't need to sleep, but I do. And drink."

"No time for that," the boy said. "Suck some energy out of the air if you need it. Or," he added with a mischievous wink, "you could drain whatever's left in your little charity project here."

183

Aleka looked at Javier, who rested with the appearance of peacefulness in the creatures' arms. Was his breath growing weaker, or was that just the bad light? She glared at the boy, who only grinned in return.

"Lead the way," she said.

His eyes gleamed as he started down the trail to the city.

Aleka followed. The smell of rot strengthened as they descended; she tried to breathe shallowly, but after a few minutes she was forced to walk with her sleeve pressed against her nose and mouth. She was barely conscious of where she set her feet, could sense more than see her guide as the shadows of twilight gathered around them. She glanced over her shoulder, but she couldn't see the boy's monstrous companions at all, their bodies having blended into the dark and only the paler shape of Javier visible to mark where they were.

Within a few more minutes, the ground leveled and deposited them on the outskirts of the city, which had the appearance not of broken stone and steel but of an enormous refuse pile. The stench was overpowering this close to the source; it penetrated Aleka's defenses no matter what she tried. She lifted her head, seeking cleaner air, but the breeze from above had died along with the light, and her throat tightened spasmodically as she took in another mouthful of the fetid atmosphere. When she gazed across the city, she found that she could still identify the tall building, if only as a black spike against the mountains' faded gray. The thought of trudging through the darkness and stink to reach the landmark made her head spin and her empty body wobble and nearly fall.

"Watch it," the boy said sharply.

A cry rose into the air, followed by a flapping sound. Aleka flinched, thinking it was more of his vampire bats, but then she realized that the ruins were alive with the bodies of huge black birds, almost impossible to see until they moved. Ravens, from the sound of their cackling voices. They held their ground against the intruders, delivering raucous choruses of warning and displeasure, but when the boy waved his hands, the whole crowd of them took off at once, blotting out the starry sky like a single bird as large as a thundercloud. Their caws returned ever more faintly until the stars reappeared and there was silence once more.

"What are they feeding on?" Aleka asked, though she dreaded the answer.

"Not what you think," the boy answered. "Come on."

He strode into the city, and Aleka hurried to catch up. She could see very little, only piles of some unknown material that glowed faintly in the starlight, but the boy seemed able to navigate without the benefit of vision. He steered them around holes that had opened in the concrete, cautioned Aleka to duck beneath the spars of fallen buildings. The smell that made her feel like vomiting didn't seem to trouble him at all. She glanced behind her and saw Javier tossing and turning in the creatures' arms, which she hoped was a good sign. Maybe the terrible reek of this place might wake him up—though when her eyes adjusted enough to the poor light to see what lay before her, she hoped he wouldn't.

The city had been transformed into a mass grave. The piles weren't tombstones, and they weren't bones, but they were the remains of bodies all the same—bodies that had belonged to human beings before they'd been taken over by the monsters that had flooded their home. In many cases, the dead Skaldi had become nothing but dust, reverse shadows of lightness that showed against the dark ground. Those must have died weeks ago. Others were more substantial, heads and tor-sos and even complete human figures with gaping chest scars and chalky gray flesh. Those were the creatures that had died recently enough to stink, the same ones the indiscriminate scavenger birds had seen fit to feed on. To produce the char-nel-house stench of the whole, there must have been thou-sands of dead bodies, tens of thousands; the entire sprawling city must have been littered with pieces of rotting Skaldi flesh that the birds hadn't consumed or carried off. It took every ounce of her strength to keep the bile that burned her throat from splattering the ground where the dead things lay, their empty shells pulverized further by the weight of her boots.

They turned a corner of what might once have been some-body's dwelling but was now little more than a pile of sticks and stones, and Aleka swallowed a cry.

A horde of surviving Skaldi walked the open space before her, twenty or thirty diminished creatures that wandered like pale, restless ghosts in the starlight. She watched as one of them stumbled and fell, its wasted frame splashing against the ground. Others were essentially whole, but they were as thin as the children of Auntie's camp during the worst of starving times. They lifted their heads at the sound of the strangers' ap-proach, and Aleka saw that they no longer had faces, as if, in their weakened state, they couldn't summon the will to uphold their masquerade. A few of them split down the middle in the instinctive prelude to the feast, but none made a move toward their prey; they either lacked the energy to attack or knew that it was worthless to assault members of their own species. Even the one fully human member of Aleka's party, Javier, wasn't enough to tempt them. Their heads drooped, their shoulders slumped, and they continued shuffling along their aimless paths deeper into the ruins of the city. Aleka watched until they'd faded completely from view, and she couldn't help feeling that they truly were ghosts conjured out of memory and sorrow and loss.

"Why don't they leave?" she asked, surprised to discover she'd said the words aloud.

The boy shrugged. "Hope. Or despair. If there's any difference between the two."

"There's a difference."

"So I've heard. Mostly from people who don't stand a chance of living to see another day."

"My mom had hope," Aleka said. "Even when everyone around her had nothing but despair. Even when *I* thought there was nothing left to live for."

"And yet, look where it got her," he said. "So it all comes down to the same thing in the end, doesn't it?"

She didn't answer. When he led on, she followed, as unsteady on her feet as the drifting creatures that had passed beyond her sight.

Few more of their kind appeared during the rest of the journey to the Skaldi leader's headquarters. When the occasional vagrant showed itself, Aleka looked away until it was gone. The smell became somewhat less oppressive as they neared the building; she guessed that the creatures closest to death had tried to escape the city and had fallen near its margin. The wreckage flowed past her in a blur, and she was neither shocked nor particularly interested when the boy stopped and announced, "We're here."

She looked across a rubble-strewn plaza at the monolith that split the sky. From this close, the tower was inconceivably huge, but also plainly derelict, with shattered windows and mangled girders showing through holes in its flanks. The canted top gave it the appearance of having had its head lopped off by a giant scythe that had sliced through glass and metal. The structure had probably stood in this maimed condition since the coming of the Skaldi, but it seemed as though it might slide into dust at any moment to join the creatures that inhabited it.

"The boss-man likes to chill in the executive boardroom," the boy said, indicating a mostly windowless level just below the structure's shaved top. "An affectation from the old days, I suppose."

They crossed the plaza, Aleka checking to make sure the faceless creatures trailed her with Javier in their arms. They did, though he had stopped squirming and lapsed into a torpid state that seemed closer to death than sleep. The base of the building was blocked by steep mounds of debris, probably what had fallen from the top, but their guide never slowed as he clambered over the unstable piles, Aleka and the shadow-shapes following. The ground-level doors had been reduced to splinters of glass, so they stepped carefully through the jagged opening, avoiding slivers that protruded from top and bottom like cruel teeth.

The interior was pitch black. Their feet echoed against the floor, which felt smoother than the concrete outside. The boy clutched her hand as if to direct her; she shook free, and he didn't try again.

"Thanks to his lazy ass, we have to take the stairs," he muttered. "Must be a real power trip, sitting up there on his throne waiting for everyone else to come at his beck and call."

With his unerring instinct or night vision, he headed for the rear of the building, and Aleka followed the echoing sound of his footsteps. Then the echoes halted abruptly, and he drew in a breath that was more like a gasp.

"My Lord," he said. "I wasn't expecting to find you here."

"That's obvious, Athan," a soft voice answered from the darkness.

Footsteps approached. The one who produced them was invisible, but Aleka had the feeling that he could see in the dark just as the boy could, and her cheeks flushed as she felt his eyes traveling over her. When he spoke again, his voice was hushed yet filled with a warmth she'd never thought to hear from a Skaldi's throat.

"My daughter," he said. "I've been waiting for you a very long time."

Chapter 15

A light gleamed in the darkness, and she saw the man's face.

Even if her mother hadn't told her that Kareem Reza had died years ago, the face that emerged from the gloom couldn't have been old enough to belong to him. In fact, it didn't seem much older than hers, with thick, dark eyebrows, smooth cheeks, and full lips. His skin appeared unnaturally pale, but there were no wrinkles around his eyes or mouth, none of the scarring or weathering that had marred her mother's countenance. Likewise, there was no touch of gray in his almost black hair. His eyes were as dark as his hair, and they gazed back at her with intensity but with none of the disdain she saw every time the boy looked at her. His inspection was simply mild and curious, not necessarily kindly but not anything like the malevolence she'd expected from the Skaldi who ruled this shattered city.

The Skaldi who claimed her as his daughter.

He raised the light—a lantern, identical to the ones they used in Auntie's camp. She looked for signs of aging in his hand, whether the normal aging of a human being as old as he had to be or the accelerated aging of a Skaldi on the verge of disintegration, but the hand was whole, unlined, pale but large and strong. The hand of a young man in perfect health, not the hand of a creature that had lived—existed—for the past sixteen years in a state of near-death.

"Aleka," he said. "May I call you that?"

She nodded numbly. The man smiled, showing the straight white teeth of a human being—abnormally straight and white, compared with the yellowed and missing teeth of everyone in Auntie's camp.

"I know this must be difficult for you," he said. "It's sometimes hard for me to fathom. I'd like to talk to you, privately if I can."

He turned his eyes to the boy, who shrank away from him. She couldn't understand why this arrogant child, with all his schemes and swagger, had become a cringing lackey in the leader's presence.

"I'm not leaving Javier," she said to the man. "So you'll just have to talk to me here."

The Skaldi leader's mouth pursed with apparent concern. He approached the creatures that held Javier, and they bowed down before him, laying their burden at his feet before backing away with their heads practically scraping the floor. The man knelt beside Javier and placed a hand on his forehead, but not in a threatening way; his body didn't open for the attack, his youthful face didn't twist in hunger or exhilaration. He simply closed his eyes and held that position for a minute, breathing deeply. Then he stood and returned to Aleka.

"I'm sorry," he said. "The damage is deep, and I doubt he'll awaken before he dies."

Aleka's heart fell. "How do you know that?"

"The Skaldi sense the presence of life," he said. "We're drawn to it, anguished to the point of madness when it comes near. But with this boy, even if one of my kind were famished, they'd pass him by. To scavenge his body would mean becoming trapped in a useless vehicle that would perish long before it could locate a viable host."

"Isn't there anything you can do?"

He shook his head, and his face seemed genuinely remorseful. "The Skaldi take life. We have none to give."

Aleka looked at Javier. The harsh lamplight seemed to accentuate what she'd refused to admit before: though his expression remained peaceful, his breath was slackening, his lungs laboring to expand. She knelt beside him and smoothed his hair, then leaned down and placed a soft kiss on his forehead. His skin was noticeably cold, and he didn't react to her touch. She whispered a goodbye and stood.

"I'm ready," she told the ruler of this place.

He held out a hand. After a moment's hesitation, she took it. Though his grip was strong, the coldness of his flesh was even worse than Javier's. Out of the corner of her eye, she saw the boy's face flush with rage, but he kept his mouth shut as the Skaldi led her across the shiny floor to the back of the building.

"You don't need to worry about Javier," the man said softly to her. "Athan won't touch him as long as I rule this city, and when we return, we can see that he receives a proper burial."

She nodded, though she felt her throat tighten. How long *would* the Skaldi leader remain in control here? Confident as he seemed, the icy touch of his hand made it obvious that he was on the verge of death—the final death, the one her mother had told her about. However he had found a way to survive for the past sixteen years, he had run out of time and had only days, maybe less, left in his unnatural existence. Was that what the boy—Athan, if that was actually his name—was waiting for? Terrified as he seemed of this city's leader, was he counting on his opponent vanishing into nothingness, clearing a path for him to take the Skaldi's place?

They reached the stairs at the rear of the building, the man's hand tightening on hers as he led the way upward. The dingy cement stairwell was similar to the one in the base where her mother had died, except the stairs went on forever, angling back and forth from landing to landing. At some of the landings, there were closed wooden doors that must have led to an interior hallway. Aleka's legs grew leaden as they climbed, the blur of exhaustion heightening the surreal nature of what she was doing. She was in the presence of a monster who said he was her father; she had come to his city at the behest of another monster who said she was a god. She still had no clear idea of what either of them would ask her to do, what power they might use to force her to carry out their wishes. Even if this thing *was* her father, she felt nothing for him, certainly not enough to do his bidding out of a sense of love or loyalty. Those feelings had ended with the death of her mother—or at least, if any trace of them remained, they would end with the death of the companion she'd left to breathe his final breaths below.

Their ascent ended abruptly at a landing where cement had rained down from above. Collapsed girders blocked the way to the next set of stairs, or where the next set would have been if the top of the building still existed. The Skaldi braced an arm behind Aleka's back to help her stay on her feet as he opened the landing door and crossed a hallway toward an empty doorframe. When they entered, she saw in the glow of the lamp that they stood in a large room, presumably what Athan had called the executive boardroom. A table dominated the space, with chairs in various states of disrepair arranged haphazardly around it. The ceiling was only partly intact, some of the panels having fallen to provide a view of the nighttime sky. A breeze shifted the dust on the table and floor, carrying the faintest odor of decay from the mortuary that had become of the city. Aleka looked out the empty frames where the windows used to be and saw that clouds had moved in, smothering the stars.

The Skaldi led her to a chair and helped her to sit, then placed his lantern on the table and sat beside her, reaching out to take both of her hands in his.

"Aleka," he said. "You must know that I never meant for it to end this way."

"I don't want to talk about that," she said.

"Of course." He let her hands go and rested back in his chair. "You want to know about me and your mother."

She waited for him to speak. He seemed reluctant to begin, turning his head to stare out the broken windows, rubbing his cheeks as if at a loss for what to say. She resisted the impulse to feel sympathy for him, reminding herself that no matter what his relationship to her might be, he was the ruler of creatures that had stolen everything from her. Father or not, he wouldn't hesitate to use her power to keep those creatures alive if he had the chance.

"I'm much older than I look," he said at last. "Or it might be better to say that the core of who I am has taken many forms over time. It confuses even me, trying to keep track of my true age. I was nineteen years old when they harvested my body for the first Skaldi experiments, but I've been remade many, many times in the almost forty years since. I exist now as I must have appeared all those years ago, but I'm not the same person I was. Kareem Reza is long gone, and yet, I remain."

He leaned toward her. Maybe it was an illusion of the lamplight, but when she looked into his dark eyes, she thought she perceived the accumulated time looking back at her, making him seem even older than he claimed.

"Yes," he said, as if he understood what she saw. "Skaldi live many lives—all of them taken from others—and in that respect, we carry within us every life we've consumed. I have the advantage over the rest of my species in that I've never taken a life other than my own, never sampled a fully human being but always relied on a succession of my own duplicates to serve my needs. Yet still, you might say I've lived thousands of years altogether. All those years, all those lives have made me what I am, even if they were stolen from beings forged in my own image."

"Do you mean," Aleka began, then had to stop to wrap her mind around what he was admitting. "Do you mean you've kept yourself alive by consuming your own…"

"Brothers?" he said. "Children? I don't know what to call them. The scientists made so many of us. All I can tell you is that within the original Reza line, there was a core group who repudiated what we were made to be, and who swore an oath to sustain ourselves as long as we could without the taint of stealing another soul. We were bred early, and that made us stronger than most; we studied the records our makers had left behind, and in so doing we learned that if we tamped down our hunger for a sufficient period of time, we were able to enter a state of short-term hibernation that delayed the starvation

195

phase, providing viable hosts for the rest. One way or another, we've managed to survive for nearly half a century without breaking our vow. But now the supply has run its course, and I am the only one who remains."

"Then you're *not* my father," she said. "Not the one who…"

"I easily lose track of *who* I am," he said, waving his hand wearily. "All those lives, all those kin, each one precisely like the others, each willingly offering himself as a sacrifice to sustain our line. Am I the ones I consumed, or was I consumed by another just like me? I can no longer say." He gave her a rueful look. "I know with certainty that the blood of my race runs in your veins. But if you're asking whether I am the Kareem Reza who knew your mother, who loved her, and who died at her hands, I suppose I couldn't have been, however much I might wish I were."

He turned his head, gazing at the city that lay buried in darkness. Despite herself, Aleka felt a rush of sympathy, something she might have felt if he truly were her father. Yet the feeling was tempered by distrust. "If you're not really him," she asked, "how do you know her story?"

"The Skaldi have traveled the length and breadth of this land," he said. "We've shared memories—or stolen them—and in the process, we've transmitted the history of our race through the generations. The eastern camp where your mother and father met was dispersed after his death, most of its members fleeing into the wilderness, where they died at the hands of roving Skaldi. Through the years since then, we've passed the story of Kareem Reza and Diana the Huntress down from body to body, and never forgotten. Maybe it gave us hope to think that one of our kind could know something other than

196

blood and death. That it could also know what human beings call love."

"I killed her," Aleka said through the tightness in her throat. "Did you know that too?"

He nodded somberly. "At my command, Athan has sent winged messengers to me each day since his escape from imprisonment. The latest team arrived this morning, and I learned what happened to your mother in the place where both you and I were born—or, in my case, reborn."

"Do you know why I did it?"

He took her hands, and she didn't pull away. "I assume it was an act of mercy."

"That's what I thought at first," she said. "But now I think it was because ... what's the point? Of living, of fighting? You know that Athan plans to take over from you."

"Of course," he said. "I've known from the moment I called him here."

"Is that why he's afraid of you? Because you know?"

"He fears me because he's craven in nature, and suspicious of anyone who wields power," he said. "He fears that I may be keeping secrets from him, and that I'll use my knowledge to destroy him."

"Is he right?"

"Perhaps."

"That's not an answer," she said. "If he's been sending reports to you, then you know everything he's done since he was freed from the base. You know he killed Didi and the others, then Mouse and Auntie and Laman and everyone else, and finally Javier. You know he would have killed my mother if I hadn't done it myself. But you let him, didn't you? You needed him to bring me here, and so you let him do whatever he

197

wanted. And now I'm supposed to … what? Think you're any different than him? Feel sorry for you because you *wish* you were capable of love?"

She tried to free her hands, but he held on. She wondered if the power lay in her to burn him, or if he claimed some kind of protection by virtue of their shared blood. She struggled briefly to call that power to her aid before giving up and letting her hands go limp in his. Really, what *was* the point? She couldn't kill him, and she couldn't kill herself. She could only watch him and his agent fight for control over her, and then serve whichever one of them emerged the victor.

"I wish for many things, as do the few Skaldi who survive in this city," the man with her father's face said. "I summoned Athan here to help me realize those wishes, it's true. If you do what I hope, I expect to see them fulfilled before the end. But even if you won't, I'll be thankful that one of my wishes has come true."

"And what might that be?"

"The wish to see you before I die."

She forced a laugh past the constriction in her throat. "So you let Athan torture the great love of your life—or somebody's life—so you could see the daughter they produced? Just in time to feed her to your followers? Thanks a lot, *Dad*."

She yanked her hands from his. He stared at them, and she was startled to see that strips of his flesh had torn loose, leaving behind bloodless gashes. Throwing himself from his chair, he stalked away from her toward the windows, stopping so close to their empty frames she had the momentary thought that he might throw himself to the street hundreds of feet below. The wind blew his night-black hair, and his shoulders lifted heavily with each breath. Each counterfeited breath.

Skaldi didn't bleed, and they didn't breathe. Whether he'd feasted on the lives of actual human beings or only on the bodies of his own twins, he existed solely because of what he'd taken from others.

"I know what you think of me," he said in a hollow voice. "I know that I disgust you, and that you would gladly sever the connection between us if you could. But don't flatter yourself with the belief that your loathing is any stronger than mine. For almost half a century, the creatures I command have left a trail of destruction for which none of us can make recompense. Though we can feel the untold millions we've slain in our own bodies, though the air we walk through is crowded with their ghosts, we can't bring them back; all we can do is despise ourselves, and mourn the suffering we've caused. For years, I've vowed that if a new path were to open before me, I'd gladly take it—no matter what I had to do, no matter whom I had to sacrifice. And now that such a path has presented itself, I'm ready to fulfill my vow. Even though, my daughter, the one I must sacrifice is you."

He turned to her, and she gasped when she saw that his scar had opened, the flesh of his face and chest peeling back to reveal the rotting flesh inside. Glass crunched underfoot; she spun to face the doorway, where she saw others of his kind approaching, ten or more of them, the stench of their diseased bodies overwhelming her. One was tall and gaunt, little more than a skeleton with long, lank hair hanging into the cavity of its chest; another was the size of a child, and it skipped forward as if this were a game, outpacing the shuffling forms that followed. All of them, even the child-shape, were badly damaged, with missing fingers and flaking skin, handfuls of flesh gouged out of their arms and legs, heads hanging by the merest of

199

threads from their necks. They were on the verge of dissolution, and yet they advanced toward her with arms outstretched and scars opening hungrily, displaying no fear of the power she possessed.

Aleka backed away from them, but she hadn't gotten far when the Skaldi leader clutched her with clawed hands. She wrestled to free herself, only to find that even this close to his own death, his grip was as unbreakable as that of Athan's appendages. The thought flashed through her mind that Athan and the Skaldi leader had been toying with her for reasons of their own, pretending to be at odds with one another when in fact they were united in a single deadly purpose. That was the last thought she was capable of as the hands of the other Skaldi grasped her and pulled her down into a darkness deeper than the grave.

"We welcome you, my daughter," the voice of Kareem Reza spoke out of the darkness. "We have awaited this moment for longer than you can know."

A deafening noise shocked Aleka back into full consciousness, the room shaking so violently she fell from the Skaldi's grasp. Her hands were cut on shards of glass as she scrambled to stand. One of the creatures—the child-shape, she saw when she looked back—sank its small fingers into her ankle and held tight. She kicked with her other foot, and the hand separated from the wrist, clinging to her ankle but unable to hold her down. She raced for the door and had almost gained the corridor when another explosion threw her from her feet. When she turned her head to locate her attackers, she saw a plume of smoke rising outside the empty window frames, smelled a sickeningly sweet burning odor as the smoke was sucked into the room. Regaining her feet, she turned and fled.

The moans of the Skaldi followed her into the stairwell. She glanced behind her as she started down, and saw that the surprise attack on their headquarters had added to the bodily damage they'd already suffered; one or two of them were left with only a single limb to balance on, while others were punctured by holes so deep she could see straight through their chests. But they were driven by desperation, and they were gaining on her, the stench of their empty bodies and the chill of their dead flesh enveloping her in a choking cocoon. She would never make it, she realized. They would catch her, and drag her back to where their leader—her *father*—waited, and then...

Something dark flew past her, and one of the creatures let out a piercing shriek. A hail of dark objects followed, each one accompanied by a scream from the Skaldi. The projectiles moved too fast for Aleka to see what they were, and she could only guess that Athan had realized what the Skaldi leader was up to and had dispatched his flying legions to fight the creatures off. She was running from one form of bondage to another, and at any moment, Athan himself would appear to claim his prize.

Another blur flew past, followed by a short scream. The body of the gaunt woman tumbled down the stairs, skidding to a stop at the landing. She lay scar upward, with something that looked like a red-tailed hawk's feathers protruding from where her forehead had been. When Aleka realized what the adornment was, she stared in wonder.

An arrow.

She checked the stairwell above her. All of the Skaldi were pierced with red-fletched arrows, some of which had crippled the creatures so badly they could no longer stand. Two of them were joined by a single arrow that had penetrated both of their heads; a third staggered about the landing, covered in arrows like cactus spines, before losing its balance and somersaulting down the steps. Aleka turned at a scratching sound and saw that the woman-creature had regained her feet, but another arrow whizzed out of nowhere and caught her through the throat, her body flipping over the railing to explode in a puff of foul-smelling dust against the landing below.

A figure emerged from the smoky cloud. A figure with streaming white hair, a fresh arrow nocked to her bow, the bowstring pulled tight against her weathered cheek.

The figure of Diana, the Huntress.

Chapter 16

This time, Aleka was sure she was seeing her mother's ghost.

"Mom?" she called out.

The blue eye closest to her squinted. "Duck."

Aleka did.

The bowstring twanged, and the arrow zipped above her head. There was a solid *chunk* as it found its target, followed by a strangled exclamation. Aleka turned to see the Skaldi leader on the landing above her, his face and body having reassumed the appearance of her father. His eyes bulged as his hands grappled with the arrow that protruded from his chest, pinning him to the wooden door.

"Come with me," the Huntress ordered, and Aleka was too stunned to disobey.

Her mother hooked the bow over her back before she started down the stairs. Her right knee was bound tightly, and she was being careful not to put weight on it. This should have been enough to convince Aleka that the apparition really was her, but she couldn't help asking.

"I saw you," she said. "In the tunnel. You were Skaldi."

"Wasn't me." She winced as her leg came down awkwardly while turning a corner of the staircase. "The germ plasma can copy anyone it comes into contact with, and it touched me years ago. I wouldn't have thought it could reproduce my current form, but I guess Athan must have some new tricks up his sleeve. I'd love to hear what he told you, though I'm sure a good half of it is lies anyway."

"He..." Aleka tried to think where to start, but there was no good place. Plus her mother was visibly laboring after the long climb upstairs, and it was much easier to use that as an excuse to say nothing. She wrapped an arm around the Huntress's waist, feeling again the strange combination of boniness and hard muscular strength, and her mother seemed to accept that in lieu of an explanation. She grunted appreciatively, the two of them moving like a single being as they fled down the steps.

"How did you get here?" Aleka asked once they'd settled into a rhythm.

"We drove. Arachne started searching for you the minute you left camp, and—"

"Auntie's alive?" Aleka asked in amazement.

"Last I checked."

"And the others?" She hardly dared to hope, but if Auntie had survived... "Laman and Petra and Tyris and the twins—"

"All of the above," her mother said. "Arachne picked up our trail, found my backpack outside the base, then used the trucks to break in. Tyris fixed my leg the best she could, which was the cutest thing—I haven't seen her since she was a little girl. They even had a spare bow to give me." She plucked the string, and it hummed a single firm note. "Not my original, but good enough, it seems."

"But how?" Aleka asked. "I saw them—they were part of the plasma. I was sure it had killed them."

"The same way you were sure it had killed me?" her mother responded. "Athan's been playing us all for fools with that shape-shifting gunk of his. If that boy would devote only half the brainpower to doing good that he spends on his little mind games…" She laughed bitterly. "Well, enough said about that."

"Who is he, Mom? For real?"

"The spirit of a child who was killed the day after you were born," she answered. "A child who dreamed of ruling the world with the Skaldi as his subjects, and who saw in you the key to achieving his dreams. I'm still kicking myself for not realizing who he was, but with the old man looking so much like the scientist who mentored him, I just didn't put two and two together. In his current state, it seems he's combined himself with others who died the same day—including his father and the people who worked on the base—to create the polymorph he calls *Aesir*. He was Laman's younger brother," she added. "And it was Arachne who killed him. So that's a burden they've had to bear all these years."

"They never told me."

"There's a lot we never told you, Arachne and Laman and me. We convinced ourselves we were shielding you from evil, but I can see now that all we did was give it time to take new forms."

Aleka listened for sounds of pursuit from above, but the stairwell was silent except for her mother's heavy breaths. "How did you get past him?"

This time, the woman's laugh was full and deep. "He and his black goo ran away the moment Arachne set off her explosives. He's always been afraid of her, and I guess being killed by her did nothing to settle his nerves."

Aleka was on the verge of asking another question when she noticed the sweat on her mother's lip and realized how hard the woman was concentrating on making her way down the winding staircase. She tightened her grip on her mother's waist, holding her upright while she hopped from stair to stair with her bad leg extended in front of her.

When they reached the ground floor and exited the relative peace and quiet of the stairwell, they entered a scene of chaos. Smoke from Auntie's explosives filled the lobby while dark bodies—human, so far as Aleka could tell—ran back and forth through the haze. She spotted Petra, Araz, Laman, and a couple of guards, but didn't see the twins, any of the children, or the rest of the adults. Tyris was kneeling beside Javier, checking his breathing and pulse, which gave Aleka a moment's hope. Then the healer shook her head and turned her attention to one of the guards who'd suffered a minor injury, and Aleka was forced to admit that in this, at least, the Skaldi leader had told the truth.

"I want to take him with us," she said to her mother. "To find a decent place where we can … bury him."

"Of course," her mother said, and that was that.

No sooner had she spoken than the smoke stirred and a small figure forced its way through the crowd, her black jacket as threadbare as ever and the silver pistol Aleka had stolen hanging at her belt. She stopped before her goddaughter and confronted her without expression in her dark eyes. She looked no different than she had when Aleka left camp—no more tired, no more concerned, no more furious. Auntie's face was like the desert she'd mastered over the course of a lifetime: flat, unchanging, unforgiving. When she spoke, her voice was the same.

"You're here," she said, as if she were calling roll prior to an evacuation.

Aleka nodded.

"That's good," Auntie said in the same flat tone. "I don't like to lose anyone."

"Auntie, I—"

The camp leader silenced her with a gesture of her hand, then turned to Aleka's mother. "This is what comes of running off like you did. I've never been able to manage this daughter of yours."

"Seems to me you've done fine."

"Couldn't help checking up on me, though, could you? Well, no matter," she said brusquely, cutting off the other woman's response with the same gesture. "Laman, see if you can restore some order around here. We're moving out in two minutes."

"I want to take Javier," Aleka said.

Auntie glanced at where he lay, her face showing a flicker of emotion at last—though only of the *serves him right* variety.

"Fine," she said. "One more child I have no use for."

She spun and walked off, leaving Aleka's face burning from the rebuke. She looked at the woman who'd left her in Auntie's care, but all she received in reply was a small, knowing smile.

"Come on," her mother said. "Let's find a stretcher and get him onto the truck."

Aleka took her arm and led her from the building, while Laman hurried around issuing orders in his best approximation of an authoritative voice. The command truck was the only one parked outside; her mother explained that they'd left the other three vehicles on the western outskirts of the city, with Kay and May and the majority of the adults watching over the children. Auntie's plan had been to move in quickly, launch a surprise attack with her last remaining grenade shells, then clear out while the Skaldi were still reeling, and so far, it seemed her tactics had succeeded. There was no sign of either Athan or the Skaldi leader, and Aleka allowed herself to hope that her camp might actually survive this ordeal.

She wondered, though, what came next if they did. Athan might have been scared away for the moment, but she couldn't believe he'd been defeated for good. The Skaldi leader and his followers—the ones that hadn't been picked to pieces by her mother's arsenal—might crumble to dust in hours or days, but she knew that they would pursue Auntie's fleet as long as an ounce of strength remained in them. She had the horrible feeling that her camp wasn't surviving so much as running away yet again—the same thing they'd been doing since the Skaldi first appeared, the same thing Auntie had accused her mother of doing sixteen years ago. The same thing *she'd* been doing for as many of those years as she could remember. How much longer could they keep running before they ran out of time altogether?

She tried to put those thoughts out of mind as she helped her mother climb into the rear compartment of the truck, then returned to the building with Laman and a stretcher. Javier was still breathing, but he didn't react at all to Aleka's touch. A few minutes after they laid him down beside her mother, the engine started with a roar and Araz peeled away from the Skaldi headquarters. He drove recklessly, veering around obstacles and bouncing the suspension through deep potholes. Crowded in the back with everyone else, Aleka caught a glimpse of the darkened city through the small window that separated the storage area from the front seat, where Auntie sat rigidly beside her driver. She had her pistol out, while her other hand was pressed against her stomach. She doubled over when they hit a particularly deep rut, and her fingers sank into Araz's arm.

"Watch it, Mario Andretti," she said in an angry undertone before she returned her hand to its previous position.

Aleka moved away from the window and gave her attention to her mother, who sat beside Javier's stretcher with her head down and her leg extended. Across the cramped space, Laman kept glancing over at them like he wanted to say something, but he remained his usual tongue-tied self. Aleka lowered herself carefully by her mother's side, then pulled her into her arms. For once, the Huntress didn't resist. She rested her head against her daughter's shoulder, her breath growing calm until the rocking of the truck and the stroking of Aleka's hand helped her drift off to sleep.

Aleka startled awake to find that she'd followed her mother into dreamland. The truck had stopped, and the rear door creaked open to reveal Auntie's face in the red glow of the brake lights. The darkness outside was total, making it impossible to tell where they were. Aleka's anxiety grew when Auntie spoke in a breathless whisper.

"Everyone out," she said.

Aleka rose to a crouch. Her mother was awake, and she accepted her daughter's assistance to climb from the truck. Once again, Laman hovered nearby as if he wanted to help, but he danced away when Auntie snapped her fingers to call him to her side.

As soon as she left the cargo hold, Aleka saw the three other vehicles lined up in formation behind the command truck. Their engines and headlights, however, were cut, and their occupants, everyone except the youngest children, stood silently by the fenders, visible only in the lead truck's brake lights. Araz cut the engine and jumped out, plunging the world into darkness until he retrieved an electric lantern from the front seat and held it high. The clouds that had moved in earlier remained in place, blocking the stars; there wasn't the slightest breeze to stir the inky cover or to relieve the smell of rot that lingered in the air. Aleka wondered why Araz kept waving his lantern at the clouds, but when she saw at last what the light revealed, she drew in a gasp.

The sky was filled not with clouds but with a web of plasma that hung less than a hundred feet overhead, denser than the flock of ravens that had taken flight when she entered the city with Athan. As she stood with her face upturned, something struck her in the cheek, a stinging blow that was repeated a second later. She reached up to touch whatever had fallen, and her fingers returned dripping with plasma that leaped from her hand and squirmed away. A moment later, she found herself battered by a deluge of black pellets more punishing than hailstones. They fell all around, striking people with enough force to knock them off balance, causing even Araz to collapse against the driver's side door. Aleka tried to protect her mother, but both of them were driven to the ground, where they lay cowering under the barrage. Within minutes, everyone was down except Auntie, who stood bent over double, clutching her stomach with one hand and the rear bumper of the command truck with the other. She panted as if trying to summon the breath to call out to her troops, but even if she'd succeeded, no one seemed to have the strength or will to rise.

In the glow of Araz's fallen lantern, Aleka watched blackness pool around the prostrate colonists like a rising flood. She feared that everyone would drown, but the plasma stopped at the depth of a few inches and began to take the shape of human figures, hundreds of them forming a circle around the trucks. Faces rippled and flowed across their ranks like waves on an endless sea, a vast multitude of faces that seemed familiar for an instant until they crashed into each other and became indistinguishable from all the rest. Aleka wondered if these were the faces of every human being who'd lived and died during the Skaldi regime, all of them captured by the germ plasma in mocking memory of the lost. Or maybe this was the fulfillment of Athan's prophecy, a world in which the Skaldi reigned as gods until the end of time.

An opening appeared in the circle of black figures, and their master stepped through. He had chosen the shape in which Aleka had first met him, the dark-garbed nomad she'd known as Aesir. He bowed in the formal manner of that being, black robes pooling around him. When he rose, he was Athan again, his face alight with wicked glee.

"It's always a thrill a minute with you people," he said. "The great escape, right? The last-second Hail Mary?"

"Athan," his brother called out shakily from where he lay. "It's been sixteen years. Don't you think it's time to let it go?"

"So speaks Lame Man, disgrace of the Genn brood," Athan said. "Trust me, Dad is rolling over in his grave."

His face bulged unnaturally, the giant's craggy visage replacing his childish features. Another ripple in the black fluid and Athan was there again, grinning widely.

"The girl belongs to me," he said. "I've wasted enough time as it is."

He was reaching down to pull Aleka to her feet when Auntie's pistol flared in the darkness.

211

At this range, the bullet must have struck its target, but the boy didn't even flinch. It was as if he'd absorbed the missile, or as if it had passed through his liquid form without leaving a mark.

"Not this time, Ash," he said, turning on Auntie with a wolfish smile.

He raised both hands above his head, then brought them down violently. Two bird-shapes burst from the black throng and dove directly at Auntie, talons extended to tear her to pieces. The moment before impact, they turned into sharp-nosed projectiles that slammed into her stomach, knocking her to the ground. She rolled over and gripped the bumper of the truck, but she seemed too dazed to stand.

The boy held a hand out to Aleka. "Now, my queen. Unless you want to watch them all die."

"You're going to kill them no matter what I do."

"Probably, but it's up to you to decide *how*," he said. "The quick way, or the ever-so-painful way?"

His pale hands flashed again, and a cluster of black tentacles streamed toward the largest of the trucks. They tore open the rear gate, the cries of the children emerging from inside. Aleka had no time to react before the appendages reappeared, this time wrapped around the stick-thin arms of the twins. They lifted the two high into the air, where Kay and May's faint voices drifted down. The darkness made it impossible for Aleka to tell what was happening until droplets struck her cheeks like rain. In minutes, the twins' screams had stopped, and the tentacles that snaked back to the ground were slick with blood.

"That's just a taste," Athan said. "I haven't even gotten started yet."

Through tears, Aleka searched for her mother on the ground beside her, only to find her standing despite the injured leg. Her wrinkled cheeks were blood-speckled but otherwise dry. Aleka accepted her hand, feeling her undiminished strength as she pulled her daughter to her feet. Laman had risen as well and helped Auntie up, though she leaned heavily against him. He brandished his only weapon—the red-handled pocket knife—like a warrior facing down a superior force all by himself.

But he wasn't by himself.

The others—Tyris, Petra, Araz, the guards, the rest of the adults—had gained their feet. The children had exited the truck and stood close behind their caretakers with sharp pieces of wood and stone in their hands. Aleka realized that Survival Colony 9 had decided to fight to protect her, even if it meant their deaths.

"It's all right, Auntie," she said. "I'll go with him."

"Like hell you will." The camp leader shook free of her lieutenant's hands and forced her way to the front of the group. "You can only kill us once," she said to the boy. "Do your worst."

She took another step toward him, her legs quivering noticeably. He raised his hands to strike, but then he paused, his expression puzzled. Looking closely at her godmother, Aleka saw that a dark splotch had appeared across the front of her camouflage pants, as if the blow from Athan's creatures had ruptured something inside her. The stain spread rapidly, darkening her pant legs. Laman seemed to become aware of it at the same time as Aleka, and he reached out toward Auntie as though to stop her from taking another step.

"Asheh," he said.

213

Auntie's face froze, and her hand fell to the sopping material. She stared at her reddened fingers in disbelief before her complexion turned pale and she dropped to her knees.

"Laman," she called out hoarsely. "The baby—"

Aleka had no time to wonder what she meant before Athan brought his hands down once more, and the camp's tight formation was scattered by the darkness.

Chapter 17

S he must have slept, because her eyes opened on a pale dawn.

It took only a moment to figure out where she was: the Skaldi headquarters. Sunlight streamed into the upper floor boardroom, but when she went to the empty windows and looked below, she saw nothing but darkness, a black pool that covered the plaza where the building stood. At first, she had the crazy thought that the salt lake had migrated, but then she realized that what she was seeing was a flood of the germ plasma, far too much of it to be a result of the uncanny storm that had stopped them at the city's edge. The dark waters moved with a will of their own, pseudopods reaching upward as if trying to climb the building's sides. Aleka could easily believe that the plasma would spread until it covered the entire city, then the entire planet. After that, it wouldn't be long before it reached beyond the stars.

She turned from the window. Her mother was there, along with the members of Auntie's colony, all except for the slain Kay and May. The group huddled on the side of the room farthest from the windows, where two stretchers lay. One was occupied by Javier, who'd been returned to the building even though Aleka could tell by his nearly imperceptible breath that he had little time to live. Laman knelt by the second stretcher, holding the hand of the small woman in a black jacket who'd led their colony for the past sixteen years.

Aleka joined him by Auntie's bedside. It shocked her to see how pale and bony her godmother had become, as if, after however many decades she'd fought off age and infirmity, the accumulated years had taken their toll all at once. Her eyes were closed, not even their dark rage remaining to challenge the bloodless cheeks and papery skin of the woman Aleka had always believed to be invincible.

"I'm so sorry, Laman," Aleka said. "I didn't know."

"No one did," he said. "Asheh wanted to keep it a secret, just in case she..." He shrugged helplessly. "This isn't the first one we've lost. But I guess it's the last."

He bowed his head and cried quietly. He didn't look up even when Aleka's mother laid a hand on his shoulder.

Aleka lowered herself to her knees, then reached out and delicately took her godmother's hand. It felt as cold as the Skaldi leader's, and as empty—nothing but skin to cover the hollowness inside. She tried to estimate Auntie's true age, but it was impossible; that was another thing the camp leader had kept secret from her. Still, she had to be far past the normal age for childbearing. Was it the blow to her stomach that had caused the miscarriage? But no, she'd shown signs of something being wrong during the ride. Which meant that, even though she must have suspected she was about to lose another baby, she'd insisted they drive on, refusing to stop even to get help from Tyris, so she could make one final, futile attempt to save the girl who'd abandoned her.

She leaned forward to kiss Auntie's wrinkled forehead. When she drew back, she was startled to see the woman's eyes staring directly at her. They burned as fiercely as always, but in her wasted face, their fire seemed less a sign of returning life than a final spark to consume what little was left of her.

When Laman saw that she was awake, he placed a gentle kiss on her cheek. "Asheh."

"Auntie," Aleka said.

"Arachne," her mother added.

"You all better decide what to call me," Auntie said. "Before I forget my own name."

She tried to smile, but it only accentuated the cavities of her eye sockets and cheeks.

"And you," she said to Aleka's mother. "I was always tougher than you. How'd you manage to get through this when I can't?"

"I had an angel to help me."

"I sure hope you're not talking about who I think you are," Auntie sniffed. "I have a reputation to keep up around here." All of a sudden, her eyes filled with tears. "Diana, I wanted to have a ... a little one of my own..."

"You still can," the Huntress said. "There's still time."

Auntie shook her head. "It's too late now."

"I've never heard the great Arachne talk that way."

"Not so great anymore, I'm afraid." She squeezed her eyes shut, but the tears continued to spill down her cheeks. "You don't know what a blessing it is, any of you. To be young."

She cried without making a sound, her tears flowing in an endless stream as if she'd held this sorrow inside all her life and was only now letting it go. Time passed without measure as Aleka stroked her godmother's hand. When her eyes finally opened again, they were sharp and bright, and the tears were gone.

"Go, both of you," she said in the commanding voice of her old self. "I need to talk to my godchild."

Aleka's mother leaned down to kiss her cheek, then helped Laman to stand. He seemed to need her support, so she wrapped an arm around his waist. Auntie frowned as they moved off.

"The fool used to be in love with her, you know," she said. "Probably still is."

Aleka had no idea what to say to that. She'd discovered more about her mother's and godmother's private lives in the past few days than she'd ever wanted to learn. "Can I get you anything, Auntie?"

"You're too old to call me that," the woman said crossly. "You only started when you were little because you couldn't say *Arachne*. You're a woman now, so it's time you started acting like one."

"I'm only sixteen."

Auntie harrumphed. "When I was your age, I was in combat training, learning how to take down men twice my size. If I could do that, you can certainly call me by my real name."

"All right," Aleka said. "Arachne."

Her godmother nodded. "That's better. Now we can talk about all the things I couldn't say to you when you were a girl. All the things that need to be said before I die."

"You're not going to die."

"I'm going to die when it's my time, not when you give me permission," Auntie groused. "So keep quiet and mind me for once."

She patted the floor impatiently. Aleka sat cross-legged and waited, but all she got for her obedience was one of Auntie's practiced glares.

218

"How much did your mother tell you about your father?" she asked.

"Not that much. Only that she…"

"Killed him? She's a little too proud of that, I've always thought. Did she tell you he was mine first?"

Aleka lowered her eyes. Apparently, the tale of her biological and adoptive mothers' romances was even more tangled than she'd guessed.

"You heard me right," Auntie said. "Your mother was young and beautiful back then—you have no idea how beautiful, looking at her now—but Kareem Reza fell in love with *me* long before she came on the scene. You know the history of the Skaldi duplicates, I assume?"

"Most of it."

"Well, I'm not going to waste my breath filling you in on the details," Auntie said. "You can ask your mother when I'm in the ground."

"Auntie…"

The woman glowered.

"Arachne," Aleka corrected herself. "Tell me about you and Kareem."

Auntie snorted. "Is that what you think this is? An old spinster prattling about her one great love affair before she bites the dust?"

Once again, Aleka had no idea how to answer.

"My life is my own," Auntie said. "When you've seen as much as I have, you'll understand that it's no one else's business what goes on between people in love. Though from the look of it," she added with a sidelong glance at Javier, "you've inherited your mother's taste for boys who are no damn good for you."

"He's only a friend."

"Of course, of course," Auntie replied. "That's what I said when I met Kareem. But you'll see what I'm talking about. You'll see how they sneak into your heart without your knowing it."

Aleka gazed at Javier's slumbering face. She recalled the moment in the tunnels when she'd thought they were about to kiss, but that wasn't anything, was it? Anything more than a childish desire to know the touch of another's lips before she died. Looking at him now, she wondered if there was something about his face she hadn't felt back then, something her heart would pine for when he was gone. She turned back to her godmother, and the woman's eyes met hers with a depth of empathy Aleka had never seen.

"So it goes," Auntie said. "Always the same story, but the only part you need to know is the part that pertains to you. I was in love with Kareem, but it was your mother who had a child with him—with him, or the next best thing. When she realized that the Skaldi would never stop hunting her to recover you, she gave you to me. I swore I'd protect you, and I meant it—"

"You have."

"Let me finish, girl," Auntie snapped. "You might think you're comforting an old hag on her deathbed, but you have no idea what you're saying."

Aleka was silent.

"I swore to protect you when you were only two days old," Auntie continued. "What I couldn't have known at the time was how much it would pain me to watch you grow, to become a real person and not just a promise. I tried to think of you as my reward—my substitute for what I'd never had with

Kareem—but it didn't work. Every time I looked at you, I was reminded of the child that should have been mine. You've probably wondered why I told you your mother was dead."

"Laman said you did it to keep me safe. So I wouldn't go looking for her."

"He was only repeating what I told him," Auntie said. "The truth is, I *wanted* her to be dead. Because then you would be mine, and no other could claim you."

Fresh tears shone in her eyes, but she made no move to wipe them away.

"Laman rejoined us three years after you were born," she said. "When he was your age, he'd had some crazy dream of founding his own survival colony, but when it came down to it, he took the easy way out, as usual. At first, I looked at him as nothing more than a nuisance—always getting in the way, never where he was supposed to be. But after a year or two, I realized I was beginning to look for him all the time, to wonder where he'd run off to when he *wasn't* where I expected him to be. And I thought to myself, maybe I could still have what your mother and Kareem had. Laman wasn't the worst looking man I'd ever seen, and though the age difference got between us at times, I grew to know him as someone dependable, someone who'd see things through. I can't remember the exact day I woke up in his arms to realize I'd fallen in love with him, but from that day to this, I've had no desire to share my bed with another, not even if Kareem himself were to show up begging me to take him back."

She reached for Aleka's hand. Though the impression of feather-lightness remained in the dry skin and knobby bones, Aleka felt the ageless strength of Auntie Spider as the fingers knitted with hers.

"He never failed me," she said. "It was my own body that failed. When we lost the first one years ago, I tried to keep my spirits up, to tell myself there was plenty of time. I grieved, but Laman helped me through the worst of it, and I came back, so I thought, even stronger and more determined than before. Then we lost another, and another, and faith abandoned me. Laman tried for my sake to put on a hopeful air, but I knew he was worried—not so much that we'd never produce a child, but that the effort to do so would kill me. I sensed his reluctance to come to me at night, and I think that cut me even worse than the babies I'd lost. Finally, I told him that if we could try one more time, I'd accept whatever the outcome was—and I meant it when I said it, I truly did. But last night, when it happened again, and I knew it was all over for me, the dream I'd held so long and so close to my heart... Well, that's when I wished I was dead, and I'd never felt that way before."

With a movement that seemed to require all of her remaining strength, she pulled Aleka to her. Aleka stiffened, fearful of harming her further, but Auntie's power was irresistible, and she squeezed Aleka to her chest the way she might have done when her goddaughter first came to her. Her lips found Aleka's cheek and kissed dryly, then she craned her neck to whisper in her ear.

"I was never a true mother to you," she said. "There was too much anger in me, too much hurt. Every time you'd disappear, I'd say to myself, 'good riddance to her,' but then I'd feel ashamed, and I'd search for you all the more frantically, chew you out all the more furiously. It got worse with each of the babies I lost, each reminder that you were never truly mine. It was as if I was punishing you for my failures, my inability to be the woman I'd always told myself I was."

Her voice had broken, the final words barely audible against Aleka's ear. She pulled out of their embrace, holding Aleka at arm's length and looking hard into her eyes.

"I don't ask you to forgive me," she said. "I ask only that you don't let what I've done prevent *you* from living. Whether it's with this boy or someone else…"

"Auntie," Aleka said. "Arachne. It doesn't matter anymore. Athan will be here soon, and then…"

"You'll face him," Auntie said fiercely. "You'll stand before him as the woman you've become, not the child you used to be. And no matter what happens, you'll remember your old auntie's words, and you'll bear your lot without fear. Promise me."

Aleka met the woman's eyes. Their expression was fervent in her haggard face. "I promise."

Auntie relaxed, and she drew Aleka into another hug. Aleka clutched her tightly, not worrying about her injuries, knowing there was nothing she could do to harm her godmother anymore. She wished she could give something to the woman who'd devoted so much of her life to keeping her safe, but she knew she couldn't give Auntie what she wanted most. Not even her own death could secure the new life Auntie had been denied.

She came out of the hug to find her mother's hand on her shoulder. The room had darkened, and Aleka wondered whether she'd fallen asleep again; she was reeling with hunger and exhaustion, and it wouldn't have surprised her to discover that she'd yielded to sleep in her godmother's arms. Then she looked behind her mother, where a milling throng of dark figures blocked the light from the windows, and where two individuals, one in the body of a man and the other in the form of a young boy, peered down at her. She laid Auntie's limp frame on the stretcher, and she knew it was too late for excuses or regrets.

"Aleka," the Skaldi leader said as he held a hand out toward her. "My daughter. The time has come."

Chapter 18

Aleka had no chance to say goodbye before Athan's hench-men closed around her and pulled her away.

She heard the sound of blows, looked back to see the members of her colony fighting to free themselves from the dark mass that hemmed them in.

"Kareem!" her mother called out. "You don't have to do this."

"I'm sorry, Diana," he said. "But I do."

He signaled, and a cordon of faceless beings grabbed the Huntress's arms. She struggled, but even she couldn't match their strength. The main body of creatures dragged Aleka into the hallway, and the last thing she saw was her mother's desperate face and wild white hair.

"Where are you taking me?" Aleka asked the Skaldi leader, but it was Athan who answered.

"To pay the ferryman," he said. "That bill's long past due."

The two of them flanked her as they started down the stairs, while their silent army followed. The majority of the creatures were composed of the germ plasma, dark and fea-tureless and rippling like water, but their number also included the few members of Kareem Reza's inner circle who'd survived the Huntress's assault. These beings were battered and broken, their limbs mangled and their faces blurred like soft clay, but their bodies tailed along as if some will other than their own were directing them.

They reached the bottom of the stairs and crossed the lobby. Beyond the shattered glass, Aleka saw the surging, boiling lake of germ plasma. It should have flooded the building, but something held it back, an invisible wall keeping it just short of the front door. Gazing at it, she knew at last what Athan meant to do with her.

She turned to the man who looked like her father. "Is this what you want? To send me out into that?"

"It's never been a question of what I want," he said. "This is what we need. Your sacrifice will open the way to a destiny none of our kind has dared dream of before."

"And once you're finished with me?" she asked. "You'll move on to other planets and do the same thing there you did here, won't you?"

He lowered his eyes. "We will move on, as we've pledged to do, my daughter."

He reached out to touch her arm, but she snatched it away.

"Don't call me that," she said. "Don't pretend any part of me came from you."

She turned to Athan, who stood watching their argument with an amused expression. It struck her that he'd turned out to be the more honest of the two—the one who'd made perfectly clear what he wanted from her, while Kareem was still seeking to deceive. Yet in the end, what choice did she have? She couldn't fight them both, and she couldn't run. All she could do was what Auntie had told her to do: face her fate without fear.

"I'm ready," she told Athan.

"Then come with me," he said. "And we'll get this show on the road."

He took her arm. His touch was surprisingly gentle, as if, now that he had what he wanted, he could treat her like the queen he kept telling her she was. She didn't look at the Skaldi leader while Athan walked her to the shattered doors and helped her outside.

The germ plasma seemed to grow agitated or excited at her arrival, cresting in a single wave taller than the building. The movement was accompanied by a squelching, sucking sound like boots tramping through mud during the rainy season, except on an immeasurably larger scale. Aleka wondered if this was what the ocean looked like, what it sounded like. If its waters were warm or icy cold, and what she would feel when the waves surrounded her. When they dragged her down to the bottom and all their massive weight pressed against her, crushing her bones while the flood filled her nose and mouth and lungs.

"You told me I couldn't die," she said to the boy.

"I had to tell you something," he answered. "Would it have made a difference if I'd told you you'd live?"

"I guess not." She craned her neck to find the top of the black wall of water, but it seemed to blend with the heavens. "How can there be so much of it?"

"It has the potential to grow exponentially," he said. "All it needed was the energy you've supplied. Join with it, and that energy will flow outward, giving it the ability to generate millions of our kind." His mouth quirked and his eyes lit with some of their old mischief. "Songs will be sung, Aleka. The gods will celebrate you in their halls for all time."

"And the other ones?" she asked, ignoring his attempt at wit. "Kareem, and the ones like him?"

"Yesterday's model," Athan scoffed. "They've convinced themselves you're going to bring them back from the brink, but the truth is, they lack the capacity to absorb the amount of power you're packing. Once it hits them, they'll burn up like a spent match. That's Nature's way: out with the old, in with the new. Evolve or die."

"You say the same thing about people. My mom, Auntie, everyone."

"Isn't it true?" he asked. "Human beings were living high on the hog, lords of all creation, thinking they had nothing to fear. Then, boom, along came something better, and in less than the blink of an eye by evolutionary time, the party was over. I don't make the rules, kiddo. I just follow where they lead."

"It'll be the same with you," she said.

He raised an eyebrow. "Do tell."

"That's *Nature's way*," she mimicked. "You're so sure your kind will live forever, but one of these days, something will knock you off your perch. Something stronger, faster, smarter. You'll never see it coming, but when it does, you'll fade into dust like everything else."

He threw back his head and laughed. "I like those odds. If something shows up that thinks it can do better than me, it's welcome to try and take my place."

He pulled her arm, and the two of them stepped within reach of the towering wall of plasma. It had settled down and was no longer sloshing as it had before, but the thought of giving herself to it still terrified her. "You have to promise me something."

"Make it snappy," he said. "Time's a-wasting."

"Leave my colony alone," she said. "My mom, your brother, all the rest of them. They'll be like ants to you once you've got the power you want, and you don't need to step on them just to prove a point."

"You're asking a lot from a guy like me," he said. "As Lame Man could have told you, I've never been known for restraining my appetites." He licked his lips with the snaky tongue, then nodded. "But okay. To the extent that you can trust me, I give you my word that I'll let them be once you're dead."

Hearing the word fall so starkly from his lips made her heart fail. "And it won't hurt?" she asked, hating herself for revealing weakness in front of him.

"You won't feel a thing," he said. "Or I take that back. Once you've started down that road, you'll feel … satisfied. Fulfilled. Maybe for the first time in your life."

She eyed him suspiciously. "What are you talking about?"

"I'm talking about peace," he said. "Or oblivion, which amounts to the same thing. Years ago, I told myself I would never let them gain the upper hand, that I'd always be the one pulling the strings. But they get to you, Aleka. They call out to you, promising something even better than power—something I can't put a name to. When it came right down to it, I couldn't resist that call, and you won't be able to either."

Aleka studied him, surprised to hear none of his customary sarcasm. Instead, his voice had taken on an odd note of wistfulness, accompanied by an expression of innocent wonder he might have worn when he truly was a child. Could it be that he meant what he said—that as a boy, he'd longed for something that was missing from his life, something he

229

couldn't achieve on his own? Or were her mother's words true: that like all Skaldi, he was so profoundly deceptive he'd deceived even himself?

"I hope you're right," she said.

"I am," he answered. "Now let's get on with it."

He gestured toward the black tide. She glanced over her shoulder at the Skaldi headquarters, but the boardroom was too high to tell if anyone was gazing down at her. She would never know, she told herself—never know if her mother was watching, never know if she approved of the sacrifice her daughter had chosen to make. Never know if that sacrifice was worth it—if Athan would keep his word and let her colony live out the rest of their lives unmolested, if the germ plasma, infused with her power and rising to the heights he envisioned, would come crashing down to earth in some far future she couldn't imagine. She'd never know anything ever again, and all she could do was hope.

She took a step forward, then another. The plasma held its position, though she could feel its eagerness, a colossal life form straining on an inadequate leash. Strange that she couldn't smell anything, the corpse-stink that emanated from the bodies of the fully formed Skaldi; the plasma had no more odor than the water it resembled. Was that because the process of decay that manifested itself so quickly in the mature creatures hadn't yet begun? She stood face to face with the wave, so close she could see beads of plasma forming on the solid wall like raindrops on the stretched canvas of a tent. Except the drops' paths weren't controlled by gravity; they left the plane of water and reached out toward her, thinning until they were as fine as hairs. The very tips of them touched Aleka's face, and though she recoiled instinctively, the sensation wasn't unpleasant at all; it was like the brush of wind-blown rain against her cheeks. She leaned even closer, so close that a reflection formed in the wave. Unaccustomed to seeing herself, she was startled by the clarity of the image: pale skin, hollow cheeks, light hair. Was it her face, or the Huntress's? The face of the new mother from sixteen years ago, before time and sorrow had reshaped her visage into what it was today? Their features might have been the same back then, and she couldn't tell in the black mirror if the double's eyes were her own gray or her mother's piercing blue. She leaned forward until her nose touched that of the phantom, which seemed to smile in response. A moment later, her face broke the plane, the waters enfolding her as they drew her into the heart of the wave.

It was surprisingly warm inside, and not the slightest bit wet; if anything, it felt soft, like another's flesh pressed against hers. She realized at once that the plasma wasn't liquid, that it wouldn't crush or suffocate her. It was a single living organism, able to support its own weight and to shape itself around her so she could breathe. Tiny filaments wiggled against her as they pulled her deeper inside, like thousands of miniscule fingers passing her from one hand to the next. She took a deep breath, almost a sigh, and the plasma copied her, shivering with apparent pleasure. Her senses remained on the alert in case this was a trick, the creature trying to put her at ease before it pounced. She didn't sense any threat, though. She felt the way she used to feel in the tunnels—as if she were seeking something, though she didn't know what she might find.

Hands outstretched, she probed deeper into the darkness. The plasma seemed content to let her take her time and choose her own path; the tendrils that caressed her body didn't try to direct her, didn't appear to want anything more than to touch

231

her. The dawn light faded to black as she wandered through the wave, but she felt neither lost nor afraid; she felt, oddly, as if she knew the way, even if she didn't know where she was going. The longer she spent in this shadowy underworld, the more she became convinced that there was something hidden inside that she—and only she—was meant to find. She was almost certain that when she found it, the answers would be revealed, maybe in the very last second of her life. But that would be enough, she told herself. It would be worth it to die, if only she *knew*.

Far away, through darkness that rippled like water, she saw a figure approaching. It moved in a slow, drifting fashion, as if it were swimming through the murky depths. For the first time since she'd entered the wave, a feeling of anxiety returned, her shoulders tensing in anticipation of an attack. The distant form appeared human in shape and size, but she knew that it was a creature born of the plasma, no different from Athan or any of the monsters at his command. If it had been summoned here to carry out his will, she would have no opportunity to flee, and her life would be over soon. Her stomach tightened as the dark figure came to a stop only feet away from her. Then the plasma drew aside like a curtain, and Aleka stared at the being that stepped through.

It was a girl, five or six years old, with long blond hair and large gray eyes. She wore an oversized camouflage uniform, its cuffs rolled back to fit her. Something about her expression, at once sober and curious, tugged strongly at Aleka's heart, and she was about to speak when she felt a light tap on her shoulder and turned to look behind her.

The wave was filled with a host of children that receded into the shadows as far as her eyes could see. None of their faces was familiar, though there were two boys near the front, one a few years older than the other, who shared the girl's gray eyes. There were hundreds of them in all, possibly thousands, and those closest to her wore the same serious, questioning look as the little girl. Aleka turned back to her and found that the girl's lips were touched by a small smile.

"Who are you?" Aleka asked.

The girl opened her mouth, and though no sound emerged, Aleka heard her words in the lapping of the dark waters.

You called for us, the girl said. *And so we answered.*

"I did?" Aleka asked. "When?"

When you came here, the girl replied.

Aleka shook her head. "I don't understand."

Come with us, and we'll show you, the girl said. *There's nothing to be afraid of.*

She stepped closer and held out a hand. Aleka took it, and felt the pulse flowing through the girl's wrist, matching her own pulse beat by beat. Just minutes ago—if time had any meaning here—she would have been worried that this was another of Athan's tricks, that he'd lulled and lied to her one final time. Now she felt certain that these children were hers, not his—that she *had* called them forth, though she didn't know how. She knew only that she'd discovered the word for the thing Athan was unable to name, the thing she'd waited for her entire life: *reunion*. All she had to do was follow this girl, and they'd arrive at a place where both of them would be made whole.

Her fingers closed around her guide's. The girl looked up at her, and her smile mirrored Aleka's as they took a step into the black water.

"Stop!" a voice shouted, loud enough to make the plasma tremble all around her.

Aleka turned to see a distant shape fighting through the darkness. She couldn't tell who it was, but in sharp contrast to the graceful, dreamy motion of the little girl, it flailed violently against the plasma like a wanderer lost in a sandstorm. When it burst into view, both Aleka and her guide fell back with a cry that seemed to come from a single throat.

It was Athan, and yet it wasn't. At the moment he appeared, it was his boy-shape, fists clenched and face twisted in fury; a moment later, it was a ravenous mouth of gigantic proportions, so huge it seemed capable of drinking the entire wave from which it had formed. The stench of the Skaldi poured from that mouth, making Aleka gag and fall to her knees. The little girl let go of her hand while the rest of the children screamed and scattered, but none of them got far before they were sucked toward the devouring mouth. Their eyes pleaded with Aleka as they hurtled past, but their bodies were breaking down into seed form, flowing like water to be swallowed by the monstrous maw. Its voice emerged again, a roar that battered Aleka to the ground while the gray-eyed girl's wail echoed briefly and was gone.

"This is mine!" the voice boomed. "All of it! You can't take it from me!"

Aleka raised her head to face the creature, and that was when the pain began.

It was a type of pain she'd never experienced before—an all-consuming pain that felt as if her breath, her life, her soul were being drained from her, sucked into the voracious mouth the way the children had been. The pain intensified as the mouth gaped wider than a thousand Skaldi's scars and figures began to issue from it, first tens and then hundreds of bodies crowding all around her, carrying the reek of the grave with them. Some took the form of human beings: Athan himself, the giant man with the craggy face, the much smaller man with dark hair and frightened eyes, Didi and the other runners, Diana the Huntress, Auntie and Laman and Javier and the twins, along with countless strangers who must have been among those the Skaldi had consumed during their long reign of destruction. Others were creatures from nightmare: black bats and carrion birds, demonic effigies with human bodies and animal faces, snaky appendages that lashed into turbulence the plasma surrounding them. The figures grew so numerous there was no room for them all, each one snapping and clawing at the others in its fight to reach her. Still they kept multiplying as if they could never get enough of the power she was providing them, the power that grew fainter and weaker as it flowed into the frothing, bubbling chaos of the plasma. The mouth was gone, dissolved into the substance it had spewed out, but she choked on the smell of its rot and quailed before its deafening roar all the same. There were other voices in the plasma, faint voices of grief and anguish, but she could barely hear them over the bellowing, and she was too weak to answer them even if she could. At any moment, she would be snuffed out entirely, her life ending not in the solace she'd found in the company of the children but in the despair of knowing that the boy had gained everything he wanted and would exact his malice on her colony as soon as she was gone.

Aleka, a last voice called out, but she had no idea who was speaking or what the word meant.

A violent force threw her backward, her body landing painfully on a mound of sharp rubble. Had the plasma cast her out, leaving her stranded amidst the ruins of the shattered city? Her eyes fluttered open, but the world around her was blurred beyond recognition. When she drew a tortured breath, she was surprised to find that the air was free of the stench of Skaldi, having returned to the dry, dusty smell of the desert. Her mind was too foggy to understand what that meant, and her eyes were closing for what she knew would be the final time. She was almost thankful that she wouldn't have to feel the pain anymore, wouldn't have to witness the end of everything she knew and loved. She let herself sink into that final thought, her eyes closing while the sound of a long, echoing wail was carried to her ears by the wind.

"Aleka."

A hand closed on her wrist. Warmth radiated from the point of contact, her forearm tingling as if she'd slept on it wrong and it was coming back to life. She fought against whoever held her, but she was much too weak to shake their hand off. The grip bore down even harder, and the feeling of warmth spread, climbing up her arm to her shoulder and chest. She gasped as a jolt passed through her, and she became aware that her heart was beating, though she couldn't say when or if it had stopped. Her eyes opened to see a shadow hovering over her.

"Can you stand?" a voice asked. Without thinking, she nodded, and a grasp much firmer than any shadow pulled her to her feet.

"We have to move quickly," the voice said. "The ruins are unstable, and we have a long way to walk."

"I can't…"

"I'll help you," the voice said. "Hold my hand, and don't let go."

Numbly, Aleka obeyed. She stood on shifting ground, leaning against the person, her legs wobbling like a toddler's. The entire world seemed to have gone gray, the ground and sky an identical shade with no solid features she could make out. The person who held her remained nothing but a darker shadow against the void, and the terrible thought struck her that it was the boy, giving her back a thread of the life he'd stolen so he could force her to witness his final triumph.

"Don't do this to me," she whispered.

"I have to," the voice answered. "I still need you, Aleka, just as you need me."

Hearing those words made her certain he was who she feared, but her arms were powerless to push him away, and her legs could do nothing but follow as he dragged her up the incline on which they stood.

They labored uphill for what felt like hours, then the ground leveled off and they made better speed. Still the terrain was treacherous, composed of loose debris that slipped and skidded beneath them. It didn't help that she couldn't see well enough to know where she was planting her feet; she would have fallen many times if not for the grip on her arm. She thought she sensed a rumbling deep below, but maybe that was only the tremor in her legs.

"Almost there," the voice spoke out of the gray. "This last part will be the hardest."

"Wait—" she said.

"No time," it responded, and they started uphill again.

Aleka's legs burned as she followed her invisible escort. Sometime during the long, arduous climb, the pain gave way to a floating sensation, and the only thing that told her she was still moving was the sound of her heavy breathing and the

237

scraping of stones as she stumbled blindly on. She tried to make out the face of the one who held her, but even with the person being mere inches from her, there was nothing to see. When she realized she couldn't feel their breath on her cheek either, she tried to push herself away, only to be held even more tightly.

"Stop," she begged.

To her surprise, their ascent ceased. Hands turned her, and the voice spoke again in her ear.

"This is risky," it said. "There's not much time, and the effort might weaken me past the point of usefulness. But you deserve to see."

A hand was laid on her forehead. Warmth rippled outward from its touch, and the first hint of anything she'd seen for the duration of their trek peeked through: a slim ray of light, as if the sun had pierced the gray fog that had descended over the world. Then the fog melted away, and daylight flooded back before her astonished eyes.

She stood midway up a towering mound of rubble nearly as tall as the wave had been. The person holding her was a young man with a thin frame, pale skin, and thick black hair and eyebrows. She sensed that she should know who he was, but the fog that had lifted from her eyes seemed to have settled over her mind, and she couldn't recall his name or anything about him. He looked at her with concern, then pointed out over the city.

A single tall building reared above the ruins, while a mountain range dominated the landscape behind. In the place where the black wave had stood, there was nothing but a shallow, muddy pool, bubbling like a cauldron on the fire and emitting wisps of smoke that were carried off by the wind. When she squinted, she realized that the bubbles were pseudopods, all of them thrashing wildly as if they were trying to free themselves. None succeeded; they burst, melting back into the slime without reemerging. There were fewer and fewer of them with each moment that passed, and it slowly dawned on her why: the pool itself was shrinking, evaporating under the late-morning sun. It shriveled from the edges inward, leaving behind a coating of ash on the dry, cracked ground. At the rate it was vanishing, it would be gone before the sun reached its apex.

"What's happening to it?" she asked.

"The organism is dying," the man answered. "Soon it will return to the desert."

"But the children," she said. "They were…"

She tried to remember what she'd been about to say, but the words were made of fog, and they slipped away before they could take solid form. The next second, the gray veil fell before her eyes once more, and she stumbled against the man who held her.

"Be careful," he said, a renewed urgency in his voice. "I can't hold on much long—"

His words ended as he collapsed against her, bringing them both down onto the pile. They slid briefly before something stopped their descent. She could feel him lying beside her, but could see nothing.

"We have to go," his voice came, much fainter than before. "There's no time…"

His hand gripped hers. Aleka had a moment to feel its icy coldness before his fingers loosened and she heard his body crashing down the pile. She would have called out to him if she had a voice left, would have searched for him if she had eyes to see. But the fog had robbed her of all sense of self, and there was nothing she could do but lie motionless and listen to the sound of the wind rising around her like the crashing of waves on a desolate shore.

Chapter 19

The tang of salt air woke her.

At first, she thought she must be dreaming of the ocean, of imaginary sand and rocks and waves. But when she opened her eyes, she discovered that she was lying in a stretcher near the shore of a lake that gleamed in the sunlight. Three trucks patterned in camouflage colors were parked along the shoreline, while adults in matching uniforms stood nearby and children splashed and shrieked playfully in the shallow water. Their cries reminded her of birds. Try as she might, she couldn't remember anyone's names, though she recognized all of their faces. A deep unease in her stomach told her that some of those who should have been there were missing, though she couldn't think who. Alarmed, she lifted herself on an elbow to look for the ones she couldn't name.

When she did so, she found that she wasn't alone. Lying close by, in a stretcher identical to hers, was a young man with dark hair and pale skin. His eyes were closed, his head turned to the side, but she could see how emaciated he was, the flesh of his face drawn against the underlying bones like someone on the last verge of starvation. He wasn't wearing a shirt, which revealed the outline of each rib, the concavity of his stomach. Even more unsettling, an open wound ran all the way down his chest, from the cleft of his throat to his belly button. It wasn't bleeding, but she had the sickening feeling that it was moving, the edges opening and closing like lips.

"Aleka."

The voice startled her as much as it would have if the chest scar had spoken. She looked at the man's face and found that he was staring back at her, his dark eyes sunken in the craters of his skull. There was an intensity to his inspection that made her uncomfortable, but she couldn't look away.

"You don't know me," he said at last. "Do you know them?"

His eyes flicked toward the cluster of people by the lake. She concentrated, tried to remember, but in the end, she was forced to shake her head.

"And yourself?" he asked quietly. "Do you know who *you* are?"

She was about to answer "of course," but his riveting gaze wouldn't let her lie. She shook her head again.

He sighed. His ribs showed even more starkly when his chest expanded, and the scar opened wider, giving her a momentary glimpse of blank gray flesh before it closed again.

"The attack you suffered earlier today has damaged your memory," he said. "The Skaldi drain life, stealing their victims' identities to cloak their own emptiness. You were exposed to an assault of far greater magnitude than anyone has endured, and though you survived, I'm afraid you may never be the same as you once were."

He turned his head away. She searched inside herself for some inkling of who she was, the life she'd lived before this moment, but it was gone. Even the attack the man had spoken about: he said it had happened today, but it felt fractured and unreal, fragments of a faded dream rather than a calamity that had actually befallen her. Something about entering a black wall of water where hundreds of children waited, only to watch them being snatched away by the ... Skaldi? She shivered at the word, and was thankful she couldn't remember that part. Still, the thought of everything she'd lost made her wrap her arms around her middle in an attempt to stifle a sob.

The man must have heard. His dark eyes found hers again, and his cadaverous face shifted in what might have been meant as a look of sympathy.

"There's one final story I have to tell you," he said. "You won't understand it just now, but in time to come, it might comfort you. I wish I could live to see that time, but my own borrowed life has run its course, and I have only minutes left. Listen to me, Aleka—yes, that's your name—and I'll try to help you see that none of this has been in vain."

He lifted himself on bony elbows to face her. The effort seemed to disturb the chest wound, which opened and closed with a convulsive movement. He drew in a sharp breath, but collected himself to speak.

"The entity that attacked you has been defeated," he said. "Seeking a limitless, immortal life, it absorbed far more energy than it could safely hold, and its cells multiplied beyond all bounds. Soon, there was nothing left for those cells to feed on—and so, in a doomed effort to survive, the organism utterly devoured itself."

He paused, his eyes roving hers as if willing her to remember. She tried, but again, it slipped away from her, leaving only the chasm of pain and loss. The man watched as tears began to fall down her cheeks, then resumed his story in a softer voice.

"I knew the creature's flaw when I summoned it from its lair and commissioned it to transport you to me," he said. "I knew that it would be unable to resist the lure of your power, and that it would feed greedily and without restraint. I knew as well that, if it had achieved its object, it would have attempted to overthrow me, for the will to dominate is inseparable from its nature. What it failed to understand is that I did not seek what it sought—that I had no intention of using your power to extend my unnatural life. I had made a pact with my fellows to end the cycle of madness that is the Skaldi way, and in so doing to atone for what our kind has done. To achieve the only true immortality that anyone can claim: an immortality of the spirit, not the body."

He gestured to the ground beside his stretcher. She hadn't noticed before, but piles of dust had accumulated there, five or six distinct mounds the size of anthills. The wind picked at them, and she could almost see them diminishing before her eyes.

"These were my companions," the man explained. "They're gone now—back to dust, back to where they belong. No more starving, no more feasting, no more hating themselves for what they were. After nearly two decades of unrelenting torment, they're finally at rest."

"But," she found her voice, "how did you...?"

"Survive?" he asked. "I partook of your power, but only as much as I needed to help you from the city once our foe was vanquished. I foolishly hesitated during our flight, and we both might have been lost—but thanks to your own companions, we were saved. It won't be long now before I join those who went before me. I was the first of my kind, and so I suppose it's fitting that I should be the last."

244

He fell silent. She tried to make sense of what he'd said, but most of it seemed to come from long ago, as if it were one of the stories she vaguely remembered listening to but had no recollection of now. There was a woman who'd told her those stories, a woman who was her ... mother? How long ago had it been, how old was she now? She couldn't remember that either.

The man looked at her keenly. His eyes, it seemed to her, were receding even farther into his skull, his skin becoming as pale as chalk. When he spoke again, his voice was a husky whisper.

"I can never thank you enough for what you've given me," he said. "Nor can I express my sorrow for what has been taken from you. You'll always be a part of me, Aleka, though you may never come to know it fully. I hope you can learn to forgive me in time, as have the other women I love."

He turned his head toward the trucks, where she saw three figures approaching. She couldn't name any of them, but somehow she knew that they were the three whose absence had worried her the most. The woman with bright blue eyes and wild white hair, a noticeable limp in her stride. The much shorter woman in the black jacket and gray braids, who stomped forward as if daring the world to stand in her way. The tall boy with long hair whose appearance made her cheeks warm and her chest melt unaccountably. It was as if she hadn't seen him, hadn't seen any of them, in years. As if she'd believed they were lost for good, and now here they were, returned to greet her as she woke.

The white-haired woman leaned down to kiss her on the forehead, the second woman following. The boy stood to the side, the trace of a smile on his lips, which for some reason

245

made her heart beat even harder. When the gray-haired woman rose, she addressed the man in the stretcher.

"So?" she said. "What's the prognosis?"

"It's as I feared," he said.

All three of the visitors looked crestfallen, but they put on cheerful faces at once.

"So you'll heal her," the gray-haired woman said. "Just like you healed me and lover boy here."

The man shook his head. "I healed you with the power I borrowed from this child. There's nothing left in either of us, and if healing is to come, it'll have to be in a future I'll never see."

At that, both women's faces fell again. The one with the white hair was the first to speak. "Then it's time?"

"Past time," he said. "If you would help me, I'd like to look on the waters once more before the end."

The gray-haired woman signaled, and a burly man hurried over to help carry the stretchers to the lakeside. The crowd withdrew to a spot farther away, where tents had been erected around a central campfire. As soon as the burly man and the tall boy set their stretcher down, they retreated as well, leaving only the two women and the two invalids by the shore.

"Help me stand," the young man said. His hair was dark no longer; it had grayed during the minute's walk to the lake, and now it was the same color as his ashen face.

The two women looped his skeletal arms over their shoulders and raised him from the stretcher. The scar on his chest opened for a moment, but it closed immediately, the line that marked its presence fading into the gray skin. He stood between them by the shore of the lake, which had turned golden in the late day sun.

246

"You'll have to remain watchful," he said to the women. "If any of the germ plasma persists at the base…"

"Don't worry about us," the gray-haired woman said. "We'll be on the lookout."

The man's body relaxed at that. He leaned over to whisper something in the gray-haired woman's ear, and she giggled in a way that was almost girlish.

"You remembered," she said.

He smiled before touching the other woman's cheek. Her eyes brightened with tears, but she returned his smile. He took her hand and put something small in her lined palm.

"You're as good a shot as ever," he said.

"My last shot," she said, her hand closing on the object. "I saved it for you."

She placed a kiss on his cheek. He cast a look at the waters, then turned to the three of them.

"I would not have you here to see me return to the salt and soil," he said. "Leave me, and let my memory be all that remains."

The women seemed about to object, but they let the man lift his arms from their shoulders. He stood by the lakeside, steady despite his wasted frame. The women stooped to pick up the stretcher with its remaining occupant, and the man faced them one last time. There was no fear in his eyes as the women turned to go.

They plodded up the bank toward the encampment. A wind rose, and there was a sound like a grateful sigh. The three looked back, but he was gone.

THEY ARRIVED AT the campsite just as a fourth truck pulled to a jerky stop beside the others, its wheels spraying sand. A thin man with long black hair and a scraggly beard jumped from the driver's seat. The gray-haired woman took just enough time to set the stretcher down before she screamed "Laman!" and bounded over to him, throwing her arms around his waist and squeezing. He flushed furiously when she followed the hug with a passionate kiss in front of the entire group, who met the display with cheers and nudges. When the poor man disentangled himself from her embrace, he nodded toward the stretcher.

"Aleka's okay?" he asked.

"She'll take a while to get back to her old self," the gray-haired woman said. "But she's fine."

"And Kareem?"

"Even better," she said. "He's finally at peace."

"I'm so glad," the bearded man said softly, pulling the woman close and kissing her much more gently than she'd kissed him. "Asheh, I'm so glad."

Aleka focused on their reunion, all the while committing the names to memory. Laman, Asheh, the white-haired woman... Nobody had said her name yet, but she expected someone would soon. The burly man had already been identified as Araz, and she thought she'd picked up the names of some of the other adults and children. If worse came to worst, she'd simply have to tell everyone she couldn't remember and let them reeducate her.

And then there was the boy with long hair, the one who made her heart thump and the blood rush in her ears. Asking him who he was would be more embarrassing than the rest, so she hoped the name would drop naturally into conversation before it got to that point.

A group of people gathered by the back of the newly arrived truck and began unloading something. They were directed by two additional people Aleka felt she should remember but couldn't: a thin young woman with light brown skin and reddish hair, and a stocky woman about the same age with darker skin and a head shaved down to stubble. The first woman was as voluble as the second was taciturn. Aleka raised herself enough to see that the camp members were unloading two more stretchers, along with a bundled form that was giving everyone a huge amount of trouble. When they finally set their burdens down by the campfire, she saw why.

The stretchers were occupied by two sleeping figures: a young boy with pale skin and long brown hair, and a small man with black hair combed over his forehead. Both of them rolled restlessly back and forth and moaned from time to time. The bundle consisted of a tent that had been wrapped around the gigantic form of a man, almost eight feet in height. The camp children stared at him as he lay on the bank, a couple of the bolder ones scampering forward to touch the prostrate giant before Asheh shooed them away. His eyes were closed, but like the other two sleepers, he seemed to be having a bad dream, his head turning from side to side while a deep rumbling groan issued from his throat. Asheh whistled softly as she inspected them.

"Well, now," she said. "Look what the cat dragged in."

"We found them in the city," Laman said. "The plasma must have expelled them after all these years."

"Do you think they're still infected?"

"No idea," he said. "They look the same as they did back then, so maybe they were in some kind of ... suspension? Does that make any sense?"

249

"No more than you usually make," Asheh said, hooking an arm inside his to pull him close. "The real question is, what the hell are we supposed to do with them?"

"We could keep them confined for now," Laman said. "Let Tyris look after them."

"Or we could skin them alive and leave them for the fire ants to finish off." When Laman gave her an alarmed look, she poked him in the ribs. "Kidding. Tyris!"

The red-haired girl came over.

"The moment we finish up here, get a crew to haul these stiffs to the passenger truck," Asheh said. "Petra!" she barked. "Any luck?"

The young woman with the shaved head went to the front seat of the truck and returned carrying a small bundle. She held it in both hands as if it contained something precious.

"Let's get on with it, then," Asheh said. "Diana, do you think this one's up for joining us?"

The white-haired woman turned to Aleka. The stoic mask from the lakeshore dropped for a moment, and grief showed in the deep lines of her face. Aleka wished she knew what had put it there, but all she could tell was that it had been years in the making. At least she knew one thing more: the old woman's name. Diana.

"I'll stay with her," Diana said. "She'll be all right."

Asheh looked dubious, but she left the two of them alone and approached the rest of the camp, delivering orders in a curt voice. Diana came to the stretcher, and with her assistance, Aleka stood and walked slowly behind the others until they reached the lakeside. There, everyone linked arms or held hands while Tyris and Petra joined Asheh at the front of the group. That was when Aleka saw that two driftwood crosses had been planted in the sandy soil, a single hole dug in front of them. Some of the littler children started crying as Tyris and Petra lowered the bundle carefully into the hole. When the two of them rose, even the stolid Petra's face was covered in tears.

Asheh stood before the others and spoke. She talked about the twins, Kay and May, who had been part of her family for so many years, and who had cared for so many children in all that time. Her voice was strong and her cheeks dry, but she faltered when she pronounced two words: *Nausikaa* and *Aristodeme*. Aleka understood that those were the twins' real names, but beyond that, she could remember nothing about them, neither how they'd lived nor how they'd died. Diana stood by her side with an arm around her back throughout the brief ceremony, and Aleka tried not to show how much it hurt to be the only member of the company who'd forgotten the ones they'd gathered to mourn.

"It's all right," Diana said when the service was over. She brushed hair from Aleka's forehead. "We'll talk later."

She stepped away, Asheh quickly taking her place at Aleka's side. Diana hobbled over to the graves and lowered herself slowly and painfully beside them. She bowed her head beneath the wild tangle of white hair, then covered her face with her hands and wept.

Chapter 20

They talked all night.

By the time they were done, Aleka knew everyone's name, discovering that all the adults except for Laman called the gray-haired woman Arachne (while the children called her Auntie Spider); that the three strangers who'd arrived in Laman's truck were his younger brother Athan, his father Udain, and a scientist named Dr. Melan; and that the teenage boy who kept glancing at her but who wouldn't approach her was named Javier. She learned the history of the camp, or colony as Diana called it: Survival Colony 9, one of the first groups of people to join together against the Skaldi. She learned the larger history of the wars, the Skaldi, the experiments that Udain Genn had conducted with Dr. Melan and Athan. Diana went right up to the present, recounting Aleka's own life over the past months and weeks, though she spared her a too-graphic retelling of what had happened in the city. When the sun rose on another day, Aleka's head was bursting with information, and she could have recited the whole story to another person who'd lost their past and who wanted to know what had happened to the world.

But that's all it was to her: a story. She didn't doubt that the events had actually happened—some of them to her—but she couldn't feel them in her brain or body, couldn't claim them as her own. Scraps of personal history floated just beyond her grasp: the twins, the Skaldi, the awful twinge in her gut when images from the past day rose to her mind. But for the most part, her memory began today, and no matter what kind of life she was able to create from this point forward, she knew there would always be missing pieces from the life she'd lived before.

"Did you know my parents?" she asked Diana.

For the first time since their conversation started, the old woman seemed reluctant to answer, turning her head away and gazing into the night. "No. They died a long time ago."

"Who were they?"

"Wanderers," Diana said. "Arachne found their bodies in the desert and took you into the colony. No one even knew their names."

That didn't satisfy Aleka, but she couldn't get Diana to say anything else about the subject, so she left it as one of the missing pieces she would never know.

She thought it might bring back some of those pieces if she could see her own face, so she asked Diana to help her walk to the trucks. With moonlight bathing the shore, she tilted the side view mirror and gazed at the person reflected there: a tall, slender woman with long silvery hair, gray eyes, and deep grooves running beside her nose to the severe line of her mouth. She glanced at Diana, who stood watching her watch herself.

"How old did you say I am?" she asked.

"Sixteen," Diana answered.

"I look older."

"You look fine."

Aleka moved the mirror back into position and turned away. For whatever reason, the first thought to enter her mind was that she looked old enough to be Javier's mother. "Can I ask you something?"

"Of course."

"How old are you?"

"I'm thirty-three. Almost thirty-four." Diana's wrinkled face broke into a smile. "So you see, it's not the depth of the scars that matters. It's what you did to earn them."

Aleka ducked her eyes. It wasn't until Diana said those words that she realized that in all last night's talk, the woman hadn't said a thing about herself.

"I can trim this for you if you'd like," Diana said. "So the gray doesn't show as much."

It took an hour to cut Aleka's shoulder-length hair with the colony's one functioning, if rusty, pair of scissors. When Diana was done, Aleka checked herself in the mirror again and found that the short style accentuated the leanness of her face and the hollows around her eyes. It didn't make her look any younger, but it did make her look fundamentally different, and that wasn't so bad.

The other members of camp were up and moving by the time Aleka had committed her new appearance to memory. Some of them cooked and served a quick breakfast, while others took down tents and packed them in one of the trucks. Diana had told her that the colonies were mobile, rarely staying in one spot for long, but even though the lakeshore wasn't much to look at, it saddened Aleka to think that they were about to leave the one place she held firm in memory.

When everyone had eaten and their belongings were packed, Arachne called the colony together. She stood while the others sat on the sand, her small frame as well as her voice bristling with energy.

"I don't like to say this," she began, "but I also don't like to keep people in suspense. Laman and I have talked things over, and we've decided it's best if we give up our leadership positions for the time being. The rest of you should stay together, but he and I have business elsewhere."

She silenced the colony's collective gasp with a wave of her hand.

"Laman's kin need help," she said. "More important, we need to keep an eye on them. From what Tyris tells me, his father and brother are starting to come around, Melan a bit less so. But there are some … unexpected developments in their recovery. Tyris, can you give everyone an update?"

The young woman joined Arachne. She cleared her throat nervously before speaking.

"Like Arachne said, the three of them are starting to respond to light and sound, though none has woken up yet," she said. "But they're undergoing some changes, particularly in the case of Athan."

"Changes?" Araz called out. "Like what?"

Tyris looked to Arachne for help, but the camp leader was silent. "Well, for one thing," Tyris answered Araz, "he seems to be growing…"

"What do you mean, *growing*?" Araz demanded.

"I mean growing," Tyris said. "Getting bigger. You remember when Laman said the plasma might have kept them in suspension all this time? Well, it's as if the period of suspension is over, and they're catching up on lost years. Athan is several inches taller than he was yesterday, and Udain and the doctor have definitely grayed."

A murmur passed through the camp.

"I can't explain it," Tyris concluded. "But there are clearly properties of the germ plasma that none of us has encountered before."

"Which is exactly why we have to keep an eye on them," Arachne jumped in. "It might be some time before we figure out what's going on, how much they remember, whether they're fully ... healed. If they are, then fine. If they're not, I don't want to let them loose among the rest of you. Years ago, there was a facility a few days' drive from here, down in what used to be Texas. We'll take them there and watch over them until we're sure they're safe."

"We could leave them," Araz said.

"We could also leave you," Arachne responded with fire in her eyes. "But that's not the way we do things around here."

Araz muttered to himself, but he seemed too scared of Arachne to say anything else.

"So that's settled," Arachne said. "All that remains to determine is who's going to take my place." Her gaze focused on Aleka's newfound companion. "How about it, Diana? Think you're ready for this?"

Diana shook her head. "I've got to be moving on. There are some things I need to attend to."

Aleka's heart fell. Diana was the only one in camp she knew at all, and the thought of being left alone with all these strangers made her feel even younger than her sixteen years.

"Must be nice to come and go as you please," Arachne said with something between a laugh and a sniff. "The rest of us don't have that luxury." She glared at Diana, who met her look placidly. "Well, then, what about Tyris and Petra? Any urgent matters you two can't tear yourselves away from?"

256

The young women shook their heads, Petra looking amazed and Tyris abashed. Araz muttered something else, but a glance from Arachne silenced him once more.

"I'll need a couple of hours to review protocol with these eager beavers," she said. "Then we hit the road."

The colony stood as one. Aleka looked beseechingly at her companion, but Diana only patted her cheek.

"You'll be fine," she said. "More than fine, unless I miss my guess."

Her blue eyes sparkled mischievously. Aleka found that Javier had approached them, which made her wish even more fervently that Diana wasn't going.

But she was. "Be good," she said, before heading off toward the command truck, where Arachne and Laman stood in conference with the camp's newly appointed leadership team.

Aleka looked at Javier. He seemed uncomfortable, shifting from foot to foot. Then he grinned. "You don't remember me, right?"

Mortification stopped Aleka's tongue. "I don't remember anything."

"I doubt that's true," he said. "There's brain memory and there's muscle memory. One's as good as the other, if you ask me."

He moved toward the lakeside, and Aleka's feet followed. The pounding in her ears had gotten so loud she could barely hear him when he started talking again.

"I could always draw from memory," he said. "I just needed to see a place or a person, and the image was imprinted in my mind and I could draw it weeks later if I wanted to. It's the same way I learned to fight."

"To fight?" she repeated, feeling stupid.

"Sure. I watched the others, Petra and the guards who were really good, and I picked it up that way. It's how I taught you."

"You did?"

"Want to test my theory?"

Before she could answer, his hand shot out and gripped her wrist. Aleka reacted without thinking, elbowing him in the gut and, when he doubled over, using his own body weight to throw him to the ground. She couldn't reconstruct how it all happened, but the next thing she knew, she found herself with a knee on his chest and a fist to his throat while he looked up at her with approval.

"I'd call that a successful test," he said.

She stood shakily and offered him a hand. They sat on stones beside the lake, Javier skipping rocks off its calm surface.

"We're all going to have a lot to learn," he said. "If the Skaldi really are gone, it's going to be a different world. Old patterns, things we have trouble letting go of, might get in the way. Maybe it's better if we all start fresh."

"It's still hard not to remember," she said. "It feels like I'm … flying. Like there's nothing to hold me to the earth."

"I feel kind of that way myself." Without explaining what he meant, he went on. "Tell you what. I'll help keep you grounded if you help me. Deal?"

He held out a hand. She couldn't stop the smile from creeping across her face as she took it and shook firmly. "Deal."

They held hands a little longer than seemed normal. When he let go, he gave a short laugh.

"Muscle memory," he said. "It'll get you every time."

They sat without speaking until they heard the voices of the new camp leaders ordering everyone back to the trucks— Tyris barely able to restrain her delight, Petra sounding almost as short-tempered as Arachne despite this being her first day on the job. Javier took Aleka's hand again and squeezed, and she knew that he'd be good to his word, that he wouldn't let her drift too far from the ground before pulling her back.

That reassuring thought was in her mind when Diana broke away from a final exchange with Laman and Arachne and started in their direction. She was using an unstrung bow as a walking stick, which enabled her to move quickly even with her leg injury. Aleka could see that she already had her pack on, a ratty bag that looked as weathered as she did.

"All right, you two," she said. "Enough of that."

They dropped hands, and Diana stood confronting them with arms crossed. Aleka was sure there was something the woman wanted to say, but long as she waited, it didn't come. Finally, and to Aleka's utter surprise, Diana reached out and pulled her into a tight hug, burying Aleka's face in her thick white hair. She held on for a long time, stroking Aleka's close-cropped head, murmuring something so soft Aleka couldn't quite make it out. Not words, she was pretty sure. Notes. A melody that was warm and soothing and sad, though Aleka had no memory of hearing it before.

The hug ended as suddenly as it had begun. Diana held her at arm's length, tears sparkling in her bright blue eyes.

"I'm not much for long goodbyes," she said. "So let's just leave it at that."

She released Aleka and crouched to rummage in her pack. When she stood again, bracing herself with the bow, she held a rolled piece of paper in her hand.

"You," she said to Javier. "There's one last thing I'd like you to do for me before I go."

SHE WAS GONE a few minutes later.

No one else in the colony saw her leave. They were too busy loading the three drowsing passengers into Arachne and Laman's truck and saying their goodbyes to the camp's former leaders. Before they left, Arachne gave Aleka a quick hug and handed her the silver pistol that hung at her side. "For old time's sake," she said. "If you need it, don't be afraid to use it." She scowled at Javier, then let Laman open the passenger side door and help her in. Though Aleka remembered nothing about the two of them, she could tell how happy they were to be together, with none of the cares of watching over camp that had occupied them for so many years. She waved goodbye with the others while the truck drove away to the south, its wheels skidding on the sand and Arachne screeching at Laman to pay attention to what he was doing. She watched until the truck was gone, and she wished them joy and an open road.

While everyone else finished the preparations for their own departure, Aleka climbed a dune and looked out over the sun-wrinkled plain until she spotted the solitary figure crossing the desert to the east. She was so far away by now, she might have been nothing but a beetle crawling across the sand, or a mirage born of the glaring afternoon. The woman was a mystery in many ways, but the one thing that was clear was that she liked to be alone. She'd made an exception for Aleka's sake, spending an entire day and night to take care of her. But now she was back to the way she wanted to be, or maybe needed to be, and there was no point in wondering where she was headed or what she was looking for.

Javier found Aleka long after the tiny figure had passed out of sight. He'd been assigned to round up the children who had been Kay and May's responsibility, and he held two of them now, a boy and a girl, one in each hand. Seeing how comfortable he looked with the little ones snuggling up to his side, Aleka knew that Tyris and Petra had made the right choice for the children's new caretaker. She decided that, as soon as they reached tonight's encampment, she'd ask the young leaders if she could help him out.

"Trucks are ready," he said to her. "You good to go?"

"Give me a minute."

He climbed the dune with the children and stood beside her. There was nothing to see, but she lingered, scanning the plain. When she turned to Javier, her eyes were wet.

"Hey," he said, "you okay?"

"I'll be fine."

They retraced their steps down the dune, Aleka holding the little girl's hand.

"Do you want me to tell you who Diana is?" Javier asked.

Aleka shook her head. "I know who she is."

"You do?"

"I don't know how, but…" She smiled. "She's my mom. The Huntress."

She took his hand, and they walked the rest of the way to the waiting trucks.

Epilogue

The old woman toiled across the desert.

She walked briskly but with a limp, her right leg held stiff and straight while she supported herself with her bow. In her pack, she carried three remnants of her past: a half-filled jar made of scuffed green glass, a used arrowhead, and a hastily sketched drawing of her daughter. Javier had captured a perfect likeness, down to the young woman's deep gray eyes. Her mother had no idea what those eyes would see in the years to come, but she was encouraged by the hopeful light that shone from the wrinkled page.

What she wouldn't give for a crystal ball to picture the days ahead! In her final talk with Arachne, her old friend had confided that she felt as if she'd been granted a second life, and she wasn't about to stop trying to have a baby until her eggs ran out. Would she get her wish? Would Laman become the husband and father he'd envisioned sixteen years ago? Aleka and Javier were obviously headed for something much bigger than friendship, which meant that she herself might become a grandmother one of these days, maybe before she reached the age of forty. Would she live to hold her grandchild in her arms? Would her path and that of Survival Colony 9 cross once more? Sixteen years ago, she'd sworn to herself that she would never see her daughter or her old friends again, and yet fate had led her to them when they needed her the most. Maybe, as the one who had founded and named the colony, she would always be connected to it no matter how far she strayed, and she would always find her way back.

And what of the Skaldi? No matter how drastically their numbers had plummeted, she'd been fighting them for too long to believe that they were all gone. Hardier enclaves might have survived—creatures that could locate another primary food source, hide from the sun's punishing rays, develop some new aptitude that enabled them to resist the decay of their species. An evolved type, the kind Athan had spoken of all those years ago. If his prediction was right, where would the new batch emerge? The Arizona base seemed a likely spot; she'd have to investigate further, checking the rail line to see if any of the plasma had been left behind. Clearly enough, it could live in a dormant state far longer than anyone, including its creator Dr. Melan, had guessed; maybe it could evolve on its own during phases of dormancy. But there were other potential hot spots as well: the Pennsylvania woodlands where her long journey had begun, the river with its life-giving fluid, the far western desert that no one to her knowledge had yet explored. Did the rail line and tunnel system extend beyond the scarred city, offering refuge to stray Skaldi that had escaped the destruction of their race? She knew in her heart that this wasn't over, not yet.

Michelle paused on a hilltop, looking back to where her daughter was about to begin her own journey.

"Aleka," she spoke to the wind. "Be strong. Stay alert. Your people will need you, and you must be prepared when the time comes."

She tucked the jar deeper inside her pack, took up the bow, and resumed her march toward the mountains that rose in the far distance.

THE END

The Book of the Huntress ends here

The adventures of Survival Colony 9 continue in
the Querry Genn Saga,
Survival Colony 9 and *Scavenger of Souls*,
both available now

Pronunciation Guide

There are a number of uncommon names in the Book of the Huntress, so I've provided the following pronunciation guide. The primary accented syllable in each name is in **bold**.

a as in *a*ct

ä as in *ah*

ā as in *a*ge

c as in *c*at

e as in *e*gg

ē as in *ea*t

g as in *g*et

i as in *i*nk

ī as in t*ie*

j as in *j*et

o as in d*o*ll

ō as in t*oe*

oo as in t*oo*

ou as in n*ow*

s as in *s*it

th as in *th*in

û as in f*u*r

ə as in *a*lone, hum*a*n

Acastus: ə-**cas**-təs

Aesir: **ē**-sûr

Aleka: ə-**lē**-cə

Arachne: ə-**rac**-nē

Araz: ə-**räz**

Argus: **ar**-gəs

Aristodeme: ə-ris-tō-**dā**-mā

Asheh: ä-**shā**

Athan: **ā**-thən

Caeneus: cā-**nē**-əs

Chelle: **shel**

Genn: **jen**

Jaden: **jā**-dən

Kenos: cē-**nos**

Laman: **lā**-mən

Lethe: **lē**-thē

Melan: **mel**-ən

Nausikaa: nou-sē-**cā**-ə

Polydeuces: pol-ē-**doo**-sēz

Reza: **rē**-zə

Skaldi: **skäl**-dē

Tyris: tī-**rēs**

Udain: oo-**dān**

Author's Note

The Book of the Huntress has been a long time in the making.

My debut novel, *Survival Colony 9*, was published in 2014. It tells the story of a small group's struggle to survive forty years after the monstrous Skaldi appeared on planet earth (fifty years according to the colonists, who have forgotten the exact chronology and settled on an estimate). I published a sequel in 2016 titled *Scavenger of Souls*, and that wrapped up the story I wanted to tell at the time.

Still, I felt that something was missing: the story of the Skaldi's arrival. I flirted with the idea of writing a prequel, but I didn't want it to be a mere lead-in to the series, with no reason for its existence other than explaining things that happen in the later books.

So I decided to write something else: a series that stands on its own while connecting chronologically and thematically to the original. Fortunately for me, I had already created the perfect character to bridge the forty-year gap, an old woman who plays a small role in the original books but who'd have been just the right age when the Skaldi arrived for the new story I had in mind. I'd written an origin scene for her years ago that never made its way into the first two books, but it became the basis for the scene that kicks *Daughter of Dust*, the first volume in the Book of the Huntress, into gear. From there, though I can't say it was entirely smooth sailing, the story unfolded as naturally as any I've told, from *Daughter of Dust* to *Dark's Dominion* and finally to *Scarred City*.

Now that the 5-book Survival Colony series is complete, I've also decided that *Scarred City* is the last novel I'm going to write for a while. I've loved creating science fiction and fantasy worlds for teen and adult readers the past seven years, but I've had to put other, equally compelling projects on hold, and I'm eager to devote my attention to them. Having come full circle, as it were, this seems like a good time to take a break.

Before I go, I'd like to thank the people who've been with me all along: my agent, Liza Fleissig; my readers, Jen Rees and Christa Yelich-Koth; my writing friends and confidantes Jenny Bardsley, Stephanie Keyes, and Kat Ross; my students and colleagues at La Roche University; my wife and children; and my friends and extended family. I also want to say a special thanks to you, my readers, for making me feel like the luckiest person in the world. Whether you've read all my books or only one, whether you first heard of me back in 2014 or only discovered me yesterday, every time you read something I've written, you fulfill a dream I've held for close to fifty years. It's you who've made me an author, and that's all I could ever ask.

About the Author

Joshua David Bellin has been writing novels since he was eight years old (though the first few were admittedly very short). A college teacher by day, he has published numerous works of fantasy and science fiction, including the Survival Colony novels (The Book of the Huntress and the Querry Genn Saga), the deep-space adventure *Freefall*, and the Ecosystem Cycle. In his free time, Josh likes to read, watch movies, and take long nature hikes with his kids. Oh, yeah, and he likes monsters. Really scary monsters.

joshuadavidbellin.blogspot.com

The Ecosystem Cycle

Only those born with the psychic power known as the Sense can survive within the planetary Ecosystem that swept away human civilization centuries ago. When Sarah, a seventeen-year-old Sensor, sets out on a mission of vengeance, she discovers that the Ecosystem is far more perilous than she ever dreamed.

The Survival Colony Novels

A desert world. An embattled remnant of humanity. A monstrous enemy that consumes and mimics the bodies of the living. And three teens who might hold the key to survival.

Available from online merchants and selected booksellers